THE BLUE HORSE

THE BLUE HORSE

Philip Miller

**FREIGHT
BOOKS**

First published 2015

Freight Books
49-53 Virginia Street
Glasgow, G1 1TS
www.freightbooks.co.uk

A CIP catalogue reference for this book is available from the British Library.

ISBN 978-1-910449-04-2
eISBN 978-1-910449-05-9

Typeset by Freight in Plantin
Printed and bound by Bell and Bain, Glasgow

the publisher acknowledges investment from
Creative Scotland toward the publication of this book

Philip Miller was born in 1973 and grew up in County Durham before he moved to Scotland in 1992. He is a multi-award winning journalist who has worked for The Scotsman, The Sunday Times in Scotland, and, since 2002, as Arts Correspondent of The Herald.

His short stories and poetry have been published in Gutter, The Island Review, Head On, the Fish Poetry Prize, Valve and Structo Magazine.

The Blue Horse is his debut novel. He lives and works in Glasgow.

Hope

'That damned painting vexes my mind's eye'

Rembrandt van Rijn, 1642

ONE

George Newhouse was in love with his wife.

But his wife was dead.

Now he was starting again. He was on a train, moving north. He opened a folded piece of paper. It was a letter from the Public Gallery.

> *Dear George,*
>
> *It is truly wonderful to have you on board. We are all greatly looking forward to working with you. It has been some time since we had a dedicated curator of our Dutch collections. And of course, we wait in great anticipation for your thoughts on Master Pieter.*
>
> *Hayley White has spoken to you about the visitors flat, I am sure. Stay there until you have found your bearings...*

The letter was from Thomas Colebrooke, the director of the Public Gallery. Newhouse would already know some of his new colleagues. Rudi, an old friend. And Dr Martinu, his old teacher.

It was brash, big Rudi, a crude man with a head like a rock, who had told him about the gallery position. The Public Galleries had needed a Dutch expert, a Golden Age curator. Martinu had been his reference. A phone interview with a man called Carver had been brief. Carver knew about the Rembrandt letter, and he probably knew, if only vaguely, about The Blue Horse. He had read the articles and seen Newhouse's papers.

Newhouse folded the letter again and put it back in his coat.

The train had crossed the border. Rain began to lash against it.

He looked out of the wet window at the soaked world. Small white farms glittered like scattered white teeth on brown hills. Low mountains loomed in the rain. Grey and white clouds drifted. Sodden sheep shivered in clumps in hedgeless fields.

The train skirted the black sea. His eyelids closed and he was asleep. His eyes moved over stones and estuaries, smooth rivers and black canals. His heart beat, and his fingers searched. He felt his mind move in shadow, through a veil, a black bead curtain, and into a sudden realm of colour.

He woke up suddenly. The train had pulled into its final station. His head was on the window, wetness around his mouth. He saw a blue night sky and the black edges of a castle on a rocky outcrop, perching over the city. He sat up and felt electric light on his eyes and face. Other passengers were moving. Newhouse squinted and his head felt heavy. The carriage smelled of sweat and cold coffee, damp cotton and silk.

Newhouse waited for people to leave the carriage. He did not want to leave with them. He sat crumpled into his thick black coat until the carriage was empty.

Up above the train station he could see a park, high lithe trees, their upper branches swaying, and a large black memorial. Its gothic fingers were black against the sky. He briefly imagined flames bursting from its spires.

He moved off the train into the cold. People moved and trains shunted and rumbled. In the black rafters of the station, white birds huddled like bunches of pale flowers. A tannoy mumbled as he reached the security barrier and, after finding his crumpled orange ticket, he walked onto the shiny-floored concourse, dragging his cases behind him. There was a taxi queue across the street. He thought of home with a sudden ache. He wanted to turn around, climb over the barriers, and go back.

But there was nothing to go back to. The house, their home, was sold.

I am just hungry, he said to himself, I need sugar. He thought of his sister. She would say: make sure you eat. Make sure you sleep.

He turned on his mobile phone and it slowly came to life. He had a voice message from someone he did not recognise. He ignored it. He had a message from Rudi Hessenmullcr. He deleted it. He had a text from his bank. He deleted it. He got in a taxi. An old tunc burbled from the cab's radio.

There was always the work. The contents of his memory, his hands, his knowledge, his experience, his training. He thought of his writing, his folios, his magazines, his catalogues and prints. There was something real there: a game that could be played with colours and words. The taxi moved through the carved ivory streets.

He saw a black figure standing on the street, dark against the crisp stone.

It was a woman, standing on a corner, beside a Belisha beacon. She wore a fur hat and coat. Her face smooth and honed like the back of a spade. She had no eyes, no nose, no mouth. Her hands were black, and held a flex, its plug swinging.

He heard a whisper his head.

Find it, find me. For you, he.

He blinked and opened his eyes but the taxi had moved on, the woman had gone.

I am exhausted, he told himself. My brain is wrong.

The taxi crawled on, and Newhouse looked down at his luggage. He remembered something Ruth's brother had said:

Tear me into new shapes, God.

Make me into something new.

TWO

I can hear the sun move, Ruth had said.

It was a good time. She lay on the grass. Her face was white with light, her eyes closed. Newhouse lay his head on her stomach. He looked at her bare feet, the legs of passing people. Light flashed on the windows of trams, whirring as it skirted the eaves of the Vondelpark. People sat in groups. They talked and laughed and ate from picnic boxes, from bags, from plastic bottles and wicker baskets. Couples walked on the grass, between the trees. Children with their parents queued for ice cream.

Newhouse's cheek lay on Ruth's stomach, hot and soft. He moved his face to hers, and his shadow fell across her.

She opened her eyes, shielding them with one slim hand.

Hey, she said.

Hey, he said. He kissed her dry lips.

Hear what?

Nothing, she said quietly.

Honey, what time is it, she said. He kissed her neck, moving up to close his lips on the bell of her ear.

The sun warmed his back. His hand held her waist.

That morning, before his meeting, they had made love at the hotel. They had lain on the floor, exhausted, silent like pebbles scoured by the sea. Two smooth, perfect stones, moving together forever under the ocean.

George? she said. His mind returned to the present, the park.

Mmmm. His mouth was still attached to her ear. Her hair tickled his nose and eyes.

Come on, she said. She began to stir. She moved her head to one side, and his face dropped to the grass. He groaned. Their short holiday was over. She had to leave Amsterdam, and he had to work. He had to go to the Rijksmuseum archives and meet Gilda, his assistant. They were working on his first exhibition. It contained most of the surviving works of a minor painter of the Dutch Golden Age, Pieter Van Doelenstraat.

He and Ruth had eaten with Gilda the night before. They'd drunk wine and eaten good food and watched the cobwebs of light shimmer on the canal. They decided on a title for the show: *The Missing Mind of Pieter van Doelenstraat*. Missing, that is, Gilda had said, from history. Many of his works were now lost and missing, too. And the title, Ruth suggested, suited the mood of the paintings from Doelenstraat's chilly, elusive Absent Period.

The Absent Period: dark paintings of empty rooms, abandoned kitchens. Empty beds and solemn, silent instruments.

It sums it up, Gilda said. Authoritative, mysterious, decisive, she said.

And it's far better than Van Doelenstraat: Lust for Glory, Ruth had said.

I was never going to call it that, Newhouse laughed.

And anyway, he said, I wasn't entirely sure of the seriousness of your own brilliant suggestions. I like the title now. It is nice and snappy.

Gilda had raised an eyebrow. What was your first paper called?

Pieter Van Doelenstraat: The Harmonious yet Distinctive

Palette of an Evasive yet Fascinating Minor Dutch artist of the first Dutch Golden Age, Ruth said, before theatrically running out of breath.

That was unfortunate, he said. It was a little long winded.

Nice and snappy, Ruth said.

Gilda laughed. I've read far worse.

No one cared anyway, Newhouse said. Not the editor, not the blessed fucking peer reviews. It shows how few people read these masterpieces of prose. We all look inwards, not out.

You're shocking, Gilda said. Plenty of people care. Dr Martinu does.

Well, he would. He virtually wrote it, Newhouse said.

Ultimately, only about four people cared about that: me, the editor, Hans, and the ghost of Van Doelenstraat, may he rest in many pieces.

George, you live in a constant state of denial, Ruth said, and poured Gilda more wine.

Humanity had vanished from Van Doelenstraat's Absent Period. But more was missing from the painter's biography. Not much was known, and much that was known was not defined or confirmed. Even some of his monographed works were disputed. And then there was his Blue Horse, lost forever.

Not even God can change the past, the priest had said. That is why the past exists, to humble even the Creator. As soon as time was born, God knew he was imprisoned, too.

Now, around them, in the summer heat, pouring from a flat blue sky, the park buzzed: cycle bells rattled, cars and trams wheezed and groaned, and on the canals, boats buzzed and slurred their way through the thick green water, the ale-brown expanses.

Stay for another night, Newhouse said. Ruth was looking into her purse, one arm out of her jacket, dark glasses pushed up on her forehead.

George, she said. No. She stood up and brushed tiny flecks of grass from her skirt. She reached into her bag and found her pack of cigarettes and opened it. She pulled a cigarette out and placed it in her mouth.

I would just prefer it if you stayed, he said.

She looked at him. Jesus. What's the matter with you?

Nothing.

He stood up. They walked to Central Station. Her train was waiting to depart. On the platform he kissed her forehead and held her body tightly.

Be careful, he said.

What's the matter George, she said. You're being strange.

Let's enjoy this moment.

She laughed.

You're really hung-over, she said, and hugged him hard. She pulled on a small woollen hat and stepped onto the train. With a turn of her shoulders she was gone. Newhouse watched the train haul itself into movement and leave the station like a slow, heavy injection.

He'd turned and walked back into the city. Pulled his phone from his pocket and rang Gilda.

You're late, she'd said.

I know, I'm sorry, he said, and quickened his step.

THREE

It was a smaller exhibition than he had originally planned. But it was, among his colleagues at least, a success. A small watershed. *The work of a talented new curator and historian,* Dr Martinu had written, albeit an in article where he did not reveal that Newhouse was aw former pupil. The newspaper reviewers had been kind. Magazines had admired it. There had been features, spreads, and a story in The Culture Newspaper. There had been some headlines: *The Undiscovered Master. Vexing the Mind's Eye, Rembrandt's Lost Heir.*

Dr Martinu had urged him to capitalize on its success, to learn even more. Newhouse had initially said no. No more could be learned. The Blue Horse was lost. Gilda van Gaal took a step back too, and said she had other projects. She said the case of Van Doelenstraat was lovely, fascinating, but ultimately a dead end.

But Newhouse had worked on. He studied the three masterpieces that were now in New York, London and The Hague. He had illustrated the delicacy of Van Doelenstraat's brushwork, the depth of his colour, his near-perfect perspective and tried to explain, in writing, in lectures, the mysteries of the Absent Period. But then there was the silence of The Blue Horse. The masterpiece that no one had ever seen. At least not for more than three hundred years. Then, one October, there had been the emergence of the Rembrandt letter.

That damned painting vexes my mind's eye.

And now a taxi climbed a hill as it sped to Newhouse's new home. The city under neon was bright and empty and clean. The cab rose over the crest of a hill, and suddenly the black sea appeared, laying like a blade of ice between the city and a hilly, far off land. Georgian terraces stood, pale and severe in the white light. Everything seemed sharp and cold, at right angles, treeless and brown.

The taxi stopped.

Here you are pal, the taxi driver said. Welcome to Scotland.

Newhouse looked at the rubber matting of the taxi floor and felt very tired.

Ok, he said.

He stood on the pavement and looked up at his new home, a second floor flat in a crescent of tall, elegant houses, with a gated, blank garden at its centre.

He sat down, on the front step, exhausted.

There were no clouds in the sky, but it began to rain.

FOUR

Newhouse was in his new office.

It was 9am. He had not slept in his flat. It had been white and clean and cold, and the boiler didn't seem to work. He had lain on his white bed and listened to the city move outside. Taxis and buses, heels scraping like knives on flagstones, low-landing planes and doors opening and closing. A terrible, dark framed print on his bedroom wall looked like a hatch into another world. It seemed to warp and weave in the night.

He had given up trying to sleep and looked at a book on Hammershøi. He looked at blurred, foggy paintings of empty rooms and the stolid backs of anonymous women. He sipped tea and thought of bending one of the women over, lifting her heavy tresses, running his hand over the curves of her linen-clad buttocks and thighs.

He thought of all the work he had done and had yet to do. He had been expecting a tiny box room as an office, full of filing cabinets and old furniture. But he was in a large room at the corner of the gallery, looking over its wide, walled, sculpted gardens. The room was dark green and an old poster for a Titian show, from 1984, was tacked to one wall. The office smelled of toilet cleaner and vacuum powder.

The gallery was a massive pile of grey stone. It had once been a school for the blind. Its portico was heavy, its pillars brutal and blackened. It was set in parkland in the west end of the city, surrounded by large silent houses and secluded cul-de-sacs. Newhouse had seen a terrible modern work by the main gate as he was driven in. A blob of excreted stone. Near the portico, there were some emaciated figures, standing in a line.

His grey computer was covered in a blue dustsheet. He looked out over the gardens and saw birds drifting on the crescent shaped pond, its surface as smooth as black plastic. They tucked their beaks into their smooth clean breasts. Nothing stirred in the city beyond. The high castle was a smudge in the haze. Church spires spiked the white air.

Birds sat on telephone lines like notes on a score.

Newhouse unloaded his books and his papers. More remained in storage in London and would be shipped up. His thesis and his dissertations, his published papers.

There was the slim green volume of Ruth's last collection of poems: *Ruth O'Reilly – The Others With Them.* He leant it against the monitor. Its spine was creased. Tiny interlacing cracks in the mossy ink.

His article on bankrupt Rembrandt's sale of arms and armour was there, too. And the papers concerning the discovery of the letter. It had been written by Rembrandt to Constantijn Huygens and he had found it, miraculously, inside a Japanese sword case in the archives of an Irish museum.

Newhouse put his feet up on the table. He heard a noise.

It was a cry. It was the gasp he had made when the letter had slipped out of the sheath. A thin, folded, slip of brown paper, sleeping inside the fractured interior of the case. How had no one found it before? He remembered scholars flying to Dublin, and studying the letter: experts from New York, from from the Netherlands. It was clearly written, smoothly signed, a dull letter about a commission, from the master to his supporter. But with something gleaming within it, fresh and unseen: those strange words about Van Doelenstraat.

Rembrandt had not written much. He was known – renowned – for the sentence in which he had described his art. *Die messte ende di naetureelste beweechgelickheijt.* It meant, most scholars thought, that he was explaining how he painted with 'the greatest and most natural movement'. It was among the only expressions about art found in ink. And now Newhouse had another.

I have a confession – I am now alarmed by the man P. v Doelenstraat – I have now seen his vision – that unnatural animal – the blue horse – that damned painting vexes my mind's eye.

Newhouse had been exhilarated. It was evidence The Blue Horse existed. Or had existed.

Now, years later, he needed a drink. His stomach rumbled. There was a knock on the door. He jumped. He dropped his feet from the desk.

A small woman put her head around the door. She had oval eyes and an oval mouth.

Hello, I'm Hayley, she said.

He recognised her voice. It was the director's secretary.

Lovely to meet you Hayley. Come in, he said, suddenly aware of his unwashed hair. His head started to itch. He introduced himself. He held out a hand, but she didn't take it. He withdrew it.

I'll get you a cup of tea, she said, looking at the floor.

Oh, OK, he said. If you have coffee, that would be great.

Of course, she said, and left.

Newhouse stared at the closed door for a while and then sat back at his desk. He took the dust cover off the computer and switched it on. It came to life. He pressed some keys. He took out a thin flat book on Jacob van Ruisdael. A minor and prolific landscape man. He used it as a mousemat. He moved the mouse with his right hand. The small black arrow on the screen would not move. The screen was blank and white apart from a tiny emblem of a waste basket and the immoveable arrow.

He sat back heavily. He wondered how he had ended up in this room, at this desk, hundreds of miles from his life, from all he had known, from his Ruth, from his home. He put his head in his hands and stared at the back of his eyes for some time. He heard a noise and another, softer noise, and then smelt fresh coffee nearby.

A steaming mug of coffee was on his desk. The door to the office was just closing. He could smell a sweet perfume. He shook as he moved the coffee to his lips. It was sweet and milky, and as he drank it, eyes closed, the idea of the day ahead seemed to get better. The sun flashed on his windows

Outside a seabird, white as a diamond, its beak a yellow blade, cawed from the top of the hideous sculpture.

He picked up the telephone and dialed an internal number. He cleared his throat.

Is that facilities? he asked. It was.

Hello, I'm George Newhouse – I'm new here: can you make my computer work?

DEEPDALE

Darkness moved over the water.

It was midnight. The club, under the flagstones, under the waterline, was nearly empty. A single woman in leather danced alone under orange and yellow, under the flickering bulbs. The beats of a disco tune thudded through the converted wine cellar. Fixtures whined and rattled. Multi-coloured perspex vibrated and settled. Behind the bar, a young man, surrounded by upturned optics and garish bottles, stared at a silent TV screen.

Deepdale sat in a corner booth, a semi-circle of fake leather seats, two low round tables with tea-lights in red bowls.

The woman in leather danced, with her eyes closed, her fingers snapping in the air.

Between his legs was a large leather case. A solid lawyer's bag. Square and bulky, multi-zipped with a combination lock. Inside was the object.

He had arrived in the city by train. Nine hours in a private carriage, with the bag between his feet. At the border, no one checked his baggage. At the station, it had been so heavy he lengthened the shoulder strap so he could wear it across his body. There were no cars in this city, and the long walk with this burden had tested his strength, his stamina. He thought, as he crossed another hump-backed bridge in the dark, of Bunyan, the pilgrim's progress.

Now his shoulders and back ached. The disco bass rippled through the floor, through his bones, through the case.

He drank his water and looked at his phone. The music's volume increased.

Deepdale was the courier. He had not seen what was inside the bag, although he knew it was a work of art. The art was not only in the bag, it was encased in another, which itself was covered in a one-piece plastic sheath. At the hotel, he had taken it out, and felt its weight. It was heavy and solid. He could feel, underneath the plastic, through the canvas, an elaborate frame, a smooth surface. He held it for a while, and fell asleep.

Now he was in the right place. The right time. The customers were due at 12:30am. He would hand the bag over and return to his hotel, a half empty hostel facing the black depth of the lagoon. He would sleep all night and have a proper breakfast. He would call his boss, find a bank, check he had been paid, and go home.

He looked out over the club. The girl had gone. A shadowy couple were kissing in another booth, their heads blurring into one bobbing dark mass. In another, a man in a suit, a little like his, sat with a bag and looked at his drink. Behind a rippling curtain of thick beads, something was happening in the far corner with three people. He could not see. Feet moved and legs moved.

Lights flashed, music boomed. His eyes felt heavy.

There was a sudden prickling in his thighs. He scratched it. It was a warm night.

He felt a sudden glow of heat between his legs. He put his hand to the case. It was cold and leather. He shook his head: he had travelled all night. He could still hear the rattle of the train in his head. He was sweating.

He looked at his phone: nothing. He took out his second phone, and texted Ana. He knew she would be awake. He told her he missed her. He typed quickly with his thumbs.

I will be back soon. This is the last for a while.

He put the phone away. It buzzed in his pocket. He took it out.

Love you, Ana had replied.

He felt something move around his ankles.

He looked down at his feet and a pool of liquid was spreading from the leather case. It was gathering around his feet.

Fuck, he said.

He lifted up the bag, and liquid dripped from it, clear and thick, orange and yellow and red in the pulsing nightclub lights.

He stood up and, holding the sodden bag under his armpit, walked quickly across the empty dancefloor to the toilets.

It was small and windowless, this far under the waters.

There were red lights and broken lights. There was a single cubicle with its door ajar, half off one hinge. There was a urinal full of brown water. There was a sink underneath a large mirror. Music buzzed and thumped through the thin partitioned walls.

He put the bag, as heavy as a body, on the sink. He looked at it. It was dry. He lifted it up, it was dry and clean. He checked the combination locks: there were all set. He ran his hand all around the bag. It was all dry, all clean. Nothing had been moved. No liquid, and no spillage. He looked down at his legs: his pale trousers were dry. His shoes were dry. He looked under his arm: no liquid, no moisture. He looked in the mirror and saw his cheeks were red, his forehead red. He felt sweat around his ears, on his neck and lips.

Deepdale blew out air from his lungs. He closed his eyes and leaned on the sink. He hadn't fucked up. He ran his hands through his hair. Everything was fine.

His eyes were still closed when the door opened. A blast of music ripped through the thick air and was silenced again. He heard the tumbled footsteps of another man. A flailing man staggered into the toilet. He was a mess, drenched, and covered in something viscous and dripping. He had a heavy lawyer's bag under one arm.

The man's desperate face looked at him. It was his own face.

Deepdale's stomach turned over.

The other Deepdale looked at him, his eyes red, his mouth hanging open, his tongue swollen and brown. Then he fell down to the floor, and lay on his side. His body a lump on the toilet's slippery floor. Black wetness clung to him. The wrinkles and sags of his wet clothes began to settle. There was silence.

Deepdale could not move.

The other man's jaw was at a strange angle. A brown liquid began to force its way through his teeth, over his lips, into a grainy pool on the floor. The head seemed to loosen, to shrink in places, to collapse. The hairline bumped and bulged. Liquid ran from the ear.

The courier was frozen, unmoving.

Something moved in the corner of his eye.

He turned to the mirror and saw his ruined face. The bulging hairline, the chin soaked in sandy brown, an ooze from the nose and ear. He looked with trembling into his own dying eyes.

Behind him, grim in the tiny club toilet, stood the mass and heat of a black beast.

FIVE

Rudi had a large head and large eyes. He was wearing a three-piece tweed suit. He was at the bar, buying them both drinks. It had been a long day, Newhouse's first at the gallery. The general director, Colebrooke, was away and his deputy, the thin, ill-looking man called Carver took the management meeting. Words were said and papers were shuffled. Exhibitions were mentioned and loans to and from other galleries discussed. The National Galleries wanted nothing to do with a proposed deal. The National in London was not returning calls.

Carver said Dr Hans Martinu was in Italy and he forwarded his apologies. Carver then turned his angled head to Newhouse, and said he was looking forward to Newhouse's survey of the Dutch and Scandinavian collections.

It is, as we know, the first time the Public Gallery has carried out a comprehensive survey since 1967, when our own Van Doelenstraat was loaned to us by the late Lord Ardrashaig, he said. Then there was the Dou and Metsu exhibition, which was already well advanced, he said.

Newhouse nodded. Oh god, Dou and Metsu, he thought, fuck.

People murmured and smiled and nodded. Carver carried on. Newhouse had been put on the Biennale Liaison Oversight Co-Ordination Committee. He did not know why. And right now, he was the only person on it.

He was also in charge of the loaned collections, he was told, at one of the Public Gallery's outstations, a country residence and gallery in the mountains called Castle House. Newhouse nodded and smiled as if he knew this already. He did not.

He stared at his finger nails. White dots on the pink bone. Mauve blood under the hard coatings.

The meeting went on and on. Carver's voice was harsh, it chopped through the air. There was talk of loans and counter-loans, displacements, re-hangs, repaints and revamps. There was talk of fund raising, corporate sponsorship, government liaison, inter-government liaison, the British Council and the culture ministry. There was talk of personnel, security, the internet, the intranet, folios, catalogues, guides, programmes and libraries.

He heard little and said nothing. His heart pounded. The Biennale; he had never been to the Venice Biennale. It was a festival of contemporary art – not something he cared or even knew too much about. This show was not even an official national pavilion, it was an associate show with no national standing. Castle House? He had never heard of it. His heart raced. Newhouse stared at his paper and watched the faint pulsing of the neon lights blur and flare on the blank page. He had been introduced to the other curators and directors, but he could only look occasionally at Rudi.

Rudi smiled back with his large square teeth, and the rest were a blur of faces, eyes, names and shadows.

He wished Dr Martinu was there. Martinu had keenly overseen his studies. He knew everything about Dutch art. He seemed to know a lot about everything else too. Martinu had met Ruth, once, and beamed at her. Newhouse remembered the smile, one of the warmest he had seen from the old man. It was as if his huge bare head was a bulb and it had suddenly lit. His round, red nose had crinkled. He had bowed suddenly and kissed Ruth's hand.

Now Newhouse sat in the pub and his friend was at the bar. Rudi was tall and broad. He was divorced. Newhouse didn't really know Rudi's former wife, he had only met her twice. When Rudi married her he seemed to disappear, and then he moved north. Now the large German was returning from the bar with two pints and a packet of crisps wedged under one arm.

The beer was cool and sour. Outside, there was a cobbled street and rows of restaurants, pubs, and clothes shops. Tourists walked slowly, eating chips out of white polystyrene plates. Newhouse sipped his beer. Rudi was talking about his new exhibition, planned for the next year, about Jesus and his Humanation. It was concerned with symbols of the resurrection in depictions of Christ's genitalia.

Rudi had his eyes closed as he talked.

A quite extraordinary example in Milan, he said, talking about a painting of the Christ, descended from the cross, painted with a large erection.

Newhouse thought of his empty white flat and did not want to go back to it.

So, anyway, Hayley, Rudi suddenly said, an eye brow raised, putting his glass on the wooden table between them.

What of her? Newhouse said.

Hayley, George, Hayley, lovely Hayley the secretary. Come on man. Newhouse noticed that Rudi seemed to be bellowing.

The pub was busy. There were men in business suits and women in business suits. There was a group of builders in plaster-stained overalls by the jukebox, who were laughing and drinking pints and chasers. There was a hum and buzz. Brass glimmered at the bar, light bent from optics and bottles.

I don't really…

She's fine, Rudi said. She has it in all the right places.

You should ask her out then.

No, you, I mean, you should chase her. She's very fine. Very comfortable lady.

Newhouse laughed.

No, no. You're ridiculous.

Rudi was smiling. He took another sip of beer.

I will have her then, he said. I need the excitement.

How long now since you and Martha? Newhouse said.

Too long, Rudi said. Maybe not long enough. But she was not the one.

He sighed and closed his eyes. He looked out of the window to the emptying street. Far too long, Rudi said. He looked down at the tabletop and traced a whorl with one stubby finger.

I might try some man fucking, he said.

Oh really.

Yes, I might have a go, It is a limited palate but a strong one. Buggery and blowjobs.

Do you love men?

Yes, said Rudi. He shook his head. But not in that way. He smiled again.

If I could entice a man as gorgeous as you, Georgeous, it might be worth it.

I am sure you could try.

Rudi took a sip and shook his head.

I'm sorry. Sometimes I do not recognize myself. I say

things and wonder why I said them. I don't think that at all. Ignore me. Darkness runs through the world. No one wants to admit it. The history of man is not an ascent.

Rudi, what are you saying?

I did not marry to be divorced, he said. I don't think she did either. But it's over now, and no going back. She's in Berlin again. I go to concerts by myself you know George. Mahler, Bruckner, Vaughan Williams' Fantasia. Maybe I should go off and run an orchestra. There are thirty opera companies at home. Thirty.

Newhouse looked at his friend's large head. It seemed heavy, carved from stone. There was almost a grain to his skin, a sense of permanence in its folds and creases.

Rudi said something more about his ex-wife, but Newhouse could not hear it.

No, she's for you, George, Rudi said, suddenly. You can have the lovely Hayley, she's all yours. All yours. God knows you need it more than me.

Thanks Rudi, Newhouse said, as brightly as he could. I will bear it in mind, I will inform Hayley that you are acting as a less than charming but wholly Bavarian match maker on her behalf. I am sure she will be absolutely... not delighted in any way whatsoever. Rudi smiled and grabbed his glass and lifted it.

Good to have you here, you know? Good to have you here, Gorgeous George. You and your reservations and hesitations.

I'm glad, at least, that you're here, Newhouse said.

George, Rudi said, and took another swig of beer. He emptied his glass.

Rudi reached across the table, and touched the ends of Newhouse's fingers. Skin touched against skin. Newhouse looked down.

And perhaps a drink for Ruth too, Rudi said.

Newhouse stared at the table.

A toast for that beautiful girl, Rudi said, and clinked his glass on Newhouse's pint.

Yes, Newhouse said, yes of course.

Tot spreken hoort noch kracht: de mijne gaette niet, he said.

Huygens the poet. 'Speech needs strength', Rudi nodded, 'I have none left.'

Newhouse thought of his old house. He thought of flower-patterned pillowcases. Bare coat hangers clinking in empty cupboards. A garden grown wild with thorns and weeds. A fingerprint on a window.

So. We are decided. You should fuck that girl, Rudi said suddenly. God fucking help me, I've tried. You can do better.

Newhouse shook his head.

Another one? Rudi said brightly, and stood up. He did not wait for a reply, and walked to the bar, slapping his back pocket.

THE BURREN

He saw her white limbs as they struggled free of her clothes. Her hands caught in tight elasticated sleeves. Pulling off her jeans in tight quarters. They both undressed in the small, cramped car, which stood alone on the headland. The car shook in the wind. The sky was darkening, rock sheets of cloud gathering and grumbling. The broad arch of beach was silver in the gathering gloom, the far hills bruise-blue, smoky in the mist. They hopped out of the car, shivering suddenly. Her legs and arms were as pale as bleached driftwood, her swimsuit a dark shadow. His shorts – bought at a petrol station along the way - were baggy, whipping around his thighs. He felt high and giddy, in the sudden cold, the salty wind, the vast horizon of the ocean below. They pecked their way down the sandy slope to the cold beach. Their feet sucked on its wetness, suck-sucking footholds and prints on their quick way to the breakers.

She smiled at him, and the Atlantic roared behind her. Her face gleaming like the moon against the wave's darkness.

They jumped in. Oh my god, she screamed. Waves hit them. The sudden cold was a numbing shock. They gasped and splashed. The tide enveloped them. Thunder cracked on the mountain.

My god its cold, he yelled. Air was ripped from his lungs. He paddled and splashed, his legs adrift.

Hold me, she shouted, her hair burnt bronze, slapped against her head, her long neck. Her eyes were black and wide. Their arms rose above the water, their fingers reached for each other. They met and tangled and pulled their bodies to each other, cutting through the ocean until they were together.

The current pulled them both to shore.

They ran laughing back to the car, their feet aching from the cold, biting from the sudden toughness of the tarmac. Lightning smashed on the distant mountains. They sat wet in the shivering car. She bent over and kissed him, her mouth, her lips a sudden flare of heat on his frozen face. He pulled her sodden dark head to his, and gripped her hard, as if he could meld them together, as if her mind could be pushed into his. He breathed her breath. They held each other. They breathed heavy. They drove back to the cottage silently in the rain. Her bare foot on the accelerator.

There were pearls of sea drops drying on her neck, and a single curl of flat seagreen seaweed looped behind her ear.

SIX

He was up early and walked to work. The city was quiet, severe and solid in clear, cold morning light. He walked along wide boulevards and through silent crescents. The stone town as hard and pretty as iced filigrees on a wedding cake. His feet slowly climbed a low hill.

Ahead of him he could see a woman, walking briskly. She had a hat that partially hung over the back of her head. It looked like a big sock. He saw a wisp of blonde hair and recognised her: it was Hayley. He sped up.

She was wearing earphones. He could hear a buzzing noise.

Hey, he said, and waved. Her eyes were wide and surprised.

They were stride for stride as they entered the gallery gardens.

Hello, she said, and pulled out the earphones.

They talked as they walked up the curving path through its large gardens to the hulking mass of the gallery. She asked how he was settling in, and he said he was still a bit lost. She asked about the flat and he said it was OK, but realised he needed to find a place of his own. He said he didn't know the city very well.

But you know Rudi, she said.

I do, he said. He smiled, and she laughed.

He's a character, she said, and shook her head. He had expected her to say something more. He nodded and said no more. They walked into the building together, past the security guards, clicked their badges on a metal plate, a double door opened, and entered the series of small rooms that were their offices.

He made a cup of tea and checked his emails. There was a long one from Gilda asking a lot of questions. He ignored it. There was a note from Dr Martinu, he ignored it. There were several from old colleagues, congratulating him on his new position. There was one from Rudi, which said: *Make sure you do something about it.* There was a message from the curator at Castle House, Dr Anna Blanco asking for an urgent meeting. The morning sun cast a lozenge of light, bright as paint, across the walls.

He had hung a print on the large main wall. It was *Christ in the Realm of the Dead* by Joakim Skovgaard. A Danish, late 19th century artist. It was a dramatic depiction of Jesus freeing the dead from hell. Hundreds of pale faces looked up to the triumphant Christ, who stood, arms outstretched, at the gates. Under his feet were writhing snakes and a crushed skull. A blonde naked woman sat in the centre of the scene. Newhouse stood up from his desk and walked across to the picture.

He knew the original was a massive painting, this was only a fraction of the size. The girl knelt in front of Jesus, her arms extended, her legs tucked under her white body. Long red-blonde hair ran from her head to the stony ground. She had a beautiful face. A halo glowed around her head. If she had been closer to Jesus, she could have been embracing him. She could have been kissing his robes. Kneeling in front of him, as a lover might.

Fucks sake, he said.

He looked at his computer. He had to write an early report on the Dutch collections. He had not even gone through them. He had not seen them, not since his interview. There were stark Dutch church interiors and icy skating scenes. There were hundreds of drawings and engravings. There was more. He had to do more work on the Dou and Metsu exhibition. He wanted to read more on Gabriel Metsu, who had lived at the same time as Van Doelenstraat. Metsu may have known him. He may have seen The Blue Horse: he could not remember when Metsu lived and died.

He wanted to sketch out another essay on The Absent Years. He wondered whether he should rename them. Absent was the wrong word. Absent suggested the artist himself was absent. But Van Doelenstraat was never more himself, never gave more of himself, than in those dozen or so paintings. The Empty Years, perhaps.

The doors to the gallery opened and people began to visit. He heard raised voices. He opened the email from Martinu sent from a hotel lobby in Milan. It welcomed him to the gallery in formal tones. It asked after his health.

I have found a letter in a private collection that may refer to your St Pieter, it said. There was a P.S. Martinu said he would return in a week. His partner, Gavin, wanted to stay on in Italy. Gavin had never been before.

Newhouse reached for a book and read about Metsu. His life and work came back to him as he read. Leiden and Amsterdam. There was a haunting painting of a sick child in the Rijksmuseum. There was a rather prosaic piece, *The Music Lesson* in the National Gallery, and a busy, minor work in Washington D.C.

He phoned another office about which Dous and which Metsus were being hanged, borrowed, loaned and conserved. He re-read an article on Dou and his pupils – Metsu was one. Nothing came close to Doelenstraat. But who had? Van Rijn and Vermeer, the Fabritius bird and the Fabritius self-portrait, that was all.

His computer pinged again.

It was an email from Hayley, entitled *Proposed Sight-Seeing Tour*

He opened it. She suggested she show him around the city at the weekend.

He wrote back: *Sounds great, you're on.*

She wrote immediately back: *Great. You can buy lunch.*

He looked up at Christ saving the dead. The kneeling woman. Her arms bare against the fleeing darkness of Hades.

The weekend seemed a long way away.

SEVEN

He could not sleep. His eyes were open. His fingers tingled. A trembling oblong of light shook on the white ceiling. He turned over and switched on the lamp. In the corner of the room his bags lay open. A bottle of wine stood on the soft chair, unopened. There was a pile of books and papers. He reached for a file beside his bed, rattling a brown tub of pills. There were notes written in his handwriting.

P. van Doelenstraat, born ?, c.1600, died —.
Trained under Bertoldt, Zwolle, 1630s, Rembrandt,
1640s? Amsterdam.
Rem.Blue Horse letter, 1642.
Ten works signed. Oil on canvas.
Figurative period.
New York: Interior with Maid, 1628 (dated)
London, Nat. Gallery: The Birthday Party, 1634/5
('The Unhappy Child')
Haag: Lady with Child, 1640. ('The Sick bed')
Dublin: Self Portrait, 1643? (c..)
The Blue Horse?
Absent period
Interior with open letter, 1646
Room with chair, 1647/8 Rijksmuseum: Table with
knives (1649?) + Room with Bed (?) Brussels: Closed
shutters (?)

He dropped the notes and looked at the mobile phone beside his bed. It was three in the morning. He turned the light off and pulled the duvet up to his nose.

Maybe he should contact the National Galleries, ask to see the *Interior with the Open Letter* again. At least it would be in good condition.

The painting was simple: there was an open dark window. A night sky with pale stars. A bare plaster wall, flaking and pitted. A tiled floor, and a simple table, with a paper knife, a ripped sheet of paper, and a folded letter, with black spidery writing on it. Unreadable writing. The signature in the bottom left corner: *PvD* in an enclosed symbol of combining letters. And in the corner of the canvass, the back of an empty chair. There was the hint of a tree bough in the window's darkened eye. The ill-lit room, the plasterwork. The illegible, much-studied letter. The ink clotted and curdled on the letter's page. And on the floor, undisturbed dust, a mist of dirt and plaster crumbs on the dark tiles, their minuscule shadows hinted at, picked out, their presence hovering over the dark surface, like pebbles scattered across a lake of black ice. It was brilliant painting. He thought, suddenly, of Johannes Thopas's *Portrait of a Deceased Girl* in the Mauritshuis, its plush, stifling red curtains and satin surrounding the peaceful, pale dead child. One hand on her chest. A girl asleep, not dead. Dreaming, not cold. But cold, not dreaming.

He closed his eyes. Tomorrow was Friday. On Saturday he would meet Hayley at the monument at midday. She was bringing a friend.

He fell into a deep sleep. He dreamt.

She was in their old kitchen, pouring water into glasses and bowls, tubs and pans. The water hit them and sprayed out. Ruth, someone like Ruth, was upset and serious, her her neck tight, her forehead furrowed. He moved to hold her and she moved away. She filled cups and baking trays. She filled eggcups and salad bowls. The water ran, and he could not hold her.

He woke suddenly to the sound of a crash.

It was light, the lamp was on the floor, its shade crumpled.

His hand hurt. A tiny frayed ribbon of white skin stood on end, newly peeled from his raw knuckle. He got out of bed and pulled on some clothes. A heavy jumper, jeans, some boots, his winter coat. He left the flat and walked into the city.

He walked slowly onto the main street, empty of cars and people, and crossed to a small park. He sat on a cold bench, colder in the dark, and looked out at the chains of streetlamps, the sillouette of the old town against the night sky, the flickering of cold lights in hotels and monuments, the glitter of distant cars.

This city was a new land, a new country. His edges felt keener, his body's boundaries more defined. Or maybe it was just the cold, hardening his skin and tightening the stitching of his bones. He sat in the night for some time. His hands were pushed deeper into his winter coat and as he stood up to leave, he surveyed the diorama into which he had been pitched: the new strange scenes before him, the alien land.

He had lifted the lids of her eyes to look into them for one last time. Dry and soft on his fingers.

And now, her body not heavy in the earth.

He walked back to his flat. He readied himself for bed in the half light.

Suddenly his mobile phone rang, buzzing and slipping sideways on the bedside cabinet.

It was Ursula, his sister in Canada.

He paused and then picked it up.

Hello there, she said excitedly. Hello!

Well hello, he said.

He smiled.

How lovely to hear your voice.

George how are you, how are you settling in – you are there now, right?

Yes, all fine, all settled in. They've given me a flat for a while, just… looking around the place.

Well I've heard it's a beautiful city. Is the festival on? No, that's not right is it? When is that on? How's the gallery?

He heard noises in the distance: a child asking for something. It was his nephew, Angus.

Ursula's voice grew more faint. Yes, yes, it's on the table, she said to her son. Two hands, please. Sorry George, Angus is trying to cover himself in juice.

How is the little man?

Newhouse was fond of the boy. He had red hair like his father, Hamish, a big Canadian with a low voice. Hamish was an architect who preferred to sail.

He is good, good: of course he's making friends at nursery, although every week brings a new cold or virus or what-have-you. He's miserable at the moment with some kind of lurgee. Angus – no.

Oh dear, poor guy. But he should be inoculated against whatever the world will throw at him.

Yes, that's what they say, But they don't have to deal with a face full of snot and runny nappies. And you? Are you OK?

Newhouse looked around the white room.

Wait a minute – I've messed up the time difference

haven't I? I'm so sorry, she said. Its tea time here.

No, no… Newhouse said. He couldn't think of what to say.

I have haven't I. Oh God. It must be what, two in the morning? Have you met up with Rudi yet?

Yes, he's in good form, Newhouse said. I had some kind of orientation thing today but he whisked me away to the pub and spared me the paperwork, the log-on nonsense, all that faffing.

You're not big on the faffing are you, Ursula said. It's super for you that the old goat is there. Are he and Martha still…?

Yes, Newhouse said. But things move fast with the German, as you know. Who knows what he is up to.

He's a one off, she said.

There was a silence, and on the line Newhouse heard clicking and a low whine.

He suddenly wished his sister was nearby.

He had not seen her since Ruth's funeral. She had come to him when he was in Rudi's car, curled on the back seat. She had opened the door, and sat down, and stroked his hair as he rested it in her lap. She had held his hand and they had stayed together, in silence, as the congregation gathered.

You sound tired. Are you eating? she asked.

They were both adopted. The love of their parents, now both long dead, had expressed itself in expensive schooling and large quantities of food.

No, not really, he said. But much better, much better, he lied. Better than before.

Good, good, she said. And what about what the doctor said.

Which doctor?

George, the doctor.

Oh you really mean the Witch Doctor.

Ursula clicked her tongue. He imagined her face at the other end of the world: rolling her blue eyes, tilting her head.

Come on now.

He lied again.

Yes, yes, I am still taking the medication, if that's what you mean. It makes me feel sluggish and dehydrated if you really want to know. But I press on.

Well, I don't know much about these things but it seems to be working, she said. And it's better than the alternative.

Well maybe so, he said.

Ursula, he added, is this a nice call to welcome me to my new home or another one of your interventions?

She laughed.

Is Hamish about to break down my door again?

No, we've done that too many times already George. It's awful actually, Hamish has done something to his hip. He did something with the wrong rope, he told me quite miserably this morning. So it's all bit stressy here: he's got this big project in Hong Kong and you know... hang it all.

Poor lamb, Newhouse said. Sounds agonising. You never want to go and yank the wrong chain.

No.

Do yourself a mischief.

Well quite. Look, I better go, she said, suddenly urgent. Angus is exploring the kitchen utensils.

Say hello to the boy from me, he said. He meant it. He could imagine the boy's soft doughy face.

I will. And look – what I meant to say was: good luck with it all, but please, please take it easy. Ease yourself into the job. Don't go at things hell for leather like you...

...I'm not going to, believe me...

…and make sure you spend time with friends, eat well…

I will eat like a prince.

Ok, Ok. I know I sound like mother.

No, you're not annoying me.

Well, I am glad you still have your sense of humour.

Actually, lately I seem to have mislaid it.

Oh George.

The clicking and the whine returned.

We all love you, she said softly.

He mumbled something. He knew he was inadequate.

You know my dreams, she said.

Yes. Vivid dreams.

You are in them still.

I suppose that is good, he said. I am glad I am vivid somewhere, if not here.

And if it doesn't work out for you George, you come here and stay with me. With us. Angus would love to see his Uncle again.

They said goodbye, and as she did, a child's high voice said something about a dog under the kitchen table.

Goodbye George.

Night night, he found himself saying.

He looked at his phone. It told him the call was over.

His sister's voice rang in his head for a short time, and then she was gone.

NEW YORK

He had been warm then. He smelled her perfume, her skin and hair. He held Ruth and she held him. Long fingers around his ribs, long fingers on the slant of his buttocks. They were small and snug on the roof, safe in each other's arms, with each other's bodies.

They both stood, a little drunk. He saw squat water towers with conical roofs, and television dishes on glinting lofts, the parallel lines of steep-sided high rises, the beads of yellow taxis drawn on strings through the humming, narrow squares of streets. He saw the Hudson shiver under the red sun, and heard the party below, a shaking attic space, an artist's studio humming with students, pressmen, marketing girls, PR fixers, academics, curators, and gallery directors. Music thumped through the roof. People were laughing. People spoke in a rumbling soup of chatter, of bass and treble, a rubble of alto and contralto. A girl screamed, a man cackled. A sea bird flapped and wheeled in the fathom of space between their perch and the next Chelsea high rise. White like a crooked arm, it swooned and swooped, down into a splatter of green - the trees and plants that burst from an abandoned railway line. They were in New York to meet her publisher. That morning, she had been writing and he wanted to see the self-portrait again. Through light rain he had walked from the underground on Park to see it, solemn in the Dutch rooms of the Metropolitan Museum.

There was his face; Van Doelenstraat – sullen and brooding between Rembrandt and de Hoogh. He had seen copies and photographs of the painting before, but not the real thing: the rough brush work of the edges, the thick ticks of white light in his eyes, the blackness of the black, shapeless background. Dr Martinu's catalogue notes, published twenty years ago, said the painter had depicted himself in a dark room. Newhouse shook his head, as he took a step back, amid the murmuring tourists, the chattering coach parties. Van Doelenstraat's head and neck, those roughly painted shoulders, hung in a black vault. No room was there, no place or space. The blackness had been worked on, painted and re-painted: the blackness had tone and texture, but no shape. It seemed to bulge and warp as Newhouse moved his eyes around its frame.

This was the man who had painted The Blue Horse. There was the Dutchman's long face, the whiskerless skin. His eyes as blue as a twist of icewater. He stood and looked at the portrait for a long time. Eventually, he struggled to see anything. Afterwards, rushing to meet Ruth, he had walked through Central Park, feeling sick. The painting told nothing of itself.

What a place, she said, looking out over the thrumming city. Sirens sounded. Boats cut through water, and cars moved up and down. Music grinded below them.

They had gone to a party at a Chelsea gallery. Newhouse had known the gallery owner from long ago. He didn't seem to be there. Dozens of people he did not know had welcomed Ruth and him in.

After a short time, she wanted to go out onto the roof.

Ignore those tossers down there, he said.

I don't know, they're funny. They take everything they do so seriously. When really…

She suddenly laughed.

Why did you ask that guy about his coat? Did you offer to buy it? You shouldn't be so rude. I wish you wouldn't do things like that.

He smiled.

He was a little unnerved, wasn't he, he said. I do that when I hate someone.

George, come on. He was just a silly boy. What was his name?

He kissed her.

You're right, he said. He was harmless.

The music got louder. A glass smashed.

It's loosening up down there now, he said. He moved his hands up her body.

She murmured and gently shook her head.

George, she said.

What?

The whole world can see.

No one can see us here, he said. No one in the world.

He began to kiss her neck firmly and she pulled away.

No, no. I said no, she said. She stood away and put her hands on the concrete of the ledge.

OK, OK.

Let's go, she said. I have a lot of work to do and this meeting with…

…yes, yes.

You don't know anyone here anyway, love, she said softly. It's a little bit of a waste of time.

It's a nice view, he said suddenly. He pointed vaguely at the skyscrapers.

She looked at him. She slightly shook her head.

Sometimes George I think that, despite all appearances, you might just be a big dumbo.

I am, he said.

I married you on false pretenses.

My pretenses have always been pretty obvious.

Evidently. She put one hand briefly to her neck.

But it is a nice view, isn't it?

Yes it is darling. You do wear your pretensions lightly, she said. That's a triumph of sorts.

Unlike yours, I suppose.

Mine are hard earned, unlike yours, Trust Fund.

Oh really. That's a low blow.

She moved to him and kissed him on the forehead before picking up her bag.

Come on, dumbo.

Ok dear, he said.

THE WIDOWER

A man in a room, working. Painting.

This was how he wanted to capture her. Her sleek sides, her ferocity.

Outside, water lapped and clapped against the red bricks. A rope was pulled on iron wheels. He looked at what he had done: the curve of her hips, the spread of her lips. Power in her legs, and the turn of her face. Her half-bared teeth, her eyes, her ears, and the shadow of her warmth. He put the brush down. He put his palette down. He wiped the blue from his fingers, from his thin wrist.

He would never see her again. Not in this time, or in any place. Only there, she would live, this new silhouette cut from the night, kicking with power on the back of the empty hand.

Framed. Restrained.

Bound by the boundaries of wood and gilt, the pentagram points of nail, board, hair, varnish and paint.

EIGHT

Hayley's friend was older than Newhouse and had short-clipped, dyed red hair. She was called Linda. Hayley had left to meet her boyfriend. Together they had seen the old town, the new town, the National Gallery, the monuments and the castle. It had rained and they had gone into a pub. Linda stood at the bar as Newhouse sat in a red leather seat.

She came back to the table with a bottle of beer and a gin and tonic. She sat down and smiled.

Terrible weather, she said brightly. She had square, even teeth and a long face. She had lean limbs and black clothes.

Terrible, he said. Thanks for the beer.

They clinked glasses. He took a swig. A sliver of lime brushed against his lips.

Sooooo, she said, lengthily. What do you think of your new home?

Where?

Edinburgh, she said.

Oh, it seems like a great city, he said. White slime on his tongue.

He was lying. That day it had seemed a cold city, with its heart long removed. Beautiful but brittle, a cluster of opalescent uninhabited seashells.

It will grow on you. You know, when I first saw you, I thought you looked a little like that man off the telly, Linda said, looking at her drink.

Oh really? he said. He wondered whether he should finish his drink and go home, lie on his bed, and fall asleep. He could call his sister.

Maybe one of those hospital dramas. Is that a stupid thing to say?

He laughed and she smiled. She looked at him sideways. She moved her hips on the seat. She took a sip from her drink. Newhouse could smell her perfume, dry and alpine. She had a large mole on her neck.

No, no hospital dramas, he said. I wish my life was that dramatic.

She smiled. They talked. He got a round of drinks, a beer for him and a gin and tonic for her.

The air began to move and vibrate, the colours around him deepened and felt heavy and bright. More people came into the bar. Rain poured in tattered waves down the gold-stencilled windows.

Linda worked for a bank. She seemed to be single, had no ring on her hand. She liked drama and theatres, liked going to see stand-up comics. She loved the annual festival in the city. She said she did not know much about art. Newhouse said he didn't either. She asked him who the greatest artist of all time was. He said The Beatles. She said, no, who is the greatest painter.

Well if you mean the greatest painter, he said, rubbing a finger around the green lips of his bottle, then there might be a tie between three.

Who? she said. She looked deliberately and hard into his eyes.

Light broke around him. It splintered off beer glasses and shot glasses, off brass and tabletops, off spectacles and ear rings, off makeup and shined shoes, belt buckles and wedding rings.

Linda pulled at her black square-necked top and he saw a sliver of white flesh on her hip.

Let's go, he said, putting his bottle down.

Go where? she said.

Let's go, he said, feeling dizzy. To another bar.

She smiled.

And I will tell you who the three greatest painters of all time are.

You will have to promise more than that, she said.

I don't promise anything, he said, grabbing his coat.

Well let's see, she said, and smiled her side-eyed smile. She led the way from the pub, he followed her, unsteady and drunk.

They had more drinks in another pub, and, as they left, suddenly arm in arm, they walked damply into rain and a darkening night.

Rembrandt, Velasquez, Vermeer, Picasso, he said, her warmth and scent drawing him to her.

That's four.

And I forget Pieter Van Doelenstraat, he said, drunkly.

She hailed a taxi and made for it.

You've made that name up, she said, and beckoned him with a hooked hand.

I wish I had.

He watched her climb, scatter-legged into the black taxi. The city was drenched in the rain. Clouds soaked above them.

He stood on the road's edge and felt suddenly as if he was going to cry.

She put her head out of the door and smiled.

He made for the taxi and got in. The seat was hard. He put his head in his hands, growled something to himself, and then wiped his hands back through his hair.

She covered his face in hers, her hot gin breath on his,

her hard lips on his, her tongue hot and pressing against his tongue. His right hand moved to her breast, and felt its warmth, its hard nipple, buttoned under the black cotton.

In the heat of the kiss, he felt wretched. But she was warm and her lips tasted of lemon. The ghost of an emotion rose and then left his mind. The taxi moved through the night, and took Newhouse and Linda with it.

Now it was morning. He was somewhere warm. Newhouse rolled on his side.

He felt his naked legs, a wetness in his crotch.

Oh god, he said. He pulled the duvet over himself and fell into sleep.

He woke again and Linda sat in a blue towel robe sat with two cups of suntan-brown tea.

Morning, fucker, she said.

He wondered how to respond, through his fog. He reached for the tea and sat up. His head swirled. He almost gagged.

Morning, he said, as she passed him a cup.

They sat in silence and sipped tea. Her legs were long. Her toes had cracked painted nails.

How are you feeling, she asked.

I feel I've been kicked down a flight of stairs, he said.

You nearly were, she said.

He looked at her. She gave him a look he did not understand.

I will be an adult about this, she said. If you will be. By the way, you look fucking awful. Feel free to use the shower.

I don't know...

I will be nice here. I'm going to be charitable and hope you were just not yourself last night, she said.

No, he said.

I'm sure you wouldn't have said those things otherwise. You don't seem like a loony. In fact Hayley said you were a gentleman.

I'm not a loony.

You were beside yourself, really, she said. I had been enjoying the night until then.

I don't know what that means, he said. He had an image of himself, sitting by himself.

OK well, she said, and smiled. To be honest, this whole debacle is a nice reminder for me not to act like a teenager any more. The craic was fun though, George. I will remember your joke about the nuns.

Oh yes, he nodded, and sipped more tea. He could not remember anything about the nuns.

Look, Linda, he said, trying to muster some depth to his voice, I think it's clear I drank far too much last night.

No kidding.

...I can't really remember much...

She sighed and after a time, she spoke.

I think, really, that's probably for the best George. Even if I'm not sure I believe it. But, you know. Don't worry. Don't worry. You were clearly... impaired. But I am sore this morning.

Oh... sorry, he said. He looked at her. A car started outside. He felt a ball of mucus in his throat.

Getting you out of the bathroom and into here nearly fucking killed me, she said, and stood up.

My back's killing me. Look, have a sleep because I have some things to do. Then I have to get going, she said.

She began to leave the room. She stopped at the door, and her cheeks reddened, her eyes narrowed.

Next time you are in this kind of situation, George, please… I don't know how to say this – just have some respect.

Right.

And if you are married, just say so, she said.

I…

Anyone else might call you a fucking wanker, she said.

She stood for a moment, and then left the room.

He sat for a while in the bed, the walls and ceiling slightly moving around his heavy head. He began to feel nauseous.

He felt the wetness in his groin again. He looked down at his crotch. He had come in his sleep.

For fuck's sake, he said. And pulled the duvet over his head.

Later, he walked home. There were cyclists on the park paths. The sun glinted on the coloured leaves. The grass was frosted, the city seemed asleep.

He had left Linda's house, and she had closed the door. He had walked down three flights of stone steps he did not remember climbing. He stepped over a pool of sick by the heavy red front door, and out into a wide street full of high tenements.

Crags and peaks of a towering hill loomed over the city. He felt suddenly thirsty.

He walked past the park, and past the tall concrete university buildings, and into a café. Newhouse ordered a pot of tea and a bacon roll.

He put his head in his hands. He thought of Ruth. The way he had traced lines with his finger on her long white back, the furrow of her buttocks, the soft whiteness of her legs.

A waiter brought the tea and the food and he drank the

tea and ate the bacon.

He remembered something from the night before. His shoulders quivered. He felt hot and cold.

This is what shame feels like, Newhouse thought.

Newhouse wanted to go back to his flat and sleep and shower, and then go to the gallery, even on this cold Sunday, and sink into the world of his work.

NINE

Newhouse was nearly at the flat when his mobile phone started buzzing in his pocket. It was Martinu.

George? Dr Martinu was shouting. There was static and whooshing. The sea was in his ear. His voice cut out. Silence. The call was over.

God's sake, Newhouse said.

The phone rang again. He put it to his ear.

George? Martinu yelled. Newhouse could hear waves and sea birds.

Doctor, Newhouse said, how are you?

George. Fine. How are you? The Dutch and Flemish survey? Colebrook lunched you yet?

He's away Doctor, and it's all quite satisfactory. Lovely city.

They spoke about Edinburgh for a while. Martinu reminded Newhouse he would need to get a flat of his own. He told him to talk to the curators at Castle House.

Call me Hans, Martinu said.

Look, George, do you have the papers on the Blue Horse to hand?

No, not just right now, I'm just walking home.

Ok, ok, Martinu said. When you do could you find me the name of that dealer from Denmark, the 1890 reference.

Ah now, Hans, that was… Langebeck.

Langebeck had been a dealer of Dutch and Scandinavian art, based in the north of England.

He had noted the sale from Langebeck of A Blue Horse by a V. Doelenstraat to a Mr Halfhouse, a dealer in

London in 1890. Mr Halfhouse had never been traced. He may have worked for Henry & Dee. The next emergence of The Blue Horse was in 1945, when it was listed as one of the works in Carinhall, the hunting lodge and home of Herman Goering, the Nazi leader. It then disappeared again.

I'm in Greece now, Martinu yelled.

Very nice, Doctor, Newhouse said. Why did you need Langebeck?

I was in the archives of the Academia, Venice, looking for something else. There was a mention by Adriano Zaraceno, Venetian, of meeting a Michael Langebeck in 1902. I thought 1890 was Langebeck. Yes. I knew it.

Yes, Langebeck died in, what, 1913?

Yes, Martinu said, anyway, in this ledger, it lists the works he was showing Zaraceno in 1902. A Rembrandt sketch, some minor Dutch works, a self-portrait by Kobke, a lovely piece I have seen in Denmark, really beautiful, and also, it says 'Shadow of a Horse, by V. Doelnstraat'

Really? Newhouse said. 1902?

March 1902.

Newhouse stood still.

Shadow of a Horse? That sounds like a new work, a different piece.

It could be our Blue Horse, too.

Hans, *Shadow of a Horse?* That sounds like a different work, a new work. Interesting, though, but...

No, no no, George. The Blue Horse is an exceptional title, an anomalous title, a very odd title, but perhaps, in all possibility, that was not its title at all. *Shadow of a Horse* sounds better, more likely, to me. The title of a study, an academic work. And it may prefigure the Absent Period.

Just think, George. It's the painting of a shadow. *Room with Chair:* that is all shadow, *Table with Knives,* the Brussels *Shutters*, they are all shadow. And *The Closed Shutters* was owned by Langebeck.

I'm not sure, Hans, Newhouse said. The dates don't work. It's 12 years out, Hans. He'd sold on to Halfhouse by then.

Well, they might do, Martinu said, they might do. He sounded vague and distracted.

How?

I will write to you. This is costing money, these international calls, he said, sounding annoyed.

Have you heard about the Hermitage, he said.

No, what about it?

The robbery, the theft.

At the Hermitage? St Petersburg?

Yes, yes, Martinu said. What other Hermitage is there George? From their archives, from their stores. A member of staff, beaten up. We don't know what was taken yet, though. You know how they can be.

No, I hadn't heard. That's terrible, Newhouse said.

It might be a boon of a kind, in the long term, Martinu said. Not for the poor night watchman, though. He's missing his eyes.

How? How could it be a boon?

There was silence. Newhouse pressed the phone closer to his ear.

Hello, Hans? Where are you? Newhouse said.

There was a crackle and sudden wind of fractured static.

Then the voice returned.

Zaraceno, the man, he didn't buy it, Martinu shouted.

The signal was fading.

No?

No, he noted it down, said it was a 'remarkable obscured work' but didn't purchase it. He put a deposit down for it, but died before he could buy it. Langebeck kept the deposit and, probably, the Shadow.

Newhouse thought; it was a different painting. The Blue Horse was in Halfhouse's possession by 1902.

I will write, Martinu said. I better go. Find a nice place to live. I am back in a week or so. Interesting, though George, it's all interesting. I have copied the Zaraceno ledger – you will see George. I need ice cream.

Ok, Hans, enjoy Greece.

George, Martinu said faintly.

Yes? Newhouse was shouting now.

Where was Doelenstraat born? Netherlands?

It's always been assumed, Newhouse bellowed.

Assumed, yes, I assumed that, the echoing voice whispered. There was a shrill whine. Then the line went dead.

Newhouse found himself breathing heavily. He was standing in front of a bar. He moved in the direction of his flat, then took a step back, and walked into the pub.

TEN

He wanted to be near the sea. The taxi dropped him at the bottom of a long road that ended in the docks. It was early morning. He was drunk. There were warehouses and cranes. Large brick buildings and one dark ship, still in the water. The taxi drove off and he realised he was cold. He stood and stared at the ground. Newhouse swayed. He looked up and streetlights glowed in strings of fuzz left and right. He turned around. There was a small square with old buildings and a fountain. The roads were empty. He wanted to see the sea. He saw a narrow street beside a warehouse. He walked into it. Lights swayed and the sky swilled. His feet clattered, his coat whispering around his heels. His stomach shook. He walked through darkness, high walls around him, the sky lead above him, closing down like a lid. The fence came quickly and he put a hand out and felt ice cold on his fingers. It was a dead end. A metal fence rose before him, its flattened post tips bent and flayed. A bare dock lay beyond it, a slab of concrete draped over the sea. Newhouse smelled salty swill and turgid pools. Oil slicks and engines. A path of bubbled concrete. A field of empty containers with open square mouths. The world was dark.

He was spent. He sat down, his back to the fence. He checked his pocket: his wallet was there. His phone, switched off. His coat was caught under him, his legs stretched out. He looked down the lane and crossed his arms on his chest. The city rose from the sea to the mountain, the dull-eyed castle. Its rock streets and icy stones lay like a hard scab over something raw and weeping.

His eyes were filled with tears. He had drunk and drunk. A volume of liquid in his stomach, swilling and bubbling. A football match had been on, and he had watched it. Little men in green and blue kicking, scampering and running. He had flicked through discarded newspapers and magazines. Features on new kitchens, on recipes, on cooks and interior furnishings. A small article about a contemporary artist called Brick.

He had drunk to the end of the night, until the lights fuzzed and streaked, and had staggered to a taxi rank. He must have eaten something on the way, his coat was stained with fat and grease, his fingers were slippery. He had dropped his phone and kicked it along the street. He had put money in a busker's hat. He had cried.

He lay in the deserted lane near the dead dock. He stared down the tunnel of darkness to the fountain square. He closed his eyes.

Their flat had been modern, a semi-circle of rooms in an old building. There were paintings in the living room. A piano in another. A wall of books, which she had arranged alphabetically, by subject matter, by the colour of their spines. Their bed had been big, low to the floor. Herbs in the kitchen, and flowers on the terrace. Brown small bricks in the wall, and small Chinese bowls on the fireplace. She would store pasta shells, twists and rice in glass jars, sealed with rubber and clipped shut with silvery clasps. She would drink tea and stir in small piles of fine sugar. She would move hair back from her face with her fingers when reading. Her eyes would dart from left to right, left to right.

She had little black notebooks for her writing. She would write in pencil in them. Pages and pages of words. She would count the beats of her verse with a finger in the air, her eyes closed.

Her heart would be hot and beating in the night. He would lie behind her, his arms around her breasts, holding her ribs and her innards. His legs on her legs, her feet on his feet. He would watch the fine hair on her lips shake as she breathed.

One day she watched birds gather on the yard.

They pecked at a sock of seeds she had hung from a branch. Her eyes wet and brown, widening and closing, her legs pulled up to her chest, her feet bare, her toenails painted pink.

The cold spread into his bones. The night would never end. The earth had been emptied.

He stared at something moving in the square. It was not a person and it was not a car. A heavy shadow, rolling on waves of its own shadow. Clattering and snorting. Something massive and fleeting, moving among the cars and flagstones, the black windows and closed doorways. It rippled and fled.

And before his head nodded to his chest, he thought he saw something clearly: a powerful animal was moving through the shadows of the dock.

BEACON HILL

They were tired from travel, and dozy in the heat. The honeymoon begun in San Francisco, continued in Seattle, and now at its heart, ten days on this Canadian island. They had a day to themselves: Ursula would come and meet them tomorrow.

My father, she said, thought of heaven as this earth, but perfected. No work, no illness, no disease.

No earthquakes or tidal waves, he said.

No, she said. Just life on earth with none of its…with abundance and peace and…

No death. No cancers.

No more dying, she said. No scarcity.

She was wearing a new green shirt.

They had rushed around a clothes store, buying shorts and T-shirts, light trousers and dark glasses as the heat wave continued. Their fleeces and woollen hats remained in their cases.

She rolled some ham and put it in her mouth.

The light was clear on the grass and high trees. The light was liquid on the soft running brook and over the pale stone of the bridges. Pure light with no clouds, glinting on swings and roundabouts, on sleeping heads of hair, on parked cars around the undulating green glades of Beacon Hill Park.

Unseasonal sun was hot on their arms as they sat at a picnic table. White cheese hard in the crumbling fresh bread, and light tumbling around the plastic wraps on salad and hams. They drank wine from a flask and listened to the park alive around them, the children playing, the low baying of goats and kids in a petting zoo behind the stand of high trees.

So beautiful here, she said. My lord.

She looked over the banks of flowers, the tall firs and trees, over to where the sun flashed on low roofs and the masts of white boats in the harbour.

Later, on Willow Beach, the breakers softly broke on the wet sand, and in a hazy distance, a mountain range white with ice and snow rose against the blue sky. Mount Baker loomed, white and jagged, massive in the distance. A sailing boat cut through the limpid waters.

So what are you thinking about it, she said.

He did not know how to disappoint her.

I think, you know. I am not sure, he said. I have to be honest. I am just not sure. It's too soon. Let's have some time by ourselves.

She looked down at her drink. She shifted her feet in the sand. Sand fell from her knees.

Well, she said. She looked out to the sea. That's you. That's you. That's all you isn't it.

Her hand shook a little.

We don't have much time, George.

I know.

It's not something we can just put off forever. You know how I feel about it.

I know, I know, he said. He wanted to change the subject.

You knew how I felt about it, she said.

She stood up quickly, brushed herself down, and walked down the beach, carrying her shoes in her hand. She moved her sunglasses from her hat to her eyes.

He watched her walk for a while and then stood up.

Accounting for another person, he thought. Thinking of another person.

As he walked down the beach, breaking into a jog to catch up with Ruth, he thought of the empty rooms, the silent nights. The cold turnings in empty beds, and the white empty kitchen in the middle of the night.

He reached her and put a hand on her shoulder.

She turned to him, her cheeks wet.

I'm sorry, he said.

That's not enough.

ELEVEN

He was at an exhibition opening with Rudi.

Get to meet new people, Rudi had said. Get to know the scene.

The rooms were almost empty, men and women in dark suits walked silently around the large white spaces. There were waiting staff in black and white, holding trays of champagne, and a small, silent bar was serving gin and tonics, vodka, whisky. A small girl with blue eyes walked, terrified, through the rooms with a plate of tiny red meatballs on sticks.

Rudi said something rude under his breath in German and then congratulated the artist, a young man with a bowl haircut, and shook his hand. The artist shook Rudi's hand and thanked him for supporting the gallery's purchase of his work. The PG had bought one of the paintings, called *Brodsky's Take On Auden 1939* for several thousand pounds.

Oh don't thank me, Rudi said, thank Mr Newhouse here, our new whizz kid up from London.

Thank you, the bowl headed man said, to Newhouse.

Oh of course, Newhouse said uncertainly. He realised he had nothing to say. He could not remember ever seeing the artist's work before.

I thought the Masters were more your thing, the bowl-headed man said.

Oh they are, they are, Newhouse said, nodding. But you are on the acquisitions committee, Rudi said loudly. I am on the acquisitions committee, Newhouse said to the artist, nodding and smiling. A ribbon of feedback slid through the room.

The artist's agent was standing on a box holding a microphone, and began to make a speech. The room, now filling up with silent people, changed as they gathered around the agent on the box.

The artist, Newhouse suddenly noticed, was standing next to a small blonde woman in a silvery dress. Her fingers were thin and small, her fingernails copper and gold. He looked at her as the agent began to chunter.

On this day, of all days, the agent said.

Outside the city was drenched in darkness, the street lamps fuzzed and smeared. The train station roared and rumbled. Newhouse looked out the window in the night.

The room started clapping, there was some cheering.

Hear, hear, Rudi was bellowing.

The silver girl was blushing and looking at her feet. Ruth used to hate these evenings, the small talk and the smart clothes.

Let's get drunk somewhere, he whispered into Rudi's ear.

You already are, Rudi said.

Births, Deaths and Marriages

Ruth Therese Newhouse O'Reilly, poet, born 7 October 1970, died 16 May 2007. Born in Dublin, but raised and educated in London, Ruth O'Reilly was an academic and writer who was emerging as a poet of great skill and quiet power before her untimely death at the age of 36. Her poems, once thought of as 'deft, funny, wise, witty' – had become deeper, longer, more complex and ultimately weightier in recent years. Latterly inspired by the depiction of women in Biblical and apocryphal works, her verse was marked by pellucid description and stark honesty as well as keen scholarship and learning. Her long-form verse 'Mary, Mary, and The Others With Them' was recently published in the London Review of Books, and was the title poem of her last collection.

Her early poem concerning the pain of a mother watching her son die, 'And His Eyes', has been much anthologized. She relished teaching others in creative writing schools in universities across the UK, and in 2001 had been writer in residence at the National Gallery in London.

It was there she met her future husband, curator George Newhouse. She was working on her first novel, The Diary of Lies, when she fell ill. She leaves her husband, George, her three brothers and two sisters and her many bereft friends.

Fr. John-Joseph O'Reilly.

TWELVE

Newhouse was working when Rudi knocked and walked in. He sat heavily in a chair.

Newhouse looked at him.

There's another party tonight, be good if you could come, a drinks thing, Rudi said.

Really? Why should I go to another party?

Yes, at Melcombes, the auctioneers, Rudi said, eyes closed, stretching his legs out. He was wearing all cord, a cord suit, a cord waistcoat, a cord tie.

It's their drinks, they do it every year, celebrate the National Sale.

Nice suit, Newhouse said, and looked back to his screen.

Rudi hurrumphed.

The Sale is rather good, he went on. The usual suspects though: Colourists, Glasgow Boys.

Newhouse was trying not to listen. He was sending a series of identical introductory emails to contacts, colleagues, old colleagues, old contacts, curators, a few contemporary artists, gallery owners, to the head of marketing at the galleries, who he hadn't yet met, introducing himself, his new email, his direct line, his mobile phone. He had written to Gilda in Holland, asking for the old press reviews of the Van Doelenstraat exhibition, which he had lost.

Sun glinted on the square pond outside. A young couple wandered slowly around its edges. He saw the flash of flesh on the girl's chest, her freckled arms, her thin hips.

Well I am going and I think you should too, Rudi said.

Well why? Newhouse said. He wanted a quiet night. He wanted to buy a television, watch TV, eat food, and sleep. He wanted to go through his clothes. He wanted peace around him, cleanliness, order.

Well there will be a lot of women there, Rudi said, and Newhouse sighed. There are also collectors, curators, owners, and people you need to be nice to.

Be nice to, Newhouse said.

It doesn't hurt to be nice George, Rudi said, his hands behind his head.

It depends how high your pain tolerance is.

I met a woman at the auctioneers annual drinks last year, Rudi said. We booked a hotel room that night. Some night.

Really, Newhouse said, watching the shadows of clouds on the rippling water outside. He briefly thought of Ruth, her legs bent and fractured under the lights of a cold swimming pool, somewhere, sometime.

She slapped me, wanted to spank me, Rudi said. She did some strange things. She squeezed my balls like they were plums, like they were ripe hanging fruit – my god, my eyes were watering, he said. She worked for an oil company, odd woman, strange female, he said. She rolled my foreskin back.

Jesus Rudi, Newhouse said, and laughed. Outside, the young couple were kissing.

Human history is a catastrophe, Rudi suddenly said. The world is an abbatoir.

Not all of it, Newhouse said.

I go into the mountains. Even there I hear the stags cry. Rudi?

Something I read. And you should read Adorno, George. Human history is catastrophe. Look at capitalism now, it is a constant affront to humanity. Think on that mad woman, squeezing my balls, biting my skin, rolling my penis skin. I hope she is there tonight, George, I hope she is. Read some Adorno, Georgio, read some Eagleton.

I've read everything by him. OK, this party? Newhouse said.

Starts at seven, at the auctioneers, we can go after work, Rudi said, standing. He turned on his heel and left.

Newhouse stared into the window.

An email pinged on his computer. It was from Rudi, next door.

Cheer up, motherfucker, it said.

Later, they had a drink in a pub near the auction house. Rudi was sweating and was drinking whisky.

What we do is so childish, George, he said.

Newhouse was looking at the catalogue for an upcoming exhibition. Hayley had given it to him before he left the office. The cover was badly produced. It had a poor font choice and tiny print. The pages were crammed with small words and pictures. There seemed to be no paragraph breaks. After page 23 all the pictures were in black and white. One of the captions on a landscape by Cuyp just said: *caption here please caption here please.* What a piece of shit, he said quietly. He put it in his blue satchel.

We are so childish, wanting to be entertained by pictures, by shapes and colours and patterns, Rudi said.

Newhouse thought of *Whistlejacket* by Stubbs. A perfect horse. Alive and gleaming.

…and this male obsession we have with meaningless productions, with details and nuances and facts and information. That is all we do, George. Gather useless information. Who cares about this and that and this and that? We do and we write it down. We live in a world inside a world, the galleries and the curators, the collectors and the aficionados, the scholarship and the curatorial insight: no one cares but us.

I'm not sure about that, Newhouse said. For some reason he thought of the blackened pillars outside the galleries, their ribbled sides. He thought of the fishtail pattern on the glass above the front door, the wires and spikes nailed into the stone to prevent birds landing, nesting, and living.

Rudi, I don't know what we are talking about.

Rudi shook his head.

We are not saving anyone's life. We are not researching cancer.

No, we're not. But someone much cleverer than us is, so that's OK. We are free to look at paintings.

Your blue horse, Rudi said, putting his glass down hard on the bar.

What of it, Newhouse said.

I was reminded of it, Rudi said, when Martinu mentioned it.

Dr Martinu called you?

Ja. He is allowed…he said was looking for your articles, for its references. I sent them.

Right, Newhouse said.

Anyhow - I saw another horse painted very blue the other day, looking for something on my exhibition of the hard and Holy penis.

Really, where?

Jesus was all man, he must have wanked, he must

have masturbated, Rudi said, rubbing a finger around the empty glass.

What blue horse? Newhouse said. He put his jacket on.

Over Magdelane, over other female followers, maybe in a white hot jet over the Apostle that he loved.

Jesus Rudi, Newhouse said. What blue horse, are you pissed already?

Not drunk. Just thinking.

Rudi looked at Newhouse. Rudi's head seemed to have grown. It was bloated and puffy.

It's not useful to you. It's Italian. It's in the Sistine chapel.

Tell me?

Cosimo Rosselli. A Fresco, 1480 something. Early 1480s.

Of course, Rudi said, all this Blue Horse stuff was done later, in my own country.

Yes, I know, Newhouse said.

They had been over the case of Franz Marc before. He painted blue horses too. He was killed in the First World War. *Blue Horse I* was in a gallery in Munich.

Rudi walked away. He tripped as he began to leave the pub.

Newhouse followed him.

Newhouse knew the fresco that Rudi had mentioned. It was a Last Supper. There were fine jugs and animals in the foreground: a dog, a cat, teasing each other. The apostles and the saints sat around a semi-circular table, draped in white cloth, their heads glowing with discs of halos. An apostle, possibly Judas, sat with his back to the viewer, draped in black. Above the supper, three large windows showed the world outside. In the far right window, Christ was crucified. A Roman soldier on a blue horse stood below Jesus.

Rudi led the way, and they reached the party. It was being held in an old theatre building on a wide street near the city centre. Brass chandeliers hung from a high ceiling. Newhouse felt dizzy as the main room thronged. There were fat men in black tie, white-faced bankers in lounge suits. PR people laughing loudly.

Ugly people doing ugly things, Rudi muttered. Newhouse nodded.

Rudi began looking for drinks, and Newhouse stood in a corner by a white pillar. He leaned against it.

A tall black-haired lady walked by in a blue dress sparkling with tiny diamonds. Music was playing, a heavy beat, slashing guitar chords. It seemed out of place. Speeches had been made, but they had missed them. A microphone stand stood untended. Seven large paintings stood on easels on a low stage. Newhouse stood on a tiptoe momentarily to look at them. Three Bellany's, two others by Doig – quite beautiful – some work he did not recognise, and a large white, black-splashed cat by Blackadder. Newhouse looked down at his feet. He was jostled. Men in suits stood in small circles, laughing loudly. The roar filled the large room. People made noise to fill the space.

He saw a lake in his head, light ripping across its black water.

Rudi returned with two flutes of champagne. Flights of tiny coppery bubbles rushed vertically and popped. Newhouse drank it quickly.

That's Colebrooke's niece, Rudi said, pointing with his glass towards the stage.

Who?

Colebrooke, fool, our blessed and wise director?

Yes I know, who is his niece?

The lovely Foster, Rudi said. His eyes were glazed.

Foster?

That's her name. Foster Flintergill. I think she's some kind of northern royalty.

How old?

Ich weiss nicht.

I didn't know he had siblings.

He had two. Twins. The brother passed away, I hear. That's her, Rudi nodded. In the blue.

Foster was the dark-haired woman in the blue slash of dress.

Her face was as long and clean as the blade of a sword. Her eyes like black stones.

What does she do?

She works for the auctioneers, down in London, I think. She must be up for the party. Sie ist schon..

Newhouse said nothing.

She is in your area, roughly, Rudi said. Something in Dutch sales. I hear.

I don't know her.

Foster Flintergill, you must have, Jesus George where have you been? Rudi said. She was the star behind that Dutch sale last year. You know?

No, Newhouse said. He had never seen Foster before. Or heard of her.

There's that fucking Pamela from the Infirmary Gallery. I want to see her naked, said Rudi suddenly. He strode off to shout at a small woman standing alone by the door.

Newhouse was accosted by a small man with a large nose and his curve-faced partner. The man was called Cameron and seemed to know about Newhouse.

Ah, the handsome Mr George Isaac Newhouse, he said.

That's right, Newhouse said. He looked around for Rudi.

Mr Newhouse of Durham, the man said grandly. Of Trinity College, of the Courtauld, of, I must add, the Chelsea High Road.

Yes, Newhouse said. He briefly felt like driving his glass into the man's face. He looked down and noticed the man was wearing a kilt.

Cameron's eyes narrowed and he asked Newhouse about a notable self-portrait in the PG, about its contentious date. Newhouse said, with a smile, that the dating was very sound, although a paper published in Germany moved it back by two years.

Cameron's voice pattered and stuttered.

Ah really, ah really, he said. He voice was like rain beating on paper. His mouth opened and shut. A little pink tongue flicked around tiny white teeth. He asked Newhouse about the poorly lit Van Meegeren.

It must be moved, surely it can be moved, I think it should be moved, it's an outrage, really, he said. I've been on to Colebrooke for years about that. He won't listen to me. If it is a Meegeren, of course, if it is, of course you and I know, George, that it may not be at all.

Won't listen, the woman said.

Newhouse nodded and smiled. It should perhaps be moved, he said, but it's not for me to say, I am only just here. Just arrived in the city.

The man closed his eyes and said, I've written a study of Meegeren.

Oh really.

It is too big, in my view, Cameron bellowed.

Far too big, the woman said.

Newhouse looked at her. He could not fix her age. Cameron ignored Newhouse. He talked about the arts council, the government support, the need for more donors, for more bequests, for corporate giving. His partner, who was wearing green felt shoes, stared at Cameron and nodded.

You seem to know a lot about the subject, Mr Campbell, Newhouse said. He turned his head. He saw Foster move out of the room and into the lobby.

Cameron. I am, as you know, on the board of the Public Gallery, Cameron said, and looked hard at Newhouse. I have been for fifteen long years.

Fifteen years, the woman muttered.

Years when we had a very strict rule. Very strict: never hire a curator under the age of 40, Cameron said.

Under the age of 40, the woman said, one of her nostrils blocked with white snot.

They both looked demented.

I must go, Newhouse said.

He reached the lobby. The scent of fresh rain, petrol and flagstones filled the large room. There were four ochre pillars and two stairs leading to the first floor. She was standing by the door, smoking a cigarette. Her shoulder blades clenched, like drawn wings, folded under the flesh.

What do you think of the Doig? she said, facing the dark wet street.

Amber-lit taxis rolled past slowly.

I'm not a fan, a male voice said.

It will be lucky to get 400, 420, she said. We should have got the Brick prints.

Top of the market, Fossy, the male voice said, top of the market.

Newhouse walked to the door. A small round bald man in a black suit was smoking with Foster. Water was dripping from the dome of his head.

George Newhouse, Newhouse said, reaching out a hand. Foster looked at him and smiled. She had a stained filling in one of her upper teeth, a discolouration. The bald man took Newhouse's fingers with a wet, plump hand, said he was terribly sorry but he needed a wee, and trundled inside.

Lovely to meet you, she said, and briefly shook his hand.

My uncle was so glad to get you. The great George Newhouse, she said.

Newhouse smiled. They both stood in the doorframe. He looked out into the night street darkness.

I understand you are a Dutch man too, he said.

I try, I try, she said, and smiled, and took a hard drag from the cigarette. You're 20th century, he said, leaving the sentence hanging.

No, 18th, 19th, she said, and turned to him.

One of her feet left a shoe and she leant against the door. Inside the room still roared with talk and laughter, clinking glass and piped rock music.

Right now I rule the 19th century, she said.

Right, he said.

Did my time at the Van Gogh Museum, Staatliche, she said.

Ok, he said.

But decided to make money. It was more fun. It still is. Melcombes has no serious rivals now.

I heard something like that, he said. He felt a chill from her.

Where? she said.

Oh, somewhere, he said.

It is, she said. I don't have to work to be honest, but what else is there to do? I like the auction trade, and it's a healthy place to be right now. New territories, virgin land. Russia, China, the new blood being pumped into the old body. That's what I'm told to say, anyway.

She laughed. And I am the doctor attaching the catheter.

Indeed, he said. He had found her and now talked to her, and he wanted to go home. It was not far.

So, you are Golden Age? she said. I heard you knew a lot about Van Rijn, Vermeer, Fabritius.

Yes, he said.

You should tell me, what is there to know about Fabritius these days? Isn't that a cold case now?

Well…

Actually. Maybe there is something we can discuss, she said.

Really?

Come inside, she said.

He watched her move inside. He thought about walking out into the street, walking home. Lying in bed. Looking at photographs.

He followed her into the lobby.

Do you know of a Dr Hans Martinu? she said.

Of course, he said, he is…

He needs help finding this blessed painting, she said.

Which?

Have you heard of Pieter Van Doelenstraat, from Zwolle, early 17th century?

Yes, I curated an exhibition of his work two years ago, he said, then regretted offering so much.

Right, OK, she said, nodding.

Well Dr Martinu is a great friend of my father. He has been looking for this work for some time.

Oh yes, he said.

He's asked me to help find it, too. Not sure where to start, but I have put feelers out. There are others, too. Maybe others with more... liquidity. Anyway, Melcombes Europe and Melcombes Asia are looking for it, she said. Melcombes US have looked, come up with nothing.

The Blue Horse, he said.

She looked at him. Her eyes were all black. There were no whites, no iris, no pupils.

Yes, Blue Horse, or something akin to that. She dropped her cigarette on the floor. Do you know about Henry & Dee?

No, who are they? he said. She must know something, he thought.

Right, right, she said.

Anyway, you hear anything about it in your travels, drop me a line, she said. She had a card in her hand. It had the red Melcombes logo on it.

I will, he said.

Your little exhibition, she said, you didn't come across this painting?

No, he said. There were rumours it was in Turkey. I am not sure of the auction markets there. It got complicated.

There is no preparatory sketch, no engraving?

No, sadly not. Not even a written description. Not

really. You will have seen my paper on it, I am sure. Just ledgers and sales books.

No? Ok, she said. Well, she said. He quickly took her card.

Is there a Melcombes in Turkey? he said.

She smiled.

I must get back to the party, she said. I hope you can stay for another drink or two.

I will, he said, and smiled.

She leant forward with her eyes closed.

He kissed one cheek and it tasted of chalk and dust. She moved away, hitching her dress up as she climbed the stairs.

THIRTEEN

He rang in sick.

Well hello, Hayley said, when she heard his voice. She seemed intrigued by something. How are we today, she said.

Not good, he said with a weak voice. I've eaten something terrible. Won't make it in today.

OK, she said. You know you have a meeting at Castle House tomorrow, I've booked tickets.

Yes, yes of course, he said. He did not know.

I will be fine.

Ok, she said. I'll email Carver for you. There is the meeting on the Venice short list on Friday, she said. Robert Hill, the curator will be there.

He woke much later, and made a coffee. He stood at the bare kitchen counter in Ruth's blue towel robe. The kettle steam rose to the underside of the shelves, and hung in bubbles and drips. He thought about Castle House. He realised a long train journey would be OK. He would do some work. He could watch mountains rise and fall.

He wandered back to bed. He stopped and saw an unopened box from London. He opened it, ripping at its brown packing tape. Inside were papers and files, notes on van Doelenstraat.

He found them, with their clear plastic binding, bent at the corner, and went back to bed.

He had not changed the sheets since he moved. The kettle clicked off in the kitchen: he did not remember turning it on. The room was warm and musty.

He found an article, published in the Fine Arts Magazine. It was short and full of holes, he thought. Some of the paragraphs made him cringe. One began: *An effortless pallid shroud of pale, lingering death prevails.*

He read the article again. One of the references had an incorrect date. Martinu had scolded him. Sloppy, unforgivable, he said.

The painting in the article was lovely. The reproduction of *The Sick Bed,* or *Lady with Child,* was clear and clean. It had been dated to 1640 because of papers and other details, but Newhouse wasn't so sure. He looked at the blues. They were dark and lustrous on the drapes. They were a pale wash around the lady's sick eyes. Light and coppery on the tiles, wispy and indistinct on the skirting board. The child's hand on the woman's hand, so beautifully painted. He had looked at those clasped hands so many times. Van Doelenstraat had not over-plumped the boy's hand, it was lean and convincing, the hand of a child grown old too quickly, a firm hand on his mother's sickly fingers. He looked closer. There were blue touches on the lady's eyes.

He looked at the lady, her full lips, her pale, yellow skin, and the drawn drapes around the four-poster bed. The glittering light on the chandelier, the lovingly painted face, her broad cheeks and dark hair, rolled up under a lace cap. The child, turned away from the viewers, grasping her hands. The woman's face, he had written, was a "moving depiction of dejected motherly love." A depiction of sickness and despair, Martinu had said. A painting about the virulence of typhus.

There were few details in the bedroom. There was the bed, a chamber pot partially hidden from view, a pair of sparely painted clogs. But there was a painting on the wall, believed to be a lost Van Doelenstraat, a rare landscape of a boat, perhaps the passenger service between Dordrecht and Rotterdam, Martinu had suggested. It also looked like another painting, one from the Queen's collection, by Aelbert Cuyp.

In his article Newhouse had suggested the child was the same one as in a previous painting, *The Birthday Party*, from 1634, also known as *The Unhappy Child*. But Martinu maintained the dates did not fit, and Casper Loritz, a scholar in Seattle, had also criticised the theory in an American journal.

Newhouse was sure it was the same child. The hair was the same, long and gold-blonde, the nose the same, small and turned up almost into a snub, the white nightshirt he was wearing had a hem stitch very similar to the crying child in *The Birthday Party*. But, Martinu had said, artists often used the same props, the same clothes, as Newhouse well knew.

You are trying to construct a narrative that is not there, Martinu had said. You are trying to weave a story from images that are random and isolated, painted years apart, with different models, with different paints and surfaces.

There is no story, Martinu had said, just separate images. Snapshots of times that may not be true, probably are not even true, probably pure flowers of the imagination, nothing to do with the real world, nothing but memories and ghosts and imaginings. Stop the false narratives, and focus, focus, focus on the details, George, he had said. You are wandering off, you are losing focus. Newhouse lay in bed and looked at the magazine, and dropped it beside the bed. The black flowers of the mind grew. Tendrils trailed in the cracks.

Light dimmed in the window. The room went dark.

He curled up in bed, pulled the duvet over his body. He was alone.

He closed his eyes tight, and saw his own eyes, flashing black on the back of his eyelids. He squeezed his eyes, and they flashed again. Black eyes, snapping open and shut.

He opened them again and reached for the magazine. He looked at the painting, the woman's eyes. He looked again.

Newhouse stepped out of bed, the hairs on his legs on end, cold in the messy room. He opened his brown leather bag, searched for something. Pens and notes and fluff on his stumbling fingers. He found what he was looking for, heavy in his fingers. He took the magnifying glass and looked at the magazine again. He looked through the glass, its brass handle cold and weighted in his hand. In the eyes of the dying woman, the blue flecks of light were suddenly large in the glass. He held it closer, the tiny dots of ink detaching from each other, becoming themselves, separate and circular on the creamy smooth white paper. He held the glass back. There it was, in the woman's left eye. The eye glassy and staring, ignoring her son, holding her hand beside her. The blue flecks of paint, five or six strokes at the most – tiny strokes, of a one-hair brush. A horsehair brush. The tiny strokes, blue highlights of a candle-sparkled eyeball. And the thin, perfectly painted head of a horse, its eye black in the slashes of paint. He put the glass down and looked with his naked eye. A beautiful painted eye, as human as his own. The highlight of light was tiny. Up close, it was the head of a horse.

For God's sake, he said, and threw the magazine across the room.

'MY DARLING–'

In dozy half sleep, she had moved her hand on her chest. Light fingers on his skin, on his neck, moving slowly, then lightly placed on his neck. Their bodies were warm and touching, warm and breathing together.

The night before, he had stood near the back of the bookshop. People sat on chairs, stood at the eaves, holding small glasses of wine. Ruth in a new dress, her eyes silver with makeup, reading poems to the human silence, to the low throb of the air-conditioned basement. Her voice was low and soft, and the heads on the back rows were leaning in. In the low light, her face looked new, the same but remade. Between each poem, the light slap of hands clapping rustled the room.

Afterwards, he sat on a step while she signed books. They had quietly lined up. A bearded youth. Two young female students. A mother with a baby in a sling, heavy-headed, past its bedtime. A man with grey vertical strands of hair.

She looked to him and smiled. He nodded to her from the step.

And that morning, as the light splashed and pooled around them, he had kissed her head. He was lightly hungover. He could smell wine on her, and the sweetness of her perfume.

So good last night, so proud of you, he had said at last.

Oh darling, she said sleepily, her eyes closed. Her head nestled snug in the crook of his naked arm.

And he had kissed her forehead, her ear, and then,

quickly, her cheek, her temple, then, his eyes closed, his lips puckered, his own arm.

Ah, he said.

Oh, he said.

She giggled. A shiver in her throat and chest.

Haha, he said. The wetness of his lips glistened on his forearm.

George, she said. Her eyes were closed.

Yes.

Did you just kiss yourself? Her voice was low and quiet.

I may have.

She giggled again.

He laughed. She laughed.

There was a silence, after a time.

I never thought I would actually catch you kissing yourself, she said, and smiled.

I don't do it as often as you would think, he said.

She propped herself up on one elbow. She looked at his crumpled face, his distraught hair. She was smiling.

I don't believe you.

FOURTEEN

Ayton-Wright was the curator of the small contemporary art wing of the Public Gallery. Newhouse saw him in the lobby, talking excitedly to Rudi and Carver, who looked nervous.

Ah George, Rudi bellowed. You know a lot about wind.

I'm sorry?

Carver shot a quick look at Newhouse and ran his hands through his thinning hair.

Haha. Nice to meet you Newhouse, Ayton-Wright said. He was small and had not shaved.

Good to have you around.

What is happening here? Newhouse asked. He had just had a coffee in the café. He was avoiding work. He was carrying a brown paper file with nothing in it.

The blowers suck, Rudi said.

Carver sighed.

We do have inflation problems, he said.

For Colossus, Ayton-Wright said.

Right.

Indeed, Carver said. He sucked his teeth. He seemed to find everything too tedious for words.

Colossus is the new park installation. By Marsipal & Wayde. Once again we have technical issues.

It's an inflatable maze, Rudi said. For the kiddi-winks.

It is for all our visitors, Rudolf. And yes, it takes a little more effort to stage than hanging a picture on a nail, Carver said.

I think this proves the universe is not neutral to our

fate, and is in fact malign. I must be going, Rudi said, and walked off.

One of the inflators has failed, Ayton-Wright said to Newhouse, and shrugged.

Ah.

It's an absolute pain, Carver said. The press launch is later today.

Shall we all get together and blow it up ourselves, Newhouse said.

Do you have enough inspiration, Carver muttered.

Carver called someone on his mobile.

Newhouse left them.

Later, as he left the office early, he saw men with a television camera walking around the side of the gallery building. He followed them. On the large back lawn stood a multi-coloured inflatable building. It had a single entrance and no roof. Generators rumbled. It gently moved. Press photographers gathered around the entrance. A party of school children in blue uniforms were bouncing inside. They were laughing and whooping. In a small crowd, journalists, school teachers, and others stood and smiled as the children fell and sprung, flopped and bounced, giggled and shouted. Photographers clicked away. Some kneeled, some lay on the grass. The structure was massive and garish.

Newhouse moved closer.

Hayley was standing with a colleague, looking closely at the structure, which was creaking slightly. They told Newhouse it would be up all summer. It had been shown in Zurich, and was an enormous hit.

I'm going in after the press call, Hayley said.

Newhouse realised he wanted to go into the structure too.

I might as well, Newhouse said.

He had loved bouncing castles as a child. He once day-dreamed, as a young boy, that the whole world was inflatable. Ursula had pointed out that no crops would grow, and also that rapid water drainage would cause immense problems for the environment. But, she had noted, everything could be very clean.

Why not do it, he thought. I could find a corner, sit and be lightly moved up and down, surrounded by unreal soft walls. It would be more pleasant than working.

The hulking maze bounced slightly as the children bounced.

Thank you, ta, thank you, the press with cameras shouted to the children.

The photographers moved away and began to take pictures of two men – the artists, dressed in black and red – against a nearby stand of trees. Newhouse moved closer to the structure. The children were being led away by teachers.

A woman he recognised as the PG press manager, Pamela, walked to him, smiling.

Hello George. I didn't expect to see you here. How wonderful. You can explore it now if you wish. Takes 15 minutes apparently.

I think I might.

The crew from M&W are going to give a 'test bounce' as well. Don't get lost now.

I shall take a ball of string, he said. She smiled.

There were three people in black and red by the door to the inflatable maze.

One approached him. She had dark hair.

Hello, are you wanting to have a look around Colossus?

I was thinking about it. Is it safe?

Yes of course it is, she smiled. We tested it on those children. No casualties and only one concussion.

Oh, he said.

Yes, poor girl, she's currently vomiting somewhere in the maze, she said. But it's all vinyl, wipe-clean.

Really?

No. Of course not.

She held out a hand.

Hello I'm Tyler, she said.

He introduced himself.

Ah, you're the new Dutch art fella, she said.

Sort of, he said.

He looked into the maze. Past the entrance was a corridor of blue and red and yellow inflated walls, with a junction at the end. In what he took to be the centre of the maze was a black cube. The whole structure seemed to rise slightly from the grass and then gently settle again.

You look nervous, she said. I'm diving in.

He noticed her more. She was small. She had bronze streaks in her black, black hair. She bent over and slipped off her shoes. She leapt onto the maze and, laughing and unsteady, made her way down to the junction. She turned, leaping and hopping, and was gone.

Newhouse took off his shoes and noticed holes in the heels of his socks. He took them off too.

He put one knee on the maze and slid off. He tried his other knee, and did not slide, then leant forward but toppled, and hit the hard plastic with his face. He looked around but no one seemed to have noticed. He laughed.

Newhouse pulled himself onto the maze, and his body bobbed and rocked. He put a hand to the bright red wall and slowly made his way to the junction. The walls rose to about three feet above his head.

He turned, awkwardly, his feet slipping, into the corridor, and made his way, bobbing, around to the right. The sounds of the garden - the press, the cameras, the children, the people - had gone. There was just his breathing, the squeaking of his feet on the inflatable walls, the groaning of the PVC structure, and its generator's roar. He came to a circular space, with two routes off it. The circle was red, the exit corridors green. He took the left route again, and slid slightly as he saw Tyler up ahead.

She was laughing. She was sitting down, legs akimbo.

Fucks sake, she said, I think I am lost already.

Me too. He realized his body was at a 45 degree angle to the wall.

You look comfortable. Fun isn't it. I am not sure children should enter here without an adult though, she said.

No, maybe not.

The walls are so high. You could spend weeks bouncing around.

And anything could be in here, he said.

As long as it's not poo, she said.

I'm sorry?

My son went on a bouncy castle last summer. Another kid had an accident in there. It was something else.

My Lord.

Exactly.

Well, a minotaur is preferable to poo, he said.

I would say so. You know where you stand with a minotaur. Which way did you come?

I'm not sure, he said. I might crawl around from here.

She had steady dark eyes. She scrambled upright and unsteadily moved around the corner.

See you in the middle, she called out.

He waited a while, not wanting to follow her. He took himself deeper into the structure. There was silence now, just his breathing and the wheezing of the generator, the slapping of his feet on the plastic floor. He took three junctions, turning right, right, and right again. The walls receded. He was in a central space, a square, with the black cube at its centre. No one else was there.

He wobbled to the cube. There was a low entrance, he had to bend to enter. He eventually crawled in.

It was black inside. His eyes adjusted to the gloom.

A television screen was in one of the plastic walls. It was detuned, a box of grey fuzz. A man was sitting on a long, low cushion in the centre of the room. Newhouse was on his hands and knees. The screen became black and then showed a series of red and white stripes, moving from left to right. Then a hand appeared. It was pale, shaking. It turned over, and its palm was hacked and bleeding. Then it turned again, and the hand was tattooed with flowers, leaves, butterflies and beetles. It turned again and in the centre of the palm was a ring. It turned again and two hands appeared, one ragged with blood, the other dripping with liquid.

The man turned to Newhouse. He face was long and pale. He looked like he was crying. His body moved as if he was sobbing.

Newhouse moved backwards out of the cube and into the daylight. He stood up quickly and leaned back against its walls, and fell suddenly to the springy floor. The plastic slapped hard on his back. His head jolted.

What the fuck, he said.

Oh dear, he heard a voice say. It was Tyler. She was leaning against the wall of an exit corridor.

I see your balance hasn't improved.

Newhouse looked around. There was no black cube.

This is…

…bit boring isn't it. But they wanted the central bit to just be a big trampoline for the children. You having a sneaky bounce?

Something like that, he said.

It's tempting. You done? I know the way out, she said.

He followed her and they quickly returned to the entrance. He looked back at the space.

They put their shoes on.

Tyler was talking to her colleagues from the M&W, and Newhouse walked away, heading home.

As he walked along the road to his flat, past a hotel and over a bridge over a white-tumbling river, she caught up with him. She was walking quickly, a large bag around her shoulders.

Hi, she said.

We must stop meeting like this, he said.

I know, she said. On bridges, in mazes, whatever next?

We are wandering through an Escher sketch.

I'm actually late for Ben's nursery she said, smiling.

Ah, right, he said. They were walking together now.

Have any children yourself? she said.

No. No.

I thought you looked well rested.

We. I never got round to it.

Wise move, she said.

They walked in silence for a time, moving up a hill and

past offices and day care centres in a clean and spacious area of the city.

I am sure someone has said this already, she said, that you look a little like that man from the television. Whathisname. Thingy. You're not related?

I can't help you. But Thingy is actually my middle name. George Thingy Newhouse. Is he terribly rich?

Well, Thingy, I doubt it, she said. He might be, I suppose.

Well, then, no, I won't claim any familial connection. I won't be harassing him for cash.

You're a spit. You should check him out. Honestly. If I could remember his name it might be more helpful. God. Anyway what did you think of the bouncy maze?

She sounded conspiratorial.

It was... different. The children will love it, he said. I'm not sure what it's doing in the gallery gardens, But...

Oh come now, she said, raising an eyebrow. Don't be such a grouch. You're only saying that because you were boinging around on your arse the whole time. Are you one of those young fogies I hear about.

I have a very poor sense of balance, he said as ruefully as he could.

No fucking kidding, she said laughing.

Don't laugh, it's a medical issue. I've been told it's an inner ear problem. It leads to my predeliction for unplanned boinging. Where's your nursery, he said.

Oh, just round here, she said, pointing into another wide, silent street.

Ah, he said, and stopped walking. She stopped too.

Look, I know you think that it is all rubbish, but are you interested in contemporary work at all? I work part time for M&W, but there's a new show at The Garage…I have some new stuff of my own there. I will be utterly shameless and give you my card. She reached into her bag.

Tyler Tomlinson, it said, with a mobile phone number underneath. *New Garage Collective*, it said.

He reached into his wallet and gave Tyler his card. She span it round in her fingers. George Newhouse, she said.

Nice font.

Thank you, he said.

How is M&W?

I'm kind of learning it as I go along. PR – it's not really me. But they're nice guys, they pay. But I feel it's not what I am here for, if you see what I mean. You should see the show at The Garage, if you can bear that sort of thing.

Of course I can. And I feel the same. Every day, he said.

I cannot believe that. I mean, have you seen one of my press releases? she said.

Are they terrific?

No they are dreadful, she said, then gestured in the direction of the nursery.

I must go. It was good falling over with you, she said. Her eyes unmoving.

He wondered what to say.

Yes, yes, he said. It was.

She turned and walked off.

He realized he was watching her walk away, and turned on his heels, and walked home.

The black cube in his mind.

Tyler's face, vivid in his mind.

FIFTEEN

Castle House was a tall, white old baronial tower with an attached manor house and disused farm, set in a tight valley of hills close to a loch.

Newhouse had taken the train, read the papers Hayley had sent, and fallen asleep.

The curator of the collections of art at Castle House, Dr Anna Blanco, waited at a small station amid fir trees. She smiled and shook his hand. He put his overnight bag in the boot of her car.

She drove.

It's a forty-minute drive and then we will hold the meeting directly, she said. We'll cover six months of work, work we haven't done, work we need to do, all those things we need to discuss, don't you think.

Yes, he said.

Colebrooke will have told you, of course.

Crags and rugged slopes stretched up to blue sky. There was bare rock, heather, fleeting sun and shadow. There were gullies and mysterious knolls, stands of pine trees and low valleys with streams and livid green knots of trees. There were low wire fences, cattle grids, and grassy junctions. Close to the castle, they passed a white washed old church, small houses with white walls, compost piles on the roadside, bright plastic children's vehicles and chicken coops.

The car smelled of a bleachy cleaner. There was a tartan rug on the back seat. Anna was short and talked quickly. Her small hands rested on the black leather-bound steering wheel.

Beautiful up here, he said.

Yes, she said. Native woodland. Deer. And sometimes we think we have seen an eagle.

The meeting was long. It took place in an old dining room People spoke and Newhouse nodded and made notes. He doodled faces and eyes and circles inside circles.

There was a problem with the hunting lodge roof. There were drainage issues. There was the damp in the games room. There were UV filters, £400 each, to be fitted in the drawing room. There were reports on the plasterwork, which was damaged in three areas. There was a request from the National Trust to digitise the castle's watercolours.

Maybe they can just keep them, Newhouse said, to silence. The meeting went on.

Now Anna walked beside him as they walked slowly from the house to the loch. The other people at the meeting had left. He saw tiny blue flowers in the shrubs, little stars of felty colour. Old footprints were hard and crisp in the dried mud. Anna spoke softly. She was talking about the Highlands, about how they reminded her of her home in Spain. Except the light, she said. And the midges.

The path opened from the trees and the lake lay before them, a vast peach blade, the sunset bleeding across its length and breadth. A white bird arched and then dipped suddenly into its lapping face.

A large ruin stood on the headland, a white and green boat was moored below it.

So beautiful, she said, what a place.

Is that the old castle?

Yes, she said, we have had offers, people wanting to

turn it into a hotel, a conference centre, a wedding chapel.

Hm.

We have denied them.

It would raise money.

And close this path to the shore, she said. And it would be a tragedy.

They talked. He asked about her life and work, and she took a deep breath. She talked clearly and openly. He nodded and said 'uh-huh' a lot. Anna's field was Goya and his times. She had written a book on Goya's Black Paintings. She had published papers on hallucinations and the art of madness.

He had read her book.

We cannot deny, she had written, *that the human lives in a Universe in which we are not important, in which we are dwarfed by scale and sense, and which could contain powers beyond our comprehension. To us, those powers may seem angelic or demonic, Godlike or Satanic. To a mind like Francisco Goya y Lucientes, they became both friends and adversaries. Great men can commune with these energies and become greater. Lesser man can be destroyed.*

When she had come to the PG, from Spain, she had been appointed Head of Spanish and French paintings. But Colebrooke, she said, had fallen out with her.

I think, simply, George, he is a big sexist, she said.

He shrugged. Quite possibly.

She was still, in title, Head of Spanish and French, but she'd been sent to curate the collections at this outpost, and a Palladian house near the border, 'as an extra responsibility'.

You should move, he said.

Yes yes, but my son is at university here, my husband

also has a good job at the Consular office. It's not easy.

Get a job at a university, he said. Catch the attention of the National Galleries.

She pulled her scarf, laced with silver, tighter around her neck.

I considered that, she said. They don't need me. Look at the money they have to spend. Not us. I have to get back now. Shall we turn around?

They retraced their steps.

The sun was setting over the far hills. The lake became pink and mauve. Distant birds rose to the sky. There was volume and silence. The world felt enormous suddenly, life a vast undertaking for two humans on its surface.

They reached a rusting park bench that someone had placed on the lakeside, and sat down.

She asked him how he was settling in, and he said he was fine.

A long way from London, she said. You will feel everything is so empty.

Yes, he said. The city did seem depopulated, emptied of crowds.

Tell me about Goya's hallucinations, he said.

She smiled. George, I wrote 80,000 words on Goya's hallucinations. You read my book.

Fair enough, he smiled. I wish I could write something as good.

He thought of the *Naked Maja*. But also the Spanish painter's depictions of his oily, musty nightmares.

There is one painting by him that used to actually physically scare me, she said, looking out over the water. She took her small hat from a pocket, pulled it tight over her black hair.

Which one. A disaster of war?

No, no. It's called *Vuelo de Brujos*.

Witches in the Air.

Yes. 1797. It's at the Prado. You know it?

He painted a lot of witches.

I don't know George, there is something remarkable there. This one: there is the sheer blackness of it. The suspended bodies of the witches, so real but of course, unreal. The blinded witness below them, not wanting to see what he sees. The deaf witness, not wanting to hear what he is hearing. Crawling on the ground like animals before something so vivid, so unholy.

I think I know it, Newhouse said. He did not. But he could imagine it.

And then, she said, the witches, wearing those dunces hats – or are they Inquisition mitres – chewing on that man's body. Gobbling on him like owls.

Newhouse nodded. Over the water, darkness was spreading. He wanted to get back to the house, to sleep deeply for the night. He was hungry. The clear air made him feel deeply tired.

And worst of all, she said, shivering, that thing in the corner of the painting. It kept me up at night. Silly to say, she said. Because there are so many horrors in the world. She stood up and began walking back to the Castle.

I would be glad to be free of Goya, she said.

They walked quietly for a time. The wood line receded and Castle House came into view. The lowering light moved down its high white plaster walls, shadows slipping down its plastered sides like slow water.

I better show you your room, she said as they moved through a gate and into the grounds of the house. The grass moved from long to short, the flowers from wild to cultivated. Flies gathered under a spreading tree. Newhouse was feeling light-headed now.

Is there a place to eat near here? He said.

The catering was awful, no? She smiled.

I'm allergic to sandwiches, he said. And the rolls, he said, were interesting, although perhaps more interesting in their former life.

There is the Mussel Catcher, a pub down the lake, she said, but it's a drive, and I will be honest George, I'm tired. There will be something in the kitchen.

How far to the Mussel bar?

Thirty minutes there and back, she said.

Look, I'll buy you dinner, he said, and looked at the lake. You deserve it, I think.

In what way?

Putting up with those idiots on that committee. Putting up with Colebrooke. And then worst of all...

What?

Putting up with me, your foolish guest.

That's quite charming, and you know it is, she said.

Supper on me, then?

OK.

He stopped and looked at her. Her silhouette small and dark against the bleeding sun.

Where do you live?

In the castle, she said, there's an apartment. It's quiet here, don't you think?

SIXTEEN

They returned late. They had eaten well.

She had talked about Spain, about the PG. She spoke about Carver and Colebrooke and their intrigues, but Newhouse did not take it all in. He didn't know the cast of characters in her unfolding drama.

He had asked her about hallucinations again. She'd said that recent research was interesting. It showed that there was a recurrence of details in psychotic hallucinations. Repetition. Also, tiny people, or small people, wandering in and out of vision, often with strange headgear. Hats and crowns, bicorns and tricorns.

How interesting, he said.

Yes, don't you think? Marching little people, with their own missions, with their own world, ignoring the distress or wonder of the viewer. Often the hallucinated peoples keep doing the same thing over and again. Lost in their own déjà vu.

Maybe Goya saw little tiny witches, Newhouse said. With their tiny hats.

Perhaps, she said.

I would write a paper on all this, myself, she said. Her shoulders sank. But I am becalmed. These galleries are the worst I have worked for. No one seems to know what they're doing. It's as if the collections in themselves are enough. They're not. And of course the best of the PG isn't even owned by the people of this country, it's that dreadful loan from that Holding Company. Who thought that was a good idea? We need to do something with them.

Showing more to the public would help, she said. Don't you think? We are called The Public Gallery.

He nodded.

The staff is not good here, she said. There is a talent lack.

Until now, of course? he said, with a smile.

She ignored him.

Did you know that Carver has been working on the same study for seven years? She said. Seven years on the pigments in the bloody... oh I can't believe it. No one cares.

Seven years, really, he said. He was not surprised, somehow. Carver looked like he could spend seven years studying a single idea. He resembled an early monk, a shaved ascetic atop a column in the Egyptian desert, blasted by hot winds.

And I think you know Mr Hessenmuller, she said, peering over a glass of wine.

Yes, he said.

Awful man. I'm sorry. He's terrible.

Newhouse laughed. He put down his knife and fork, crossed them on a plate smeared with steak blood.

Yes, Rudi has his moments, he said. He knows a lot about his...

I'm sorry, she said, and shook her head. He is one of Colebrooke's men and a terrible person.

I'm sure, I'm sure, he said. He didn't have the energy to defend Rudi. She ate her food quickly.

In that painting, the floating witches, he said.

Yes?

What's in the corner?

A horse, perhaps a mule.

He looked at her.

It looks like something from the Inferno. The very Devil in the flesh, she said.

He drank more wine.

Your work, she said.

Yes?

That Rembrandt note, of course, she said. She spoke as if she was leading up to something.

Yes, the Armour Note, he said.

How would Rembrandt have seen the painting? The Blue Horse? Did he own it?

He nodded.

We just don't know.

Was it exhibited?

No, not that kind of economy. We don't know. But we know he saw it, commented on it, was disturbed by, we can only surmise, its quality.

When did he see it?

We don't know that either. The note is not dated. Perhaps around 1641, 42. Around the time his wife Saskia died.

Hmm, Anna said.

She drove them both back in silence. The woods were dark, and beyond them, the lake was black and solid. The car's lights flicked over distances and closeness, over sudden flashing proximity and then lurching far surfaces. At the castle she walked him up wide wooden stairs to a large white bedroom, fresh with new linen and clean sheets. There were pale walls flowing with the pattern of green-leaved wallpaper. An en-suite bathroom scented with lemons. Anna quickly bid him goodnight and walked away. He wished he had said something kind to her, but he did not. Newhouse sat on the bed. He heard Anna's footsteps, and then nothing.

He heard footsteps again, from another place. Something, creaking on the floor above. Anna had said there was a drawing room for herself, and one for guests. He looked around the bedroom. It was empty and clean. Paperbacks were placed neatly beside the bed. A large cupboard in the corner. He heard the footsteps again. He looked in his night bag. There were pills and painkillers in brown plastic bottles. He took them out and put them beside the bed.

He wanted to talk to Anna. He was not Rudi. He was not Colebrooke. He felt the need to say sorry for something, although he was not sure what. Before Ruth, he had rarely said sorry. She had taught him that apologising made him feel better, even if it did no good in the end. All words lost in time, all emotions and regrets, thoughts and feelings, lost in time.

He swallowed hard, stood up and left his room.

The hallway was dark, lit by a single light on the wall. There were heads of deer on the wood paneling, and large portraits of the ancestral family. Pale faces in the darkness. A painting of a small lizard on a lead held by a lumpy-faced child in a bonnet. Stairs led upwards into further darkness.

The only noise was his feet on the staircase carpet. The soft and heavy tread of his legs. He moved up into the dark. He reached a landing but there were no doors, just more stairs. He moved up again, lit by a single light on the wall, between the teeth of a bear's head and the beetle-armoured eyes of a stag, its horns spread and waiting.

Again, on the landing, no doors, only a large wooden

trunk and, in the corner, a curl of new, stone stairs leading upwards, its ascension occluded by a swiftly turning wall.

He leaned on the banister, and looked back down the staircase. He could see the steps descending. There should be a door into the room above mine, he thought. But I don't know this place. There must be another way.

A light suddenly came on over the stone stairs. They were white washed and clean. A red rope ran up their side. He smelt damp and mould. And something earthy and brown.

He moved up the stairs. His feet scraped and tapped on the stone. He trudged up and up, round and round, holding onto the rope, the steps tightly wound around and around its central axis. He climbed up, the spiral of the steps so tight he could not see ahead, could not see down. He climbed and climbed. The steps seemed to become tighter. The light, he realised, was coming from nowhere. The light came from the stone itself. It was bright and crisp and fell harshly on the grain of the steps, on the thread of the rope, on his pink fingers and brown cords. He moved back, to step down, but could not. The stairs and the walls were too small, too tight. His head swam. He stepped up, and the walls widened.

He had climbed too far. This was too high. Higher than the castle was, higher than the battlements. He moved up and was standing suddenly on a plain open landing. He stepped onto it, and there was a wooden door.

He pushed at it.

He was in a large stone room, square and open, its plaster walls black with damp. The room stank. It filled his nose and eyes. Mould soaked the plaster, it sagged from the ceiling. But the windows were open and it was day outside. White and blue moved there, beyond the frames.

Newhouse put his hands over his eyes. He stepped into the room. Spores in the air floated like drifting seeds. The room stank of the moisture and the rot.

In the centre of the room was a construction, a large pile of rotting straw, black with tiny mushrooms, fibrous outcrops and fungus. The brown and black mass sat and sweated in the fungal reek.

The room was silent and stinking. The mould stung his nose and his eyes. He moved to a window, to look outside. All he could see was light and air. He thought he heard boats and sails, the swallow of water, the slap of waves, and the shouts of men.

As he moved, the pile of straw suddenly shifted and something black and large arched a strong neck. The walls of the room throbbed. The dampness and the blackness thickened and burnt. He choked and gasped. His eyes closed. And opened.

He was in the dark.

A light came on, harsh on his eyes. His back hurt, there was a throbbing pain above his buttocks.

Are you OK? A sleepy voice said.

He looked into Anna's eyes. He realised he was lying on the stairs outside his bedroom door.

George? Are you OK? She was leaning over him.

He looked at her. His hands were wet. His throat felt clogged and sore.

I'm really not sure, he said.

Have you fallen?

I have fallen.

SEVENTEEN

It was morning and the sun was bright through the lead-lined panes. A tall crooked tree leaned across the window.

Newhouse lay under the covers, exhaustion rolling over his legs and body. He felt the small of his back. It was tender, a little swollen around the spine.

He remembered the dark stairs, the light stairs, something of the room.

Newhouse turned over. Much of the night before seemed indistinct in his mind. He did not remember taking pills. He must have. He had fallen down a flight of stairs.

Anna had helped him stand up, had walked him into his room. She had seen an opened bottle of pills beside the bed. She had taken the bottle and put it in a pocket of her gown, and given him a glass of water. As she bent to him, he had seen her breasts under her nightgown, a single mauve nipple, and the smell of her hair had filled his sore nostrils, entered his eyes and mouth. After she had gone, and he had crawled into bed, he had dreamt of women and bodies, open mouths and smooth legs.

Now in a foggy half-sleep, he thought of Cara, a Welsh girl. She had been the first girl he had kissed. She had brown hair and grey eyes and had been two years older than he. He had fumbled with Cara's friend, Janice, at a party later that summer. Janice also let him feel her breasts. They were in a back room. New Order was playing on the hi-fi. There was a copy of Van Gogh's cornfields on the wall. He remembered how strange her nipples had felt, how tight the skin under and around them was. He had kissed her brown neck. She had smelled like honeysuckles.

The first woman he had fallen in love with had been Ruth.

He saw her face, heard her voice. A fragile memory returned, unbidden.

It had been a holiday.

There was white wine: limpid honey in small glasses, a tidy sunny square. Blonde stone was smeared with stripes of light. Dappled sun on wooden shutters. A clarinet played in a nearby bar. Signs swung in a light breeze: L'Antre Potes and Bistro Gourmand, Chat Perche and Bar Felix.

The pores of her skin were open in the sun. Light ran along the copper wire hairs on her ears, her neck.

I just don't feel well, she said.

You're hungry.

No, I feel sick. I feel terrible.

You're tired. Have more food.

No, I need to lie down.

And then, later, there was blood on her teeth on the wet bathroom floor. Staring white eyes. A fragment of a tooth, sharp like an ancient arrowhead.

Lying on blue bedsheets, white slime on her tongue. Her eyes rolling. A grey metal box with blinking lights beside her bed. Rust in tiny red rings around its controls.

A tube bulging under her pale skin.

Doctors whispering in another language as nights passed under fluorescence.

EIGHTEEN

He met Rudi for a drink before they both headed to the Public Gallery.

Rudi was telling him about a work he was including in his show, the massacre of the Theban legion. It was a depiction of a Roman legion that was crucified for refusing to sacrifice to pagan gods. The picture was medieval. It showed hundreds of martyrs nailed to crosses. In the foreground, twisted white bodies writhed on enormous thorn bushes. All their heads were ringed with thin halos. There were at least sixteen martyrs in the frame, Rudi said. Sixteen was a holy number among the Theban Christians, he said. Or maybe Upper Egypt.

That was not made for Thebans though, Newhouse said, or the Upper Egyptians?.

Of course, of course, Rudi said.

Gruesome, Rudi.

It's delightful, wonderful, its remarkable, Rudi said. It's a masterpiece. It's a Sadean thing.

Where is it?

Somewhere in France, Rudi said, it's a minor piece. I saw it in a book, *Christian Mythology*, by Every, in a bookshop near the border. I went for a drive. There were no women to be seen.

Newhouse nodded. He said he had never heard of Every.

A monk, I think, Rudi said.

Monks, self-mortification, the celice, the knots of whipping, he said.

It was another cloudless day. Whitewater glistened under the road bridge. They were both wearing light suits. They walked past Colossus. It seemed to be closed. A white sign had been stuck to its sides. It was too far away to read.

Shame, Rudi said.

What's happened? Newhouse said.

A series of almighty clusterfucks, Rudi said.

Right, Newhouse said, nodding. Sounds painful.

I haven't been sleeping, Rudi said.

No?

No.

A special meeting had been called at the PG.

Colebrooke was back from a holiday and wanted to speak to all the senior curators. An email from Carver said attendance was under a three line whip.

Colebrooke wore a striped suit, a gold and black waistcoat. He was tall and broad and had grey, feathery eyebrows and a thin, grey moustache. He did not look like Foster.

His interests were straight forward. Impressionism. Monet and Manet. Raphael. French Empire style. He had been in charge of the PG for so long, several staffs had come and gone. He was now unmarried and spent his holidays in Thailand and Singapore. He occasionally had cold sores. He owned a house in the islands. Someone had once spread a rumour he and Carver were lovers. His voice boomed and he smoothed his moustache between utterances.

Colebrook did not wait for all the curators to sit down before he began. There was one chair short. Rudi leant against the wall.

Colebrooke rolled a black pen under his fingers.

Carver was wearing a new tweed suit. His neck was red. Two late arriving curators, both men, stood by the door. A lank fart drifted and settled.

I will be straight and honest and open and candid, candid, candid and to the point, Colebrooke said, at top volume.

He went on.

As we know, Lady Ardrashaig, may she rest in a long and restful peace, died eight years ago. Through fair means or foul her collection, the Ardrashaig Collection became part of a financial instrument called Ardrashaig Holdings. They own the paintings and up until this doleful point, we have had cordial dealings with them and their chief executive, Murray Murrey. However, they have now informed us...

He sighed deeply. He shook his head, theatrically. He pulled suddenly at a white hair which hung from on his ear lobes.

...that the 160 year history of those paintings being on the walls of our blessed, small but perfectly formed Public Gallery are over. Three will be sold at auction, the rest will be permanently loaned to the new £1 billion gallery in Doha.

Shit, someone said. Jesus, a few others said.

Carver closed his eyes, put his hands to his face.

Holy Lord in heaven above, someone said.

That is the entire fucking core of our fucking collection, someone said. Those paintings are the only way we can compete with the National Galleries.

Language, please, language, someone muttered.

Yes. 14 paintings, 7 masterpieces, Colebrooke said.

There was a sudden silence.

Seven outright masterpieces, seven, seven masterpieces by our reckoning, Colebrooke bellowed.

I need water, someone gasped.

Game Over, Rudi said. He crossed his arms. What a heavy rainfall of utter bastards.

Why? Someone asked.

In the letter Mr Murrey said the new building in Doha is a finer gallery that is *forward facing and public facing*, I quote. New, bright, clean, with strategic objectives and *'Connector Lines more in synergy'* with that of the blessed Ardrashaig Holdings.

No one said anything,

The basic, basic, basic plan, Colebrooke said, is what? What is the basic plan now?

There was more silence.

I need a brandy, Carver said.

The paintings for sale would be bought by a Russian or a Chinese businessman and never seen again, Newhouse thought.

Someone spoke.

If we come up with a new plan, an attractive objective, a self-realisation, redevelopment and restructuring, can we convince Ardrashaig Holdings to change their mind?

A room of sick faces.

Never ride the lonely road, Rudi said.

What we have here is target exhaustion, one man said. And that does not compete with shareholder value.

We have advocacy issues, another said.

People were speaking but not listening.

We have to capture the wow moments, the head of press and marketing said. We have messages that need to be heard. We have no narrative. We do not have the prestige of a national gallery.

There is no turnaround to tell. There is no come back. There's no opposition, no antagonist, someone muttered.

That is shit. We have a clear antagonist, someone said.

We have no face in the market.

Another man said: There are protocols and guidelines in place. Clear rules and boundaries. They cannot be changed, cannot be crossed.

A woman said: We need to target our targets and engage with them.

We have no natural audience. We have no national resonance.

There is localised dissonance. There is dissonance in our narrative.

Newhouse said to himself: I once had a dream, but that dream has gone.

George, Carver said, what's your take?

We need a narrative, an over-arching story of our own, he said quickly.

Everyone nodded. Carver narrowed his eyes.

We need a target, a goal, and then a narrative completion, he said.

A few people nodded. Rudi began to smile.

As his voice spoke, he saw pale blue flowers in a bowl in a sun filled room. White folded linen on a clean kitchen table. He saw her newly laundered underwear in a small pile on their bed. Her saw her fingers, splayed on the mirror. Her mirror; circular, blue, with three red fish swimming around its pale blue, sky-blue circumferance.

He spoke and at the table people listened.

What we have is a crisis, and we need to explain it,

make it clear, clarify our position, their position, he said.

We are the goodies, he is the baddy, Rudi said.

We have to find something to placate and pacify, Carver said.

Rudi said: Find the Blue Horse and save yourself.

What? Newhouse said to him.

Rudi raised his eyebrows.

I said nothing, young prince, he said.

No? Newhouse said.

No, people said. He said nothing.

The meeting went on. Decisions were taken.

It came to an end after five hours. Sandwiches had been eaten, two rounds of tea and coffee.

Carver said: *The Herald* has called. They've heard something.

Fucksake, someone muttered.

Brandy for me, Carver said.

Colebrooke said something to Newhouse as he staggered from the room.

I need a word, George, he said.

NINETEEN

Colebrooke's office smelled of lavender. On his large desk Newhouse saw a marble cigarette dish, an Art Deco lamp and what looked like a polystyrene box with a baked potato inside it. Colebrooke took off his jacket, which had large patches of sweat in its armpits, and sat down. There was a window behind his desk. The frame of his body was a black silhouette.

Cherie, his secretary, came in with a small tray with two coffee cups on it, some cream, a pile of brown biscuits.

Colebrooke nodded and the secretary left.

How are you finding things? Colebrooke said.

Well, today has been challenging, Newhouse said. Unbidden, he sat.

Sit down, Colebrooke said, from his shadow.

There was a silence. Steam rose in dragon tails from the coffee cups.

I will cut to the chase, Colebrooke said.

OK.

Cherie had left a plummeting trail of ionised perfume. It was slowly drifting in a ribboned sheet of tiny droplets to the thick red carpet.

I want you to meet Murray Murrey, talk this disaster over with him, Colebrooke said.

Newhouse nodded. His mind was a blank.

You're new, he doesn't know you, and there's no baggage. You have a London reputation, they like that, these fucking people.

Right.

I think, to be honest with you George, he's a bastard.

Yes.

A fucking bastard and a cock, too. This is what we are dealing with; the dregs of the world. I won't say that old cliché. That they know the price of everything and the value of nothing, I won't say that.

Indeed.

I cannot believe they are doing this to us.

Yes.

Colebrooke's shadow was shaking. His hand rose to his black head and fell again. He drank from his coffee.

I want you to meet him, anyway, offer him a list of things we can do to try and change his mind. Withdrawing the pictures will tear the heart out of our gallery.

Newhouse nodded.

We would be reduced to a provincial sideshow. We would have to merge with the National Galleries.

If they would take us, Newhouse said.

Yes, you are of course, right. I can't imagine they need us, Colebrooke said quietly. More real estate for them to deal with, and pictures of less value. Newhouse nodded.

You would be heartbroken, George, to see that those paintings sold, would you not? To some Russian murderer? To one of those porcine hedge fund reprobates? To some mobster?

It would be a truly terrible thing, Newhouse said.

What do you think of what Tavish said?

I... Newhouse did not remember what Tavish said.

He did not know who Tavish was.

About us becoming a warm and welcoming node, Colebrooke said.

It's... certainly a point he made, Newhouse said.

Colebrook nodded.

George, come back tomorrow, I will have a file put together, a series of offers. I need to speak to the Minister. I need to speak to Carver in private, to the British Council, to the Art Fund, to some other fuckers. I need to attend a conference in Mexico City. I am due another holiday.

OK.

Thanks George. Obliged. Hayley will get you the stuff you need.

Newhouse stood up.

By the way…

Yes?

How is the Biennale decision?

We are deciding.

Good good good. I like Macpherson. I can take or leave his Systemic works. But his porno paintings, very good. Freud, Bacon, Rusche: all there. Max at the National in Denmark compared him to Klimt.

Ok.

Good work, good work. Come by tomorrow, we will arrange the Ardrashaig meeting.

Newhouse walked to the heavy wooden door of the office.

George?

He turned around. Colebrooke was standing, hands in pockets, looking out of the window.

What do you know about that painting, the horse?

Newhouse felt his shoulders tense.

In what sense?

Where is it? Is it real? Is it even out there at all, somewhere? Martinu seems to think so. If you could… I mean, if it were… even if no money could be raised to buy it… it would be a coup.

Colebrooke stuttered and stopped.

I don't know if it is out there somewhere, Newhouse said. And the chances of finding it…

Yes yes of course, ridiculous notion, Colebrooke said.

If I did know where it was, Mr Colebrooke, I would be a rich man.

There was a thick silence.

Fine, fine, fine, OK, Colebrooke said.

Colebrooke turned his back. He held a finger in the air.

Why, Newhouse, did Rembrandt write that note, do you think?

Well, as you may have read…we will never know.

Of course, of course, Colebrooke said, and folded his arms.

He looked out of the window, motionless.

TWENTY

Ruth on the beach.

Three fish in the shallows, swimming in a circle, chasing each other's tails, on and on, round and round.

His computer beeped and he woke up. His eyelids slid over his eyes, and opened.

Anna had emailed. She had meetings in the city and wanted to meet him again. He sat in his office. Birds fluttered over the park. People entered and exited the portico of the galleries. A young couple kissed. He emailed Anna back and said he would meet her the following evening.

He worked. He looked at the file on Macpherson, in his mind the best artist in the Biennale short list. He remembered seeing one of his Porn paintings, a large oil work of a still from a pornographic movie called *Dirty Debutantes*. It was oil on canvass, it was beautifully painted: reminded him of the feathery touch, the fleshy immensity of Titian's *Diana and Actaeon*. He had taken the profane, the sinful, the wrong and made it beautiful. The woman's face had been sorrowful, gorgeous. Above her prone body, Macpherson had painted: *I Am A Delicate Flower.*

Newhouse brought up Macpherson's CV on his computer screen.

Crawford John 'Brick' Macpherson
Born Glasgow, 26/09/1970.
Cowcaddens High School, Glasgow School of Art,
degree, Fine Art Painting, and MFA.

Degree show: Rudiments at Glasgow Third Eye Centre (group show)

Group shows: Transmission Gallery, 87839 gallery, Sensation, White Cube.

Short listed Becks Futures, 1999 for 87839 gallery show, Angel sculptures.

Solo: Glasgow, Tramway, 2001: 'Damnation' – 40 oil paintings, replicas of hardcore pornography stills, with text.

Short listed Turner Prize, 2002 for Damnation and second show at Arnofini, Bristol: Atrocities.

Move to New York and Seattle on one year Thurmond residency (2003).

2004 - Show at Schwartzer Gallery, NY, Burmont-Carroll Gallery, Portland, series of 'schematic' paintings based on American football terminology and US sports culture.

Wins Turner Prize for Double Stick Trips Y Bunch, Retrospective exhibition at Weyland Sword Gallery. Changes names to Dabrickashaw (Brick) Macpherson, homage to D'Brickashaw Ferguson, NY Jets player. Tate Modern buys HB Option X Slant and 34 2 Man Under Ted Spy.

Double Stack, TE Flash, Fourth and Long sold at auction, Christie's, NY, for $2.3m

2005 – Reconnaissance at Tate Modern: mixed media, video, photographs, re-staging of Renaissance masterpieces using actors, non-actors. Vatican buys 'Pieta – again'(stabilised film) for undisclosed sum. National Gallery, London, buys 'Assumption – again' (stabilised film) for £1.2m.

Lives in Glasgow, Berlin, Ischia (Forio).

Newhouse got back to the flat early.

His clothes were still in his suitcases, piled on a chair in the bedroom or in the washing machine. There was no food in the fridge or the freezer. He sat at the kitchen table and the small lights flickered over the range. There was dust and stains on the laminate.

He stood up and walked to the living room. He had spent no time there. There was a folded train ticket on the coffee table and the gloom of drawn blinds. A television with a black screen sheeted in dust. An empty book case. Dust drifting in fields. Newhouse sat on the sofa and closed his eyes. He thought he should clean his bed sheets, change his pillowcases. He thought he should clean the bathroom, clean the kitchen. He should take a suit to the dry cleaners, cut his nails, have a bath. He swung his legs up on the sofa and closed his eyes.

He thought of his new job, the projects and the research. He thought of his review of the Dutch collection, barely begun. He heard the radiators click. He heard cars move on the street outside.

He sat back, and suddenly he slept.

He woke. He was hot, sweating. His suit was shapeless and wet. He felt dizzy. Time passed in a smeared paste of light. The toilet flushed. He was on the floor of the bathroom, the extractor fan roaring, holding his knees to his head. There was water on his cheeks. He looked up, into a field of glare, and it glared back at him.

Now he was in the hall, lying on his side.

Now he was in bed, his pedalling legs pulling at the sheets.

He turned over. He shivered. He scratched his face. He pulled at his trousers and his jacket. The jacket caught on his elbows, the lining ripping on his shoulders, catching on his fingers. He was hot, he was tingling, his toes fizzing with some kind of spiking pain. His trousers slid off, fell to the floor.

After deep sleep, he woke again. He felt cold, pulled the sheets up again. Outside the day was breaking, a thin pink light, the sound of cars and buses. Birds singing. He closed his eyes, his stomach rumbled loud and long.

His body spun into twinkling darkness. He saw planes of colours shifting and spinning, life spun out in webs and lattices, understanding and intelligence inhabiting unreal light and impossible angles.

He woke. The window was open. His clothes were all over the room. His suit arm was ripped.

It was 8am.

He stumbled to the bathroom. The light was on, the fan wheezing. There was water on the floor, and a swirl of watery blood in the pan.

He sat on a kitchen chair and breathed deeply.

He heard something. A swish. A rattle.

Find it, find me. Instead of you, he.

He looked into the dark hall. Something was moving. A long purple leg, a hard black hoof. The shimmer of blue-silver. Something large and solid moved into the doorframe.

The long face of death, its black eyes unblinking. It turned and was gone.

TWENTY ONE

So, George, here is the Zaraceno material and some other interesting notes, Dr Hans Martinu said, pointing to a large blue file which he had just dropped on Newhouse's desk.

Martinu was back. He smelled of Cologne, fine clothing.

Thank you, Newhouse said.

Zaraceno: an interesting family, Martinu said, waddling over to the window, looking over the grounds, which were drenched in summer rain. A small pool of water gathered on the window ledge.

I feel, for one, your painting is still in Europe.

The Blue Horse? Newhouse said. He looked at the file but did not want to touch it. He was meeting Anna in the Café Royal at seven.

Newhouse said: Why is that? After the war, after Karin Hall, it could have been taken by anyone, Hans. It could be in Russia, in America, in South America. It could have been shot, burnt, vandalised, destroyed. We don't know how big it was, or even what it was painted on. I did say, years ago now, that it is a dead end. Why go back to this?

You're being grumpy, George. Less grumping, more thinking. How is the Dutch survey going? What do you think of the Breenbergh landscapes?

Shoddy.

He wanted Martinu out of his office. He had meetings all day. He still felt shaky.

Trifling, yes, Martinu said. A minor painter. But we have so many of them. No wonder that Ardrashaig mob is moving on. But what a disaster.

The wind tacked and rain battered against the windows. As soon as something becomes a commodity its actual value is erased, Martinu said.

Newhouse nodded.

Have you read this new study by Wycliffe.

No, what study. I thought he had been defrocked.

Wycliffe had been a peer of Martinu, a fearsome mind in his field. He had recently lost his position at his university.

Yes, a sad situation. St Andrews did not know what they had there. But anyway, he's having it published, self-published I think, Martinu said.

What's it called?

I have it at home. *The Double Walker: Occult Nodes of Being in Art,* Martinu intoned. I think it will be a key contribution to this rather interesting Parallel Art Theory movement.

Fascinating, Newhouse said, with as much interest as he could muster. What is an occult node?

Anything can be. And perhaps you should be interested.

I am more interested in my new job swirling down a plughole.

Martinu nodded.

I warned that fool Colebrooke about this new Ardrashaig arrangement when the Lady died. She had a sense of grandeur, the larger sweep of things. The nation state and the avalanche of time. She understood the worth of things. She once said to me: 'It is no more my collection than it is the moon's. I inherited it, but that is more chance than true ownership.' Murray Murrey? A crass, greedy fool. An accountant.

Rudi says Ardrashaig Holdings is within its rights, Newhouse said. He says the PG has done nothing for them, or the pictures. And look at the state of them.

Martinu snorted.

Rudi has a big thick skull with nothing in it. He is all tip and no iceberg. No wonder his terrible wife left him. His opinion of women is appalling. What is his grand project? Paintings of Christ's penis. I mean really.

Newhouse sighed.

George, let us think of The Blue Horse's size, and of its materials, Martinu said. He opened the file, and pulled out a printed email.

Here, he said, from the Zaraceno exchanges in 1913: *Shadow of a Horse, oil on canvas, 20 inches by 23 inches. Poor condition. Signed, bottom left, VDt.*

Newhouse held out his hand. Martinu handed over the sheet. It was the scan of a document, printed from an email attachment.

Hans, I am being serious. Why do you persist with this, Newhouse said.

He looked at the sheet.

There were words printed on the page, but Newhouse felt he could see the painting in his mind. It existed there, and did not need to be real. He knew it had never been described. But he could see it anyway: the grave skull, black pits for nostrils, black ivory eyes glaring from the darkness of a doorway, its flanks only wings of smoky night glittering and glinting. The heavy head, nodding with power in the eaves of his mind.

Hans.

Yes?

I have been having very vivid dreams, very real dreams,

Newhouse said.

Are they troubling you George?

Newhouse looked at Martinu. His face in folds of brown and pink. Yellow under his eyes.

Yes. I wonder if…

It probably means you are close to something. Your mind is grasping for it, but cannot yet see it, bear it, Dr Martinu said.

Newhouse looked down at his hands. They were shaking.

TWENTY TWO

I'm not quite sure where I'm going, Newhouse said.

The country rolled past the train window. There were low fields and old fences, unkempt bushes and ragged trees. The train line ran near the coast, a ragged line of cliffs, and the northern sea, silently swelling, beyond, to the horizon.

Did you read my email? Hayley said on the other end of the phone.

I'm sorry, Newhouse said. He heard a pen tapping.

The train felt very old. The seats were thin and cold. The ghosts of old graffiti smeared the windows. He was heading south, to the border country, to meet Murray Murrey at the former estate of Lady Ardrashaig. He was wearing his good suit, and had bought a new briefcase. He had a new haircut.

Hayley said he should take a taxi from the station to a lodge house on the edges of the Ardrashaig estate. From there he would be picked up and taken to Murrey.

Why couldn't we meet in the city?

This is a pantomime. I have a walk-on part, he thought.

Hayley said nothing.

Where is Colebrooke?

Meeting with Ministers, she said.

Couldn't Carver have done this?

Carver is with Ministers.

OK. Thanks Hayley.

The phone line was dead.

Now the train rattled and wheezed and then stopped

at a small town station. A gold crenulated design hung from a shabby grey roof. He left the station, found a white private taxi and gave the driver an address.

Time washed over him. The murmur of the taxi and its small radio lulled him. A small heater belched warm air. He thought of the Netherlands, its glinting canals, water saved from the sea. Land cut and shaped and added to the land, a continent extended into marshes and swamps.

He thought of Van Doelenstraat, alone and freezing in a small tiled room, painting his empty rooms, rooms with dust and grit and dank air, shredded curtains and greasy glass, the empty gut of loneliness. Hands working, dabbing back and forth, from palatte to canvass and back again. Dab dab, the empty rooms brought to life. A life without a wife, without hope. Plaster crumbling from holes hidden in brick and mortar, and shadows, more shadows. And outside the greasy whorled window, horses cracking on cobbles, and the winches winding, and clouds tearing bright on water, slow water, sunk with deathly barges.

The taxi stopped, and Newhouse paid, and he stood outside a squat lodge house in the middle of fields and woods. The sky was a malleted white. He looked into the windows, but they were black. He pressed a brass doorbell, and he heard it ring, but nothing happened. Somewhere over the fields, a gun sounded.

The low drone of distant traffic.

He remembered, as a boy, lying in moss in woods, his father walking dogs, Ursula running alongside. He would stare at the stones beside his head: the stones don't care for me, they don't care for time. The moss on the stones does not care, the earth around the stones does not care. The woods do not care, nor the muddy banks, nor the river.

He waited and leant against the lodge door. A car drew up, long and black.

A window slid down, and a long pale face topped with curls of white hair looked out.

Mr Newhouse, he said.

Newhouse climbed inside the car. Inside was dark and lush. Leather gleamed. Rosewood and silver.

A window slid down between the front seats and the back. The driver moved the car off, and said: We will be with the Mr Murrey most presently.

Great.

He looked out of the tinted windows, into darkened fields.

What did you think of the Lodge house?

I— it looked fine.

There was a document for you on the kitchen table, did you not pick it up?

The door was open?

Yes, sir.

No, I thought it was shut.

The document was for you.

Can we go back?

No, I'm afraid not.

What was it?

I don't know. Mr Murrey's secretary told me to leave it for you there. I left it there.

The door is always unlocked?

No one lives here, the driver said. It is perfectly safe.

The window slid up again.

The car drove on, and came to a thick wood of conifers, and turned into a long drive guarded by smoothly opening electronic gates. The car crunched up the drive, to a cleanly massive house. Behind the house was more bulk and shape; more bricks and buildings, outhouses and gardens and walls, and, as Newhouse stepped out of the car, the hum of heavy generators, shaking with electricity.

TWENTY THREE

There was a long white hall made of marble and glass. There were open doors at the far side of a large empty space. The walls dissolved into light, flickering with the shadows of garden trees. Out of the light, a young woman in a blue dress suit came and shook Newhouse's hand.

The woman said she was called Margot and she was Murrey's secretary, and that he should wait in another room. She asked whether he wanted tea or coffee. He asked for tea. He moved into the other room, the light touch of her hand on his back. His eyes took a while to adjust to the gloom. There were no windows.

Around the walls were hung shabby copies of eight religious works by Poussin. The originals hung in a small room in the National Galleries. He stood and looked at a Biblical wedding scene. The colour control was poor, the varnish too heavy.

A good copy, he said to the woman. Do you know who did this?

He looked around and the door was closing; the woman gone.

A fire was set up in the grate but unlit. Two heavily embroidered chairs sat either side of it. He sat in one, putting his briefcase at his feet. The carpet was threadbare in places.

He opened his briefcase and took out the documents. They had been written by Colebrooke and Carver, amended in part by Rudi and made readable by Newhouse, with Hayley putting it all together. A copy had been sent to Ministers. The document was a case for keeping the Ardrashaig Holdings collection at the galleries. There were several headings and subheadings. There was the historical case, the national case, the local case, the heritage case and the legal case. There was an argument from patriotism, from nationalism, from humanitarianism and from the viewpoint of 'Western Civilisation' (heavily revised by Rudi). There were case histories of each painting, and how the galleries had cared for them, conserved them, and judiciously loaned them in return for other masterpieces. This section, whose composition was not helped by the PG's faulty and poorly organised internal administrative documents, was written by Newhouse. The final section was a faintly emotional plea from Colebrooke and the Minister, with derogatory remarks about the Gulf States written at the last moment by Martinu. It was a solid document in shape and size.

The final section also included three promises which Newhouse was fairly sure Colebrooke could not fulfil: a capital project: a new gallery extension especially for the collection, a promise to tour the treasures once a year to the other cities, and, every five years, a tour of key world galleries, including six-month stays in the new galleries in Dubai and Qatar.

The door opened, Margot came in and Newhouse stood up.

I'm terribly sorry about this, she said.

Newhouse could not place her accent. It sounded somehow metallic.

Mr Murrey is delayed, she said, I'm sure he won't be long. Would you like tea or coffee?

He had asked for tea before.

He's at another property, Marvell House. But it's an hour's drive. I can only apologise.

Right, Newhouse said. An hour?

I'm terribly sorry.

Well, this is not ideal.

It's a Holdings matter.

So is this, he said.

She stared at him.

Is there a bigger Holdings matter than this?

I'm sorry, I'm not 100% certain what the business of your meeting is, she said. But I can get you some tea.

She turned and left the room.

Newhouse sat down and stared at the unlit fire.

He looked around the room. He waited for a few minutes then closed his briefcase and left the room, back into the light of the hall. There were several doors, and a staircase he hadn't seen before.

He saw someone sitting on the steps at the far end of the hall, leaning on the stone balastrade that led down to the grass and trees. As he stepped closer, he saw it was a young man, dressed in a white shirt and jeans. His hair was long and shaggy, a mess of brown and caramel and blonde. He was staring out into the garden, smoking a cigarette. He had bare feet.

Newhouse walked up to him and looked out at the garden: a lawn, flat and lush, trimmed and neat. Beyond were high hedges, conifers, distant glass glinting on greenhouses, and the tingling scent of ponds and pools.

No luck, no luck, the man said. He turned around to face Newhouse, tapping his cigarette on the stone.

Hello, I'm George Newhouse.

Yes, the gallery man, the man said. He face was pale and blotchy. He had some teeth missing.

The man reached out and weakly shook Newhouse's outstretched fingertips. His eyes opened and closed quickly.

Hi, hi, hi, Laurence, he said. Good to meet you.

I'm here to see Murray Murrey, Newhouse said. Laurence squinted and took a drag from the cigarette and nodded.

But I don't seem to be having much luck.

Me neither, me neither, Laurence said, and stood up. He put one hand to the small of his back and stretched. He moaned.

He will be a while, I've been told, Laurence said. Newhouse saw a tooth missing at the front, several at the back of his mouth.

He's at Marvell House, Newhouse said.

Ah yes, of course, of course, Laurence said. He threw the cigarette stub into the glittering grass. He reached for a crumpled packet from his back pocket and offered Newhouse a fag, then put another in his mouth.

I'm waiting for him, too, as it happens, as it happens, he said, his eyes twitching. Nice day though, isn't it. Nice day for it. What's in the briefcase?

An argument, Newhouse said.

Ah yes, of course, of course, Laurence said. His shirtsleeves were pulled long and buttoned tight. The argument, yes. Well I have a few of those myself, he said. He was beginning to sweat.

Do you like poems? Laurence said.

I used to, Newhouse said.

The Magus Zoroaster, my dead child, Laurence said, *Met*

his own image walking in the garden.

Newhouse heard footsteps echoing in the hallway. He looked back, but it was empty.

Forty bedrooms, Laurence said. Forty bedrooms here.

Forty? Newhouse said, peering into the hall.

Or fourteen, Laurence said. A lot anyway.

Do you live here?

Laurence was crumpled over the stone parapet.

No, not anymore, no, Laurence said quietly, moving his head from side to side. Smoke shifted around his blotchy face.

I did and then I didn't. I didn't and then I did. I live in town, in the smoke.

London?

Used to. Used to, Jack. Had a place. Had to come back though. City's not for me, he said, shaking his locks, looking hard into the garden, squinting. Too much time on my hands, too much to do. Quit it for the old country, you know?

Newhouse nodded. He picked his mobile phone out of his pocket. He had missed a call from the office. He had a text from Rudi. It said: *Remember dinner tomorrow night, 7:30 at my place. Bring a bottle. Bring a woman. Read the Art Newspaper on Flemish sale? Heard about Hermitage?*

You waiting for Murrey too?

No, no, no, Laurence said, stretching again. He chuckled, No. You are, not me.

Okay.

I have his number, Laurence said, I can call him anytime. He answers. We talk fine, we talk all the time.

Can I have his number? Newhouse asked.

Laurence looked at him, his eyes moving quickly.

Yeah, sure, he said. He took an old flip-up mobile phone

from his pocket and recited a number to Newhouse, who tapped it into his.

I need a walk, Laurence said, and moved slowly down the stone steps to the garden. His white feet sunk into the green. He padded slowly, bonily, across the grass, smoking, then walked through an arch in the hedge and disappeared.

Newhouse phoned the number. A dialling tone rang and rang.

A man answered: Yeah?

Mr Murrey?

Ya what?

Sorry, is this Murray Murrey?

Who is this?

This is George Newhouse, from the Public Gallery.

How did you get this number pal?

From Laurence?

Who? Do you want something?

I don't know. Laurence gave this to me, look I think this is a mistake, Newhouse said. He shook his head.

Fuck off will ya, the voice said. Fuck off. If you want more, call me back.

The line went dead.

Newhouse sat on the step, his heart pounding. He heard footsteps somewhere in the house, echoing down a hallway he would never see. The sun glittered on many windows, seared the blades of grass, and heated the stone underneath him. Faint smoke rose from a distant bonfire, stoked by a stick held by an unseen hand. Dust drifted on old paintings, and a car was started in the drive. He looked up into the sky.

Murray Murrey would never come.

THE LAKE

She had sat there, at the long white table, her finger moving over the map. She had planned their journey, following a path on roads, back roads, motorways and country lanes.

Ruth took a pencil and traced the route. They would be driving down the coast until the main road shook inland, moving through low marshland, and then into sudden high hills, a long lake, a winding, high-sided valley, and then they would enter the market town, where they would see a horse show, a fair, and maybe stay overnight. She wanted to see the horses, the local ponies.

Does that sound OK?

That sounds good.

We don't have to if you don't want to.

No, that's fine.

He was washing up, suds spattered on his shirt and forearms, his legs bare, his boxer shorts faded and tatty. The sun gleamed on pale crockery, on the remnants of their breakfast on cooling blue plates. Last night's fire was silvery ash in the black-mouthed hearth. She was in his shirt, drawing circles and patterns on the map.

He was late with his paper on Van Doelenstraat, she was late with marking and revisions. Neither of them were sleeping well.

Now the car eased around a long lazy corner. White stones marked its edges, either side, spiky grass tufted in the marsh. Ruth was driving. He turned the radio on. It played music for a while, and she turned it off.

Had such a strange dream last night, she said.

I have to remember it, write it down.

He didn't answer.

It was all mirrors and reflections. I was standing on a beach, watching you walk through the frame of a mirror, she said.

Right.

It was my mirror, the blue one. I had made some kind of deal for you but I don't know what it was, and anyway you were ungrateful. You didn't thank me for it. I felt aggrieved but... there was some kind of miscommunication. We couldn't understand each other. And then you walked back through the frame and were gone.

Are you sure this was a dream?

She shook her head slightly.

Yes. Well anyway. I guess it's true how boring other people's dreams are.

Yes, he said.

They drove on further.

So what's in this town?

I told you.

What's there?

Horses.

Horses?

Ponies, it is famous for them.

Do you like horses?

What else is there to do here?

Ok, he said.

I had a horse once.

Ok.

Their bags were jumbled on the back seat. He looked at them. He would be reading and writing again tonight. She had been writing too.

He looked at Ruth. She sucked her bottom lip.

They drove in silence, and the air thickened. As the mountains came closer, low clouds rose and a mist crept over the fields.

The mountains were sudden and vast. A sudden dropped curtain of rock.

Do you mind if we stop? she said.

What for?

I need some air.

She brought the car to a halt we know. The air was thick with hazy rain, and they were alone as they walked silently down to the lake.

The lake lay solid and deep blue.

She walked ahead of him, towards the water's edge. He looked around at rolling low mounds covered in spiky bog and tough brown grass as high as their knees.

The mud sucked at their shoes and they hopped from tussock to tussock and rock to rock, steadily moving towards the murmuring lake's edge that lapped slowly and silently at the shore.

She walked ahead, her jeans, brown-stained with mud and soggy from the rain. She got to the thin pebble beach and, with her hands in her pockets and her hood up, walked slowly to the edge of the water and stood still.

He heard rain on the hills as he got to the beach, and the grey pebbles crunched under his feet.

She stood with her back to him for a while. As he approached her, she turned around. Her cheeks flushed with chill.

Great, isn't it, she said.

He walked up to her, nodded and said: It's cold.

She rolled her eyes.

Why are you being like this?

Like what?

You're being a dick.

I am cold.

I know you have work to do. I have work to do, too.

It's not that.

What then?

I'm OK.

She turned her head, and he saw a raindrop fall on the pale coral arch of her ear, and run through and past tiny pale hairs, past a pale brown birthmark, down its slender length. He moved behind her as she looked at the lake. He felt the warmth of her body and moved his arms around her.

She flinched.

Please, she said, get off me.

He held her.

George, she said.

He held her.

George.

He held her.

Please.

Light drowned in the nameless lake, dying in its fathom of shadow.

LAS RESULTAS

The darkness of books. Rows and rows of bound wood. Lines and lines of bound paper. Leather and string, cardboard and pulp. Bound and inked and stitched and filed. Sullen and dumb witnesses in wood and brass. The bookcases loomed, the pictures between them, soaking in the night silence.

As if under water, with no light beneath the waves, Dr Hans Martinu read and worked. In his leather chair, its marching studs dull under a single light, it was 3.03am. Gavin was not yet home.

A crack of coal spat in the grate. Low flames flicked in shadows on the ceiling. Each flame with its shadow, divided.

In the opened pages on his knees, plates of the paintings of the artist Van Doelenstraat. Newhouse's artist. There were two empty rooms, finely rendered. One with walls of flaked plaster, a bed, a stool, a jug, Delft tiles, a closed and shuttered window. On the right page, its print pulling away from the paper at the corner, a living room: a large cupboard, a chair with a tapestry slung over it. A dull chandelier. A map of the Netherlands on the wall. Closed shutters, again. Red brick leaking through cracked plaster. Damp patches in the corners and stained paint at the skirting board. Beautifully painted, preserved, and empty.

A minor but superbly talented painter. Like Fabritius, perhaps. But that Rembrandt letter had changed everything. And Newhouse's work, holding up an obscurity to new light.

The Blue Horse would be found. He knew it. It was close.

He closed the book, marking its place with an envelope printed with a red M. on the envelope, there was a line written in pencil. It was swiftly written, while his other hand was on the telephone. An international call.

Encased. Plumbum. No corrosion. No electric. Ductile. Open Hand r/v.

The fire was low. Coals crumbled. His cat was somewhere in the house. The rooms were silent. Outside a car came close, then passed.

He needed a piss. He moved slowly to the bathroom. In the dark he lifted the seat and peed into the lavatory. He felt the hot liquid leave him. His back relaxed. He needed to sleep. Gavin would be home sooner or later. He could have the spare room.

Martinu moved in the swimming darkness, back to the library. He needed the book. He was looking for his cat. Where was it?

He opened the door, and walked in.

In his chair, a body.

TWENTY FOUR

Newhouse was at a dinner party.

There was Rudi and his new girlfriend, Iona, and three more couples whose names he could not remember.

Then there was a thick set art dealer called Santopietro, and his wife, Gillian.

They had eaten pink fleshy salmon and then some tough lamb. That was hours ago. Wine had been drunk, port and prosecco. And brandy and gin and tonic.

The night had spun by as time slewed around the crockery and fine glasses. Newhouse sat next to Gillian Santopietro. She'd just moved to the city to work at the university. She taught medieval and early modern history, and was researching religious archives in the Low Countries. Rudi said he had put them together so they could talk about those dreadful Dutch people. Gillian had a deep voice, like a radio announcer.

They talked about the Netherlands, and tried to find academics they knew in common. She'd met Dr Martinu once.

A frightening man, she said.

I think sometimes he scares himself.

Newhouse felt tiredness creeping through his body. He drank more.

Did anyone ever say, she said, smiling, as wine was repoured into their glasses, and her husband was in the bathroom, that you look very much like that actor from the television? I cannot place his name.

No, I can't say they have.

You really do, she said, shaking her head, looking at her wine, one hand to her neck. I wish I could remember his name. What is his name?

I assume he is known for being late, hungover and dishevelled, he said.

She put a hand to his hand.

No, George.

Santopietro barrelled back to his seat and sat down heavily, with a sigh. His hands were wet and he wiped them on his trousers.

So, George Newhouse, he said, you are the original Dutch prodigy, I hear.

He knows more than I, Gillian said. About art, at least.

Newhouse had taken some pain killers.

You trump me on ecclesiastical history, he said.

Now, now, Rudi bellowed from the other end of the table. Don't inflate that fat English head of his. The bastard.

People laughed. Gillian smiled at her empty plate.

You're embarrassing him, Iona said.

And the conversation moved on. Newhouse drank a gin and tonic. Someone put a CD of Sinatra on. Rudi stood up, buttoned his waistcoat, and paused the music to announce that he and Iona were now engaged. Everyone laughed and smiled. People clapped. Santopietro wandered across the room, lit a cigar and blew the smoke out of an opened window. Iona looked at the floor, moved her feet in a short little dance and then half-ran to the bathroom.

There were handshakes and backclaps. Newhouse smiled and nodded at Rudi. Rudi looked at Newhouse and nodded back. Iona re-appeared, her eyes red.

Newhouse looked at Iona again. He had not met her before. He remembered Rudi saying he had met a woman at the opera, at a business function in the interval. She was small with white blonde hair.

Her apartment, which Rudi appeared to have already moved into, was enormous, with pictures hung on blood red walls. Chandeliers were slung heavy from high ceilings. Her father had run a piping company. Now he was dead and she did nothing. She was a trustee, ran Friends' societies. She briefly wrote a column for the local evening paper on her gilded life. She said she saw Rudi at the Usher Hall during the overture to Parsifal, and was smitten.

In her low tone, leaning over, Gillian told Newhouse she was looking into occult practice and church responses in the Netherlands.

It was not only a phenomenon in Latin countries, she said, scraping a small spoon around a glass that had contained black chocolate mousse.

There were dozens of strange rites in the 1630s, 40s, 50s, she said. But the Dutch are less theatrical, there is less levitating and the throwing up of frogs and nails and such like.

Where? Newhouse said.

In the towns, she said, in Breda, Utrecht, Groningen.

Delft?

Very possibly. I haven't gone through it all yet: the records are so voluminous, she said, shaking her head. It will take me a while, of course.

Of course, he said.

But what a city we have here, she said, we feel so lucky to have landed here.

Indeed, he said.

Rudi and Iona were dancing to the music, and another

couple joined them. Iona held Rudi's thick arms, he held her slim waist. They stared at each other. It dawned on Newhouse that Rudi was wearing a cummerbund.

Gillian stood up and walked across the room with Santopietro to the large open window: the city glowed with electric light, with the swell of low clouds lit with orange haze and the buzzing fug of street lights and traffic. The castle stood in blue spotlights, as if cut from ice and granite, displayed on its rocky shelf.

Newhouse was beginning to feel sick. He had to travel to Glasgow the following day to finalise the identity of the Biennale artist. He was sure they would choose Brick Macpherson.

He left his seat and moved to the bathroom. It was long and white and clean. He staggered a little, his knee rapping on the bathtub.

He stared at his face in the mirror as he washed his hands.

Newhouse saw faces drifting and dropping, shaking like moths, like summer insects fluttering and flashing before a night candle. There was a terrible vacuum in his stomach. But he also felt a sense of pale anticipation. As if something was about to happen, and it was not necessarily bad, or worse than had come before. He wondered if he was eager to know what it was.

He dried his hands in the bathroom while music played and people shouted in the next room.

He looked back into the mirror. There was darkness, a doorway, the stark frame of an empty easel. His heart pounded. He blinked. He looked into the mirror again, and only saw his face, tiny burst blood vessels in his eyes, his hair a little too harshly cut, the trace of an old scar near his left eye. He clenched his teeth and looked at them, white and straight. He stuck out his tongue, it was pink, spotted with furry white, a tiny coiled hair near the middle. He pulled it out.

He could hear Rudi roaring next door.

He tucked in his white shirt, straightened his suit, and went back to the dining room.

Ah, gorgeous George, Rudi shouted. People smiled and laughed. One of the couples was kissing by the open window. Iona was laughing with another woman. Gillian was sitting beside Rudi.

So Rudolf, George said, filling a glass with red wine. How are the loincloths of Christ?

Gillian frowned.

Rudi here, Newhouse said, is studying the penis of Jesus.

The Humanation of Christ, Rudi said, loudly. There will be a book, there shall be a show. It's going to seriously affect the courses of modern Christology, he said.

You should see the Krug, the Maerten van Heemskerck, Newhouse said, looking at Gillian. She smiled.

Extraordinary, Newhouse said.

Revolutionary, Rudi suddenly yelled.

Tell me more, she said to Rudi.

Well, he said, red-cheeked. He winked at Iona, who was moving around the room, pouring spirits into glasses.

In Jesus, they say, God became a man, a whole man. And a whole man was a penis, and after three days, it became erect. Erect! he shouted. People jumped in mock surprise.

Newhouse ran his finger around the top of his wine glass. He heard, above Sinatra's glossy croon, the faint chime of a glass-tone as he eased his flesh along the rim. Gillian was staring at him.

Now Jesus was circumcised, of course... Rudi was saying.

Newhouse raised his eyebrows. He looked at Gillian. Her husband was talking to a man by the stereo system. They were talking about something that involved sizes, volumes, lengths and measurements. Their hands rose and fell, holding invisible boxes, sketching trapeziums in the air. Gillian was sat still, her body facing Rudi, her eyes on Newhouse.

...There are paintings where the Madonna is pulling back his clothes to show his manhood, there are erased erections, there are crucifixions where he clearly has a hard-on.

Rudi, Iona scolded softly.

When they hung men for witchcraft, Gillian said, looking at Newhouse, they would often have erections. The blood flows and fills the tissues.

Jesus loved Mary Magdelane, someone said.

He was a man, a real man, Rudi said, nodding. Ja. He lost his temper, he scolded, he was ironic, he was grandeloquent, he was mystical and poetic, he was sarcastic: he loved, he lusted. And he had a big fat dick.

Oh Rudi, Iona said, smiling.

Gillian looked down at her fingers.

God sent his own Son in the likeness of sinful flesh, Newhouse said.

What is that? Rudi said.

Romans, I think.

You know your New Testament too, Rudi laughed.

Conversation moved on. More people came to the table.

Someone asked Newhouse about Brick Macpherson. He said he was a very skilled painter, among the finest of his very fine generation, but possibly wasting his talent on replicating pornography.

What kind of pornography? Gillian said.

All kinds, he said.

Hardcore?

Yes.

Like what?

Some violent, some tasteless, some depressing. All extreme, almost medical.

She nodded.

People talked about house prices, about nursery fees, about the other city: its corruption, its gangsters.

I'm going there tomorrow, Newhouse said, slurring. The edges of his eyesight were gauzy and red.

Remember to take your own soap, someone said.

Someone asked what Newhouse specialised in. Newhouse looked at his glass while Rudi explained his great knowledge of Dutch art.

George is the kind of person who gets excited about local Delft painters of the early 17th century, Rudi said. Little Dutch men painting maids and dockers.

It's true, Newhouse said.

Like who, George? Rudi said, taunting a little.

Oh, I don't know, Newhouse said. He thought of Pieter Steenwijk, Egbert van der Poel, Balthasar van der Ast.

Someone really obscure like Reynier Jansz, he said.

Rudi laughed.

I'm not familiar with him, Santopietro said.

Reynier, that's a nice name, Iona said.

Jansz was Vermeer's father, Rudi said loudly. George

here is being clever.

Not only that, but a weaver, an art dealer, pub owner, Newhouse said. But he was Johanne's father, yes.

I've never heard that before, Gillian said.

George specialises in people no one has ever heard of, Rudi said, like his precious Van Doelenstraat. VD. He was truly remarkable: he painted pictures no one has ever seen.

Oh come on. These are all just made up Dutch names, Iona said, blowing smoke from a small cigar into the ceiling, you're making them up.

Joos Barneveld van der Flughafen, Rudi said with a rough approximation of a Dutch accent, Tulip van der Bicycle, he shouted. People laughed. Iona giggled.

Newhouse downed his drink then stood unsteadily, and walked to the door.

The talk carried on behind him. The hall was shadowy, sliding off his eyesight. He walked into the loo, but someone else was there.

The bath was full of dark liquid, a woman lay in it, her back to him, her head away from him.

The bathroom door closed behind him.

The bath, full of blood, the white body within it, upright, unmoving, breathing.

He was not breathing.

The neck moved. The head began to turn. An eye. A nose. Another eye. A red mouth. Gaping.

The face turned to him.

An open mouth with no teeth. A red maw. The black red of gum holes, bone ripped from the pulped sockets.

Lover, this is my face too.

Ruth's voice.

He moved back. He opened his mouth to shout but

there was no noise.

He felt a body behind him and he suddenly fell.

There was a shriek and some shouting, the sudden weight of a body on top of him, and then beneath him.

He was lying on top of a scrabbling body. Pain spiked in his back, his legs. There was a woman underneath him. It was Gillian. Other people stood about.

Rudi was suddenly in the hallway, laughing loudly. Noise splintered off tiles, off the chandelier, off the colours of the room that were hurtling around Newhouse's sore head.

For god's sake, Gillian said, and pulled her feet from under Newhouse. She stood up stiffly, pulling her skirt down, straightening herself.

Fuck's sake, man, Santopietro said, unsurely.

Newhouse lay in the hall by the bathroom door. He could see a collection of gathered feet and legs, ankles and socks.

Rudi knelt beside him. More wine, vicar?

I think I need to go home.

Gillian said something sharp to her husband, then knelt down too. She put a cool hand to Newhouse's head.

You are feverish.

He's pissed, Rudi said.

I fell over, Newhouse said.

I know. On me, Gillian said.

I'm so sorry, Newhouse said, and tried to sit. Rudi roughly pulled him up, and leant him against the wall.

The group of people had moved away.

You look terrible, Gillian said. He saw her face. She looked concerned.

Did I hurt you?

No no, she said.

Don't worry about that, man. Gillian's used to fat old Santo sprawling all over her, Rudi said, and staggered off.

Newhouse said he needed to sit down. He and Gillian moved to a sofa.

You gave me a shock, she said.

He looked into the bathroom. It was just a bathroom. Pale tiles and a toilet, a sink and a shower. No bath. No bodies.

For fuck's sake, he said.

What?

For God's sake, he said.

He felt something pulling at his eyes. And at his chest. Like a child, his lower lip began to quiver.

Gillian patted his hand.

I'll call you a taxi, she said.

He stifled a sob.

I can't take it, he said very quietly.

She didn't hear him.

I cannot do this anymore.

TWENTY FIVE

The door was knocked and Hayley entered his office.

Sorry about the delay, cartridge needed changing.

Thanks Hayley.

It needs a binder, I think.

It's long, he said, and smiled. She did not smile back. Can you send that attachment to Mr Rudolf, Mr Carver, and Mr Colebrooke please.

Of course, with the painting as its front page?

Yes, *Interior with An Opened Letter* by Van Doelenstraat, 1646. And that title: *The Netherlands and Low Country Collections, a Summary by G. Newhouse.*

She left the room. He sat back in his chair and took off his shoes. It had taken a while. There were problems in the archives, problems with categorisation. Some etchings had been listed as drawings. A de Hoogh drawing was actually missing.

He had been drinking too much.

He looked out over the gallery gardens.

Collosus had been removed. Carver had mentioned an enormous bill, some kind of cancellation fee. He briefly thought of Tyler, her face and her voice.

His visit to Glasgow had been short: he left the train, walked to a coffee shop, and met with three other curators, the producer, Hill – a nervous man – and a press officer. Everyone agreed Brick Macpherson should represent the Gallery at the Venice Biennale.

The city's noise had been deafening: buses wheezing, an underground rumbling, people shouting, a press of cars winding slowly around a central tarmac square.

There had been high buildings, 1960s office blocks, sandstone 19th century banks which now sold clothes, coffee, furniture. Marble columns on computer game stores, colonnades around shoe shops and chip shops. There were bulky policemen in paramilitary uniforms: armour, truncheons, gas guns and tasers clunked on their belts.

Newhouse spent the meeting leaning in to hear what the others were saying. He found that he had to shout when he spoke. It seemed the whole city was shouting. He heard yelling and shrieking in the streets. A white noise of bellowing, bouncing off crumbling brick and concrete. It felt like a city that was howling. As if somewhere a great mass of people were being crushed by masonry.

This week he had to go back there to meet Brick at a studio. He'd made arrangements with an assistant, a Ms Boyd, over the telephone. Brick had an idea for Venice and would be able to tell him about it. It was too complicated to explain over the telephone.

Newhouse figured the budget for Venice was a third of what it should have been. He hoped it would cover what Macpherson thought he could do. It was not more porn, Ms Boyd had said, and it wasn't more schematics. It has more to do with God, she had said, then hung up.

Perhaps it's a scale painting of God, Rudi suggested.

There was a small pile of post on his desk and Newhouse went through it after he had filled and put on the electric kettle in the corner of his office. He could hear it rattling and moaning as it heated up. There were press releases and subscription reminders, there was a bill for his predecessor and, at the bottom of the pile, a handwritten envelope from London. He recognised the writing, and put it to one side. His chest felt tight. Hayley knocked at the door and walked in.

He looked up, annoyed. Behind Hayley he could see the bulk of Rudi, his face was flat and white.

George, I am so sorry. We have had a call from the police, Hayley said.

What about? Newhouse said, his pulse quickening. He pushed the envelope further away, under his computer keyboard. The small white kettle was bubbling and shaking. Steam gushed up the wall.

It's Dr Martinu, Rudi said, stepping around Hayley, who was holding her hands, looking at the floor.

What? Newhouse said, standing up.

He's dead. He has been found dead at home, Rudi said.

I am so sorry, Hayley said, and fled.

Newhouse looked at the floor. The pattern and bindings of the carpet shifted and moved. The tiny linked bubbles of wool and polyester shook and shimmered. He looked at his desk, and the envelope's edge glinted from under the keyboard.

Rudi sat down heavily, and lit a cigarette.

Fucking hell.

Newhouse pulled at the envelope and opened it. A slim folded piece of paper slipped out, and sliced a tiny cut on his thumb.

Blood welled and dropped.

He opened the letter. It was from John-Joseph, Ruth's brother. He looked up and Rudi was staring out of the window.

Dearest George,

It has been some time, I know. Perhaps time is what we needed. But now, perhaps, fate has intervened. I have found something you may be interested in.

TWENTY SIX

Martinu had been dead for days.

The Doctor had been expected to turn in his catalogue notes for an exhibition that summer, but had missed his deadline. The galleries had called but there was no answer. A neighbour noticed his lights were on, his curtains undrawn. When the police found him, he was dead in his armchair.

Hector Carver, who had known him for more than thirty years, identified the body. No one could find Martinu's lover, Gavin. He did not return their calls. He did not return his emails. Martinu had no next of kin, no family.

Carver had sat in Newhouse's office. He looked even thinner and more boney than usual.

And the terrible thing about his eyes... he said.

Newhouse said, Go on.

They found him... when they found him, after those days, they found his face had... well, Warren had eaten his eyes.

Oh my god, Newhouse had said. He temporarily thought Gavin's name was Warren.

Then he remembered Warren was Martinu's cat.

Yes, Carver said. Warren was found under a cupboard.

Where is he now?

In a pot, I imagine, Carver said. Or buried in the garden.

Anna called Newhouse at work and said she was devastated. She said she knew how much the Doctor had meant to him. Newhouse said thank you.

I'll maybe speak to you soon, then, she said.

I'm quite busy, he said.

OK. But let's meet soon. We have things to talk about. What things?

The galleries, what is happening, of course. Do you not think?

Yes. My diary, it's busy, he said. And Martinu has been found dead.

I know, you must be upset. But we must do something. Nothing is happening with Ardrashaig. There is no dialogue. Something has gone seriously wrong. I don't understand the lethargy. What's happening?

I don't know, Anna.

I don't know either. We should meet and talk. I'm so sorry about Dr Martinu.

I'll see. I have this Biennale thing. This review of the Netherlandish collection. It's all so…

OK George, I get it. You're busier than me. Well, call me. I'll be coming down for meetings, she said. I think we could meet. We could get together with Pamela Hardcastle, with Sergio at the Portrait Gallery, even Paul at the National Gallery of Modern Art…

And do what? he said. They have their own issues.

Talk about what's happening to the Public Gallery, she said. Form a working group. We can brief the press. We can brief the politicians.

The press know what's going on, he said. The politicians know what's going on. They have no money either. The papers. The BBC have done something or other. I don't know.

Right, she said quietly.

There was a brief silence. Then she asked: Are you OK?

Yes, fine.

Because that night at the castle. I worried.

I'd had too much to drink. And those pills. Bad combination.

Nightmare combo, my son says, she said, lightly.

Yes a nightmare. But, no processions of tiny people yet. No hats.

He could hear her breathing.

Look Dr Blanco, I have to go, he said.

George, she said. Her tone had changed. Her voice hardened.

What?

I'm disappointed. I thought you were a serious person. You are not a serious person.

What do you mean?

About this terrible mess.

OK, I have to go, he said.

Let's leave it, let's do it? like that then.

Must go.

This is a disaster and no one is doing anything.

What is there to do, Anna? There is nothing we can do. It will be terrible yes, you're right, nothing is happening. The paintings will go. And then we'll survive.

There was a silence.

I am disappointed, she said.

I'm sorry, he said. He put the phone down.

His email pinged.

It was a message from Carver. Martinu had left a file on his desk, marked for George Newhouse. Its title was: The Blue Horse.

LOS ANGELES

Not long after Ruth's funeral, he flew to Los Angeles. He had a job interview at the Getty.

He woke in a large bed, a TV on, muted but flashing brightly. Clear sunshine glowed in the window. Heat on his flesh. Fresh white sheets held his legs, fresh pillows gave under his head. He closed his eyes, and saw caves of crimson and red.

He propped himself up, naked. The light was on in the bathroom, an extractor fan humming. His suitcase stood unopened on the floor.

He put on pants and opened the blinds.

A sheet of light from east to west, a scattering of pale houses, and a vast wall of blue sea, silent, a mile away. A jumbo jet lowered and came into land at the airport, nearby. Yacht masts bobbed in a marina. He could smell fresh bread, drifting up from the kitchen.

Newhouse sat on the edge of the bed and flicked through dozens of TV channels. A sports channel showed highlights of a gridiron game the night before: in a massive bowl of light, enormous men in pads and glinting helmets hurled themselves at each other.

At breakfast he sat near the white wood verandah, but not on it. He had drunk a lot on the flight, his head was heavy. His hair was too long, he had grown a scruffy beard. The owner of the hotel smiled and served him coffee, muffins, pancakes, syrup, different kinds of fruit, and soft fresh bread, its crust like linen, its dough tacky and sweet.

He walked out into the sunshine. There were no clouds

in the sky. The blue shook with lines and worms, jags of shape skipped from eyeball to eyeball. The city lay inland, its motorways and hotels, its drags and malls, they all hummed and buzzed somewhere behind him.

He had been to Los Angeles before, visiting galleries and collectors. He had stayed in a hotel with what seemed to be a crew of mutilated bar staff, men and women with plastic faces, rubber breasts, strange amphibian smiles. He had phoned Ruth from a stone telephone on the 15th floor, in a hot tub, laughing about plastic surgery, discussing silicon, about the price of modern art, about their life together. But that was some time ago.

Here, in this seaside suburb, detached from the city by marshes, by disused land, and the thunder of the airport, there was a single street with a bank, a juice shop, a coffee store, some shops, some restaurants, and a long view of the Pacific. A lifeguard tower stood black, as if drawn by heavy pencil, etched on the wide gold beach. Breakers lapped in a fizzle of white.

The sidewalk moved under his light feet. His fingers tingled. He stopped in the juice bar. He ordered a coffee and sat at a small wooden table and reached for a newspaper. A man in shorts and a baseball cap worked on a laptop. Two women slumped together on a sofa, drinking coffee. He looked to his pocket, but found only his room key. He had left everything behind.

His mobile phone was somewhere in the Thames, tumbling in the tide, lost in the silt and sand.

The coffee arrived and he stared at it as the sun rose to the height of the sky. There were twenty-three points of light in the glittering cup, tingling around its ceramic curve. He counted them. He thought of his telephone, drifting in the currents. Swamped plastic under the rust of the handrails, the crumbling red brick in the darkness, bobbing under waterlogged timbers, the salvage yards and the listing barges, choking with dread weed and mud.

He drank quickly and walked in the heat to the beach. He felt unsteady, drunk. He had no hat and his skin began to tingle.

Another jet pulled in to land at LAX.

He smelled running shoes and latex. Someone ran past.

Newhouse hung his head. He smelled his sweat. He smelled his body. He curled his arms around his legs. He was tiny. The world rolled under him and he felt no weight. He and the sand were alike, he and the grains of sand: the sea rolled up to them and returned. He could be moulded and dragged, crushed and encircled.

He opened his eyes. The sun like a vast fire.

Newhouse glanced at the bikini girls, looked at the joggers, saw the sunglasses of the lifeguard, watched the slumped fishermen on the bridge toting their rods into the blue sea, saw the sandwich seller on the coast path, the rustling dog walkers, the tiny white birds, eyeless on the current: they all knew nothing of him.

The skin of the bikini girls gleamed.

Shadows flitted across their bodies as the small white birds flew.

Newhouse slowly rose to his feet. He brushed the sand from his clothes. He walked back to the hotel.

It was clean and warm. Fans turned slowly on the ceilings. Fresh coffee sat black on the sideboard.

Newhouse walked into the kitchen, took a pastry, and went to his room. He opened his laptop and found a menswear shop in the city. He thought of going there, ordering ten new suits, ten new shirts, new shoes and new ties. He ordered room service.

Newhouse showered, dressed, walked out and got a new haircut, a fresh, wet shave. The razorblade scraped across his neck. He took a taxi to a mall, and bought new aftershave, new soap, new skin conditioner. He sat in the dark and watched the TV in silence. He watched planes stacking, rolling, and swooping in to land. He saw lights at sea. He saw cars roll slowly along the road. He saw people walking slowly on the sidewalks.

He picked up the receiver of the telephone beside his bed, tapped in a number, and called it.

It rang and rang.

He put the handset down.

He called it again.

It rang.

Newhouse called it again.

His home number. Their home number.

No one was going to pick it up.

It rang and rang.

He called it again.

TWENTY SEVEN

Martinu's file was made from grey cardboard. It contained several sheets of paper: notes, some scribblings that were hard to read, some photocopies, a faxed statement from a museum, an old ledger of a Parisian art dealer, a copy of a file with *US MILITARY* as its heading.

Newhouse pulled out the military file first. He looked at the document. It was dated 1945. It was the notes from a meeting with a Soviet commander, who had been given Carinhall, the palace of Goering, as a present from the Kremlin.

Carinhall had been built by Goering and named after his dead wife. It lay north east of Berlin, in the Schorfheide forest. Commander Leonid Rublev said the vast weight of art that Goering had plundered from Europe was already gone from the house when he received it. The most valuable of what remained would be taken to Leningrad or to Moscow. He said the Red Army found a chaotic, destroyed scene when the palace was discovered. Large, rolled up paintings had been found buried in the grounds. Many works were burned by the Nazis before they arrived. Large piles of ashes studded the gardens. Locals found objects in the nearby lake. In the straggling grounds, statues were smashed, marble women and men broken from their pedestals. White heads lay in the dark grass, splintered legs stood jagged on granite plinths.

The Reichmarshall's house had been razed – all that remained of the Nazi's palace, modelled as a vast hunting lodge, was a gable end, standing alone, and his daughter's playhouse, a tiny model version of the Palace of Sans Souci. Goering, Rublev explained, had the palace detonated before the Red Army could reach it.

Rublev listed the art works that remained. They were found buried in fireplaces, behind plinths, in a garage, which the US, UK and French forces could add to the repatriation committee for artworks – most were Dutch, Flemish, and German works by anonymous or obscure artists. Some signatures could not be deciphered.

On the list was a work that was found when a fractured plinth had collapsed.

The report said:

> *We have been confounded by one particular matter worthy of note. Our soldiers found a sealed box of lead inside an unmarked Italian marble plinth for a statue of a horse. Inside the box was a framed painting, with the title: The Blue Horse by Peter Van Dolenstraat [written in English]. However the face of the canvas had been covered entirely by a blank layer of a soft metal. On the back of the canvas our experts found a painting of a family, untouched. They believe it dates from the mid-17th century. It has been passed to Moscow.*

Newhouse read an attached note by Martinu: *BH never reached Moscow, listed in sales document, Paris, 1948, Halfhouse & Melcombe Paris office, damaged work by PVD (1650?) sold to prvt collector, 1100F.*

Newhouse's mobile phone buzzed on his desk top.

It was Tyler.

Hiya. Tyler here. Recovered from the maze? it said. *Sorry*

*late notice but its Garage drinks tonight, at the show.
You're welcome to pop by.*

Drink and show sounds good, he texted back quickly.

He left the Martinu file on his desk and shut down the office lights.

Only the screen of his computer glowed in the darkness as he pulled his coat on.

He felt something move in the air. Something was wrong. Cold air ran thinly over his hands, his cheeks. In the corner of the office, a darker bulk stood. There was nothing there. No filing cabinets, no bookcase. Now there was a blur of blackness, darker than the shadows. He screwed up his eyes, his hand moved to the door of the office. His hand moved in the air but did not find the handle. The darkness was solid, its shape changing. He flicked on the light.

The room was bright, clear, its corners and edges sharp. Nothing was in the corner of the room. No darkness, no shadow. Just the hinge of wall and wall, a sharp junction of stones built hundreds of years ago, covered in plaster and wallpaper.

He shut off the light and left the room. He realized he was breathing heavily.

He thought of Martinu's papers.

He thought of Martinu. His old flat, where once they had drunk many drinks and talked about art and artists, about theories and histories – bunking and debunking, gossiping about galleries and museums. Already it seemed so long ago. He saw his face, but could not fully recall the size of his mouth, the colour of his eyes, the way the skin hung on his cheeks, the colour of his thinning hair.

His friend's size and warmth and shape were already

lost to him.

As he walked down the dark road, looking for a taxi, he thought of his sister. She had once been afraid of the dark. They had all been afraid of the dark.

He went through his numbers on his mobile phone and called her. Eventually a distant shrill noise sounded, like a phone trilling in a bucket at the end of a corridor.

Hello?

It was Ursula, heavy and sleepy.

Oh fuck, he thought. He had ignored the time difference.

Hello? she said again. George? Are you alright?

He wanted to tell her about the darkness. About how scared he had been. But he suddenly couldn't.

Yes, yes, he said, trying to sound happy.

Are you alright? she said again. What are you doing?

Sorry, sorry, I will call in the morning – your morning I mean – sorry I have fucked this up. I just called to say, you know, hello.

No, no, it's fine George. Hamish is away and I am dozing. Wait a second.

There was a click.

What's the matter then?

Nothing, he said.

Right, she said. She sounded unconvinced. He knew she was unconvinced.

I just wanted a chat, he said. Maybe some normality.

What's not normal for you, she said.

I... nothing. You know what it is? I think I am just a little homesick, he said. But that's nonsense. Sorry. I will go.

No, no, it's not at all, she said. Are you sleeping? You know what Mother would have said.

No, not really. My job has got a bit complicated. I didn't really appreciate what a mess this place was in.

She yawned.

New jobs tend to be like that, she said. You'll take a while to get used to it. Look, your first job, you were so young. You still are. Hamish has been in Hong Kong for a month. On and off. His back is giving him all kinds of jip. But anyway, homesick George – what for? For London, you mean? You could move back. I'm sure the National...

No, no. I don't mean that. You know what I mean. It comes and goes. But it mainly comes.

Of course, she said.

There was a silence.

That is natural. It's to be expected, George.

He was still walking through the dark city. His footsteps and his breathing were all he could hear.

If you need a break, you know we are here. I would come and visit but...

No, don't even think of that, he said.

He said nothing for a while and neither did she. He walked on. The roads were empty. Not a taxi on the streets.

George, she said. Do you mind if...

Sorry, you sleep. And say hello to the boy for me.

I will. If you need help, you know we can help. I can help. Are you drinking again? Is that it? You're not drinking are you?

No, no.

You sure?

Noooo, you know me, he said. I follow orders. And before you ask, I am eating fine.

Hmm, she said. You better be. I must sleep now, early start tomorrow: Angus is suddenly into horses. So we are off to ride a 'horsie'. Well, a pony.

Newhouse nodded.

Goodnight George, don't worry about the time, you call whenever and wherever.

You are a long way away, he said.

I know. I know. I think of you, she said. Good night.

Bye bye, he said.

The line clicked. He was alone again.

He wondered if he would ever speak to his sister again.

TWENTY EIGHT

The taxi stopped outside The Garage and Newhouse stepped out.

A group of people were standing outside its doors, drinking and smoking. It was a large, old industrial building near the docks. Music was pulsing inside. Fresh, chill night air in his mouth and nose. He saw the young people laughing, the lights strobing through a crack of the doorway. He heard the laughter, felt a strangeness, and decided against going in. He turned to take the same taxi home.

But the car had gone.

He quickly began to walk up the hill, back to the city.

He arrived at a junction and waited for the lights to change. Cars crossed before him. Light fell across the pavement. It came from a busy, white-lit café on the corner.

Someone was waving at him behind its windows. It was Tyler. She was sitting with some people around a cramped formica table top. She waved again and smiled. Her friends squinted out, into the darkness.

He walked towards the café. Music was playing loudly, people were shouting. The servers behind the bar were shouting.

George, Tyler shouted. She looked flushed, drunk. She waved again.

Hi George, she said, and beckoned him to her table. Her friends smiled.

Good evening. I was just going home, he said, dimly

waving to the street outside.

I'm sorry I missed the show, he said. He was now standing at the table, her friends a bank of blank faces.

Well, I am deeply offended, she said. Come and join us. Shove up, Simon.

No, no, Newhouse said. He was standing and they were sitting.

No bother, someone said.

Actually I am off, so you can have my seat, a man said.

Well…

Me too, said Simon.

Yes, early night for me, a woman said. She smiled at Tyler, who blinked rapidly.

Newhouse now wanted to stay.

And then there were two, Tyler said.

Newhouse was still standing. Tyler said goodbye to her friends. She hugged her female friend. She blew a kiss to Simon, who blew one back.

Newhouse sat down. A waitress came and he ordered a coffee.

So, she said. So you didn't see the Garage?

I didn't… I couldn't get in, he said.

That's a shame, she said. She looked down at her drink.

Yes, I am sorry, would have loved to have seen your work, he said. I will.

Oh really, she said. I'm not sure it's your kind of thing. But surely a curator from the Public Gallery can get into a tiny little art show.

He looked at her face. She had dark eyes, dark hair. She checked her phone. She answered a text message.

Well the party was fun so you missed that. That's my babysitter, Ben's OK.

How old is he? Newhouse said. His coffee had arrived. He filled it with sugar. The café was loud, full of drunk people, some from the Garage party, others from the streets. A television up high in the corner showed autumn trees, a clear stream running over smooth rocks.

The babysitter? She must be twenty.

No, your son.

Three, she said.

Ah right.

Three and a bit.

I have a nephew, he is a handful. He lives in Vancouver. Angus.

How lovely. Yes, it's a busy age, three. That's a shame for you that he lives so far away.

It is, he said. He thinks I actually own all the paintings I work with.

Ben thinks 'talking on my phone' is my job, she said.

How was your show? he asked.

Well, Mister, you should have seen it yourself.

She smiled and looked down at her drink and stirred it.

He asked her what she was working on now. She said paintings, enamel on board. Streets and buildings, houses and carparks.

You know Hammershoi, of course, she said.

He nodded.

I love his London paintings. The empty streets.

Beautiful, he said. His late works.

Exactly, she said. I studied him at art school. Totally in love with Hammershoi. I have taken his warehouse painting from 1909? You know it? I've taken that one work, and just run with it. Copied it, really. So yeah, that's what I'm doing right now.

Why enamel?

It reminds me of my father.

Ah.

Your father still around? she asked.

He and Ursula's father was long dead.

No, I never had a father. I was raised in a cave by a pack of twelve wolves.

She looked at him.

Oh no, not again. I meet a lot of your kind, the wolf children.

Well, it's a growing phenomenon. I would admit it stunts your social skills. But wolves are terribly interested in the arts.

She nodded. He liked the shape of her face. Her lips.

So, he said. I'd like to see your enamels. He looked at her ringless slim left hand.

She nodded and smiled.

I guess all the artists you usually deal with are pretty dead most of the time, she said.

Rather than being dead pretty, he said.

He wondered what he had said. Her face was calm and unreadable but she looked at him.

Oh ha ha, she said.

It is often much worse than them being dead.

What's worse than being dead?

They are the undead. Spectres, some of them, actually.

I feel that way every morning, she said.

Tell me about you, he said. Now we've covered my lupine past, what about yours?

They talked. She was from London, from Highbury. They talked about her art school, also in London.

So after art school, what did you do then? he said.

Actually I had a 'moment'. I just… I just thought: fuck. I am not an artist. This is not me. So I went to Europe.

This is Europe.

OK: yeah. Right. She rolled her eyes.

There was a silence.

Sorry, I'm being a dick. He shook his head. All that was left in his coffee cup was brown sand and bubbles.

Yes. Stop being a dick. Anyway yes so I went abroad. Taught English as a foreign language. The usual thing. Spain, Madrid. Then Italy. Moved around. Then, you know, got into things again in Amsterdam. Moved away from my old stuff, got into new stuff.

Amsterdam, he said.

Yes, love it. So there was this artist collective. Fabrika. We put on shows. Got invited to places. Then… jeez, well, Ben came along.

What happened… is the father here?

The dad is fine but he is not here, no. He is fine. But it wasn't planned. I was freaked out, he was really freaked out. Then this job at the Festival here came up but…

Her voice was low. Her eyes dark.

…turned out it wasn't a job. I don't know. I fucked up. I was pregnant. The dad went back to Holland. It was pretty complicated there for a while.

Newhouse stayed quiet, let her think.

So anyway, I wasn't sure what to do. My mother came up. It was kind of mortifying but – you know. She and dad got me this place. I had Ben. She left again. Dad left again. They want me to move back. I was dead against it…but now, I like it here.

OK, he said.

So you know: I do the mum thing. And I do the artist

collective thing.

The Garage, he said.

Yes, well remembered, she said lightly. You're so clever.

I know my stuff. I've got this contemporary art scene thing taped.

I could tell. It must be your corduroy jacket.

What's wrong with it? He said, looking down. It was old.

Anyway, there's another big show at the Garage this summer. You can't wimp out of that one with some lame excuse.

I won't wait to the summer. I'll see this one. The big one: you'll have some work in it?

I guess. If you can call it 'work'.

She laughed a little.

Of course it is, the most important kind, he said.

What, more than being a curator of dead Dutch people?

Oh, well, it's not that important. How could it be.

Tyler's phone buzzed.

Ah shit, she said.

Your son? he said. He thought of Angus, hurtling around his sister's home.

Yes I am afraid so. I must go.

They moved outside, into the neon and the dark, the low moan of cars, the high stars. She went first, he followed her. He realized he was looking at her body.

Well, I had better go, she said.

But... he said. He did not know what to say next.

They were standing close together.

But what?

Why did you not mention all this before, he said.

What, she said.

That you're an artist.

Hilarious, she said. She smiled.

Why didn't you mention you were such a dick.

Their heads moved together swiftly.

They kissed and he felt her tongue in his mouth. His hands moved through her thick hair, around her face and neck. She put her small hands around his waist, put them inside his jacket as they kissed. They parted and kissed, parted and kissed, and then parted again. Their lips softly clicking and smacking. She was warm. She smelled fresh, her skin was clear and soft.

She pulled away.

Ok, she said. She smiled.

Right, he said, her taste on his lips. The smell of her sweet black hair.

She wiped her mouth and looked down at her boots.

I have to get back, she said.

She smiled. Look, a babysitter is waiting for me.

That's fine, that's fine, Newhouse said. He raised his hands. He felt relieved.

But he wanted to kiss her again. He wanted to hold her body.

Look, I will... she said, and then waved, slightly, and walked down the street.

He waved at her back. He looked at her shoulders, her legs, her body.

He walked quickly home. The darkness around him.

He returned to his empty flat.

His life had not changed. His body had not changed. His memories had not changed.

TWENTY NINE

It was late and had been a long day.

Newhouse had several files about Crawford 'Brick' Macpherson on his desk, and his publications. He looked through his early work, fine oils in a small show called *Rudiments*. His natural technique, his obsession with the quality of surface, not only the beauty of the image, was very evident. And Macpherson possessed draughtmanship of the highest quality. He could probably trace a perfect circle with his wrong hand. His handling of paint, tone, surface and scale were exceptional. He got a first from the Glasgow School of Art, and the highest mark for a portfolio in the school's history. Then he went into seclusion, he told a listings magazine which had championed him, to produce something *that would break the world's face*.

He emerged with 'Damnation'. His series of oil paintings based on stills from pornography had been a press sensation, as well as his commercial watershed. Macpherson had by this point moved to New York. He had chosen some images for their shock value, for sure. Others were more distant, almost abstract. The painting itself was fine, the technique absolutely sure. Like Richter, Macpherson was almost too fine, too photographic. But Macpherson had painted *She Wants Love* more than twenty times: those eyes, the smear of flesh between them, were haunting, were real.

Newhouse looked at an interview.

Q: Why did you choose pornography for your

inspiration? You've repeatedly said you hate pornography.

CM: I do. It is not inspiration, it is revulsion. I cannot think of anything more malign, more pervasive, more evil than the pornographic industry. There is pornography, there is the military industrial complex, and there is the banking industry, and each are evidence that the Gnostics were essentially correct.

Q: [The Gnostics were an early Christian sect] In what way?

CM: That the creator of the world, of the material world, was not God, but the Devil. That no loving God lies behind earth, behind the universe. And how can you say that isn't on the money? Have you seen the scale of human suffering outside the west? And in the west, we take the most delicate, private, human thing - sex, love - and feed it through the meat machine of porn. Porn is despair written in human flesh. You don't have to read Dworkin to know that porn is evil. Because, the thing is: it works. Men wank to it. They want more. The orgasm drive is insatiable. And the Devil wants us to behave like that, like fucking animals. You have to remember: the devil tempts us with what we love the most.

Q: Do you believe in the Devil? In Satan?

CM: I don't have to.

Newhouse flipped through Macpherson's *Schematics:* almost abstract works, based on the patterns and strategies of American football, the gridiron game with which Brick had become obsessed. It was at this time, in the mid-2000s, that he told people he wanted to be called Brick, after one of his favourite players. *The Schematics* were also popular, but less so with critics than the public. An American billionaire bought a dozen.

There was another interview, with *Re-Cast/Re-Make* magazine, a quarterly written in English, published in Italy:

"American football," he says, laconically, as he looks across the pristine harbour, "is a haven for me, mentally. It is pure. It is beautiful. It is what all sports should be: the balance of brain and brawn, of violence – and if sport is for anything, it was siphoning off the innate violence of men into something else, something more beautiful, more uniting and, yes, entertaining – and intellect. The violence and the grace, the accuracy and the complexity, the simplicity and the structure. It is all there for me. I never expected anyone else, I mean, anyone else from outside America, to see what I see in it. But it seems people do – they know purity and beauty when they see it. My prints for that stuff keep selling. The prints alone are buying me a new house!" He pauses and takes another swig of his carbonated water, a bead of sweat ambling down his close-shaven skin. "I was brought up to appreciate soccer, football: but really, how can one admire a sport where the use of hands is forbidden? Is that manly in any way? The US have done many bad things, but the turbulent soul and ingenuity of its people can be seen on the gridiron, where all sport has reach its apex."

Macpherson was now suddenly very big in the States. He moved away. His girlfriend, Una, had a baby. He bought a house on an island off Italy, Ischia, and came back to the art world with his *Stabilised* films.

These were video works, or films, but with no movement, only the faint breathing of the models, who posed in exact, or deliberately, almost-exact, poses from Renaissance masterpieces. Again, the show – *Reconaissance* at Tate Modern – was a press sensation. One end of the Turbine hall at Tate Modern was filled with a gigantic digital screen, where *Pieta-Again* was displayed, a replica of Michelangelo's Vatican *Pieta*, with two models, all white – white clothes, white skin, white eyes – enacting the marble pose, against a depthless black background.

Newhouse did not care for video art, but he, like the thousands who visited *Pieta-Again*, many Christian bus tours included, was impressed, even if it was just by the size of the work: a glowing, sepuchral piece of deathly theatre.

Newhouse looked at Macpherson. A black and white portrait, taken by Una in Ischia. He had a hard face, lean and long, but with a shaved, domed head. His eyes were large, soft, with long eyelashes. He had two small pale scars near his mouth. Curls of hair sprung from his sagging T-shirt. Black hair covered his forearms. He looked like a boxer, a footballer, perhaps a hard-tackling midfielder. Macpherson was wiry, tough.

And his Venice project? The proposition was light on detail. It involved his *Stabilised* film, which slightly disappointed Newhouse, mainly because every art student from Aberdeen to Brighton now was using Stabilised Film, and would have a RELIGIOUS THEME, the project document said, in bold capitals.

Macpherson had, Robert Hill said, been filming a lot of model's hands, feet, legs, arms, and heads, all seperately. He had sent assistants to film storms, hurricanes, volcanos and mud-pits. No one seemed to know what he was doing.

Newhouse had signed off on a press release which said Brick Macpherson's Venice piece would be *a moving homage to the Christian tradition of the West, a spectacular work that will provoke as well as profoundly move and challenge assumptions about art, faith, film and the act of creation itself.*

But no one really knew what Macpherson was doing at all.

MOTHS

There had been moths in her apartment. Tiny flakes of golden brown, fluttering silently across the white walls, they shimmered in and out of the shadows, flickering shreds of sawdust.

She was standing on her soft springy bed, half naked, dead drunk, flapping at a fleeing moth with her left hand. The timorous creature was a shred of light dizzy around her pale fingers. Her hair moved around her shoulders, sliding over her bones. Ruth's slim white back glimmered in the lamp light. It was nearly morning, and Newhouse would have to go home soon, face the day, and his girlfriend.

Fucking moths, she whispered, sozzled. She turned her head to see him, lying under her sheets, her eyes bright and sharp.

I can't fall for you, George Newhouse, she said.

He stared at her, a tingling dread gathering in his guts. He was drunk, too. His head was heavy, his eyelids heavy.

Earlier, it had been McInnes' leaving drinks, and nearly everyone from the Gallery's management were in the pub near Grosvenor Square. It was a small hot pub. Men in suits stood outside, leathered, with pint pots in their pink hands.

Ruth, writer in residence, had arrived late, with her friend Celia, swinging a small purple handbag. Newhouse told his girlfriend he was going to be late home. He had not said why, or where he was going to be. He could barely look at Ruth, as he drank with other people. He drank with McInnes, with the department secretary, with staff he had never met before. They bought McInnes whiskies and pints, and Newhouse drank gin and tonic and looked over at the fireplace where she stood.

Blue, blue veins laid in her, like wires of sky.

He staggered to the toilet and looked in the mirror: he was young then, with longer hair, with tight skin, with broader shoulders, and less gut. His suit was new, his shirt was clean. The night air, as he smoked outside, smelled of newness, of air that had not been breathed before, thoughts that had not been thought, fresh feelings slipped into old blood vessels.

Later, very drunk, he stood with her at a whirring jukebox, undergound, dark and damp, with music blaring, people shouting. Ruth stood close to him as, glazed, they watched the wheels of song titles blur past. They stood for a while, in the darkness, the cards spinning and spinning.

And she put her hand on his, and he said to her: You are the most beautiful woman I have ever met.

I am glad you said that, she said.

They kissed on the steps of St Martins in the Fields, her mouth hot and wet, his hands on the soft warm flesh of her hip, under her breasts.

Now he was dressing slowly, after she slept, after the moth had been chased, after he had showered in her tiny bathroom, and watched the city wake from her small balcony. A white church tower was high, fluted and pale. Down below, shapes and patterns were painted on a schoolyard. Lights blinked in the city towers. Traffic muttered, and the river slowly moved through trees and under bridges.

He looked at her before he left. Her face was sure

and still, her eyes turning behind her lids, her mind lost in dreams. One arm was long and lean, cupping the warm pillow where he had lain. Her hair was splayed and sprayed. She breathed in and out, in and out.

THIRTY

Rain was pouring down. Great slugs of rain slapped off the train as it lurched through brown fields, past blocky housing estates, choked pools and grass-stained slag heaps.

Newhouse was reading his notes on Brick Macpherson, looking at images of his paintings, his stabilised film, his bristling profile.

He dropped the folder on the table. Rain, pinned by the train's speed, formed a second glaze. The world warped and shook in its measure. There were sunken brown fields, broken walls. The trackside was thick with thistles, weeds, nettles and black thorn bushes. The world passed, it seemed, slower on one side than the other, as if the train was veering through viscous air, tipping it and bending its path.

Newhouse found himself waking up, his head resting on the cold window, dribble on his mouth. He had been asleep.

There was a fire suspended in mid-air.

The train had passed a wide plain with a vast refinery burning at its centre: tall towers of black, spurting ribbons of flame into the rain. Newhouse watched as the train cut through rubbish-strewn fields, past half-built housing in brown sites, past an abandoned stone yard, a car park of cement mixers – flat-tired and rusting, like red dead hippos – piles of masonry, ripped plaster board, abandoned cars.

The train pummelled through a tunnel and emerged on the outskirts of the sprawling city. Huge piles of brick and concrete, powder and panelling stood either side, as the train passed demolished high rises, levelled schools, a red field of mud and standing water. Low hills were covered in housing, in pebble-dashed blocks, in low high-rises stained with damp, dark weepings below windows, as if the windows were crying with rot. Cars moved slowly on streets shot with holes. People walked slowly, loitered in bus stops, stood, pale faced, alone, on corners. In the distance tall high rises stood pale against dark hills.

The train entered another tunnel, dark enshrouded him, and Newhouse smelled eggs and sewage as it entered the glass-shelled station.

He was there to meet Macpherson, to confirm the Venice show, to meet with his agent, with press officers, with the show's producer Hill, with Brick's gallery – The Contemporary – to assess costs, talk about insurance, transport, parties, press strategies.

They would talk about Venice, about the pavilion – a dry neo-classical box in the Giardini, wedged between France and the UK. A newspaper had published an article about Macpherson's show. He had, so the report read, videoed hundreds of men, some of them naked, making them stand with their feet together, their arms outstretched, their heads in different positions. He had, it is said, videoed the homeless and the drug addicted. He had gone into jails and videoed prisoners and warders. Macpherson and his team had gone to Hawaii, to Seattle, to Chile, to Russia, to Ascension Island, to video storms and volcanoes, cloud formations and wave movements. He had ordered 560 small, tailored plasma screens, each to be interlinked, each identical in size, each rimmed with black plastic. He had bought a sound system from a Dutch DJ that had enormous bass bins, thunderous sound. Macpherson had refused, so far, to explain what he was doing, apart, in an email to Martinu, from saying he was creating the first masterpiece of the 22nd century.

Martinu's funeral was at the weekend. His partner had not been found. There was talk of some kind of police investigation, although – Carver had said, passing Newhouse in the corridor – the post mortem pointed to a "massive stroke. Savage. Bigger than the usual. Rather severe." Newhouse thought of Martinu and then thought of Tyler, the curve of her back, the black hairs between her eyebrows.

He had not heard from her. It had been a week. The past was being cut away from him. Only Martinu and Rudi had met Ruth, and now Martinu was gone, his eyes eaten away. Rudi talked only of Jesus and his exhibition, and was drifting into another life, drifting into some other mental sphere.

Recently, Newhouse had mentioned the Russian file to Rudi, who, he suspected, was only half listening. He had mentioned Goering, and Rudi had looked up from a spreadsheet with one eyebrow raised.

Strange enormous fat man, of course, Rudi said. But, you know, a greater looter of art. Like the Visigoths, he raped Europa.

Yes, Newhouse said. I had never thought I would touch the Third Reich with all this, but they did steal so much.

You should approach one of the spoliation committees, They have information on all kinds of things not held in regular places.

Good idea actually. Maybe I shouldn't be surprised.

George, they loved Dutch art. Goering was a fat drug addict and lousy general, if he hadn't been so lousy the war might have been longer indeed, but he did a remarkable turn at Nuremburg.

The trials.

Yes, he was like another man. He was completely different to his last days. He was clean, spoke clearly. Nearly talked his way out of it.

No.

Yes, seriously, look it up. It was like he had a new brain, or he was a twin brother of himself. But anyway, must get back to this fucking nonsense: we've gone over budget with our penis show. We need a budget extension. A penis extension. Glad you got another piece to your puzzle. A puzzle, which I may add, with great love in my heart, brother, no one gives a fuck about.

Thanks, Rudi, he said.

Later, Rudi emailed him:

I saw three headless men playing at a ball/ A handless man served them all.

What do you mean, Newhouse wrote back.

You are King Arthur's Sir Pellinore, Rudi wrote, *going mad searching for the Questing Beast.*

You're a silly and ridiculous man, George wrote back.

The Contemporary was based in an old redbrick warehouse near the river. It was seven storeys, with small windows and a flat roof, a single entrance up a concrete ramp. Newhouse buzzed the entry button and a woman's voice answered, and, with a click, a windowless metal door opened.

It was cool inside the stairwell. He walked to the lift and pressed the button. It was silent. He adjusted his suit, looked at his file. The lift did not move. He pressed the button again, and nothing happened. He walked up the stairs. The Contemporary was on the fourth floor. He reached it and the door was locked. It had a sign on it: *Knock to Enter.* He knocked. Nothing happened.

He walked to the landing between the fourth and the fifth floor. He stood by the window. He was above nearby buildings now, looking down over the river. The far bank was a scramble of waste ground, a single, windowless black building stood alone, its roof bursting with weeds. Three black high-rises, one of them with metal over its windows, stood beyond, as did cubes of low brown box housing. A black Victorian bridge writhed with traffic. The city spread for miles beyond, a grey and brown blanket of fuzz and confusion. On a far hillside, white high rises stood pale, windows flashing.

The door on the fifth floor opened. A thin girl with long black hair stood in its frame.

Hello, are you Mr Newhouse?

Yes, that is me, he said, smiling.

I'm sorry, the door downstairs is broken. Something electrical, she said. She had a straight fringe from temple to temple. A long nose and large eyes. She wore a hooped jumper that fell below her knees.

Is Mr Macpherson here? he asked.

No, not yet, she said, raising her eyebrows.

Can I come in that way?

Yes of course.

He walked up the steps and followed her through the door. The room was large and walled with red brick. An iron staircase in one corner led down. The room was full of recording equipment: video cameras on stands, large lights, booms and light baffles. There were cameras in cases, on their side on the floor, laid on plywood tables.

In one corner there was a three piece suite covered in pale throws, a desk, a computer, a hi-fi, and a coffee machine. A kettle stood on the floor next to a large red open tin of biscuits. A large stone basin was full of dirty cups and a tray of abandoned chips.

The girl wandered over to the computer and leaned into it, looking for email.

I'm sorry, I'm Ivy Boyd, she said, shaking his hand. Welcome to Glasgow.

Ivy, I'm George, he said. She smiled.

We spoke on the phone. Nice suit George.

He looked down at it.

Brick says suits are the out-turned inner skins of dead and calcified minds.

Right.

He has his made in Hong Kong, she said.

She offered him a cup of tea while he waited. Mr Macpherson would be coming with his agent, the owner of The Contemporary, Justin Callahan, and his assistant, Sabina Fenton.

Sabina Fenton, he said. The name sounded familiar to him.

Yes, she's an artist too.

Oh yes, I remember. She painted strange little portraits, unfinished, partial, dominated by olive greens and terracotta, odd pinks and smears of emerald.

But since her accident, Ivy said, and shrugged. She filled the kettle at the sink and turned it on.

Newhouse felt light headed. He looked at his watch. Macpherson was ten minutes late. He moved to the sofa and sat down and read his notes.

Ivy sat on a stool at the computer, humming, flicking through emails.

I work for Justin, she said, unprompted, not Brick. Do you know Brick?

No. Not yet.

You work for the Government?

No, the Public Gallery. I'm actually out of my genre here, he said. My thing is Dutch and Flemish art.

de Kooning, Mondrian, she said flatly, typing into the computer.

Rembrandt, Vermeer, Fabritius, Van Doelenstraat.

She turned and smiled.

Oh the old gluepots, she said, and turned back to her computer. Do you know Silver, the journalist?

The name is familiar, he said.

He loves all that stuff, that old buffery stuff. The oils and the varnishes.

Well, I'm a buffer, he said.

Thought so, she said, tapping the keyboard.

But it is easy to lose yourself in surfaces, he said.

Ned's a friend of mine, she said. He might be there tonight.

What's tonight?

The Contemporary opening? The Copy Desk?

Ah right, he said.

She said it was a new space, an old bottle factory, and a group show.

He nodded.

The light suddenly darkened outside. The sky seemed to clench and pause. Then rain poured in slinging grey sheets. It rattled on the roofs, it battered on the roads below.

Christ, Ivy said.

What terrible weather, Newhouse said.

He stood up and walked to the video equipment. Beside the wall were stacked small white boxes, each with the same packaging. He looked at one: a compact digital screen, colour. It had attachment ports on each side of its frame, which was barely a milimeter in width. You could join dozens or hundreds of the screens together to make bigger screens.

These are interesting, he said.

Yeah, they are the leftovers. We're sending them back.

How many has he used?

Hundreds, she said.

The rain smashed against the windows. Cold drilled through the walls.

That's where your budget has gone, she said lightly.

He looked at her. She was still tapping on the computer.

How are they powered?

That's been the problem, she said. I'm sure Sabina will tell you in great detail. They need to be individually attached to the mains, they don't work on batteries. We tried to find a model that does, we found one in Chile. Brick didn't like the screens or the size or the frames. He wants the frames like you see – almost invisible – and the screen of the highest quality, the very highest. I mean he insists on the best or the thing won't work. Of course.

Of course, Newhouse said. Macpherson was now nearly 40 minutes late.

So Derek is out in Venice now looking at the wiring issues, she said.

Ah yes, someone said a technical person was at the Giardini already.

Yeah, Del's done Brick's stuff since whenever.

Can we contact Macpherson or Callahan in some way?

She shrugged.

Ivy called Callahan's secretary, then Callahan, but had no response. Brick did not have a mobile, and Sabina did not answer hers. Newhouse needed to get back to his office, to work, to plan a trip to London. To prepare for Martinu's funeral.

His mobile rang. It was a number he didn't recognise. He moved away from Ivy, who was eating a biscuit and drinking coffee, looking out over the rain-lashed city.

Hello?

It was a female voice.

Hello this is George Newhouse. Is that Sabina?

No, Sabina? No George, it's Gillian.

Newhouse could not think of a Gillian. His mind raced over empty ground.

Gillian Santopietro.

Right, he said.

You met me at your friend's party? The loud German?

She sounded amused.

Hello Gillian, he said.

Well it was some party, she said.

Newhouse said nothing.

Well Mr Newhouse, she said.

She spoke again. I have found something in my work which I think, although I'm not sure, relates to your own area of expertise.

Oh really?

Yes it's very interesting, and a little frustrating, too, she said. He could hear her breathe. He could hear her fingers move, slightly squeaking, on a plastic phone receiver.

You were absolutely correct about Delft, anyway, she said.

Was I?

You asked me whether there were any occult incidents in Delft in the 1640s or so, she said. I was in the Netherlands last week, and found a very curious reference.

Really? Of an exorcism?

No, no. But, also, yes, she said.

She explained it to him.

The world outside receded into fog and mist.

In 1645, she said, there was a report in the church records of Delft of a minister who was asked to say prayers over a group of objects in an empty house.

Objects?

The Dutch document was damaged and badly written, she said. But it seemed to suggest that the house, which had been rented, had been abandoned, and the contents within it had 'frightened or unnerved the residents of the street involved.' They had reported black walls, a persistent smell of rot or 'death scent', if that was translated correctly. They blamed the renter, an artist, who had left over night. The minister had been brought in by the owner of the house to, in a sense, exorcise the belongings so they could be taken away and burnt or sold. Which they were, except for one item.

Where was the house?

On Vlamingstraat, close to the River Schie.

Newhouse felt light headed. His stomach turned over.

Do you know which house number?

I don't think so. Let me check, Gillian said.

Newhouse imagined her bent over a photocopy of a water-logged ledger. He imagined damp on her study walls, water pooling around her ankles, spores in dark corners, droplets hanging on broken spider webs.

There was a growl of thunder outside, and a flash of

lightning.

Fuck, Ivy shrieked, and looked at Newhouse. Her black eyes like buttons in a white sheet.

No, no number George, Gillian said.

Thanks for checking, he said. Could you email me that document?

Of course, she said. Do you want to know about the item?

The item?

He thought of the minister, praying over Van Doelenstraat's belongings, his empty double bed, the bare table, the threadbare carpets, the misty brassware, the rusting knives and forks, his abandoned clothes. Red bricks outside, and the water hitting the buildings side, lapping and slapping.

There was one item that was mentioned in the ledger, she said. It resisted all prayers, it said. Even prayers to St Michael and the Virgin Mary.

Yes?

A painting, it says, *The Equine Spirit.*

Equine Spirit, he said.

Yes, that is what it says. It says the church officials took it to the sea and *disposed of it with haste.*

With haste?

Unless I'm reading it wrong, she said. Which I'm not.

Read the whole passage to me?

Due to this unease and unhappiness in the residents of the Vlamingstraat, Minister Jol performed his prayers over the belongings. All were saved, but the vexed painting of the Equine Spirit resisted even the most Holy appeals. The town men and Minister submerged this most blackest item into the sea, where it will reside with the wrecks and the ruinations.'

Wrecks and ruinations?

There it is. The next reported exorcism is of a man in Delft two years later, he died from the prayers, Gillian said. Seven frogs were pulled from his mouth.

Seven frogs?

And a candlestick.

He thought for a moment. He could hear her breathing.

Thank you for this, he said.

Is it of interest to you?

It is.

Newhouse realised he was now sitting on the floor.

Email me the document. I have to go.

Newhouse suddenly wished he could call Martinu and tell him.

You OK? Ivy said.

Yes, yes, he said. I just had some bad news.

I can't get hold of anyone, she said. She shrugged. I'm really sorry about this.

He was sat on the floor. The rain smashed against the windows.

I just need a drink, he said to her.

Me too, she said.

THE CARD GAME

The black and the white, the gold and the silver. And below each face, a name.

The dark wood and the dark pigment, solid and unyielding. The last face was his own last face, and his hand shook a little as he dabbed at his eyes, dabbed a little, stroked a little, on his hair, his long chin, the scars and the blemishes.

Her face was at the centre, as he remembered it, in all its beauty and its loss. The most beautiful child of her race.

Their faces below hers, at the table, in their skirts, their smocks, the faces of the little boys, his little babies.

All held cards. For him the King. For her the Queen, and then in their children's hands, empty cards. No shapes or patterns. The emptiness of an empty future.

And so, in turn, he painted out the Queen, with thick white paint. The face and then the hands, the patterns, the chevrons and the dice.

A thick brush pressed over her eyes.

And she was gone.

And over it turned on the easel.

And there the horse stood.

Bone rider, its eyes, holes to the pit.

Picked fine, backwards in gold at its razor hooves:

The Lord of this World.

THIRTY ONE

Have you read this little book by Wycliffe, Rudi said, as they walked through the park of the Public Gallery.

No, Newhouse said. Martinu mentioned it, before.

Santopietro lent to me, the hairy old fucker.

The day was hot and the sun shone on new green leaves and thick stands of trees.

As they neared a door in the boundary wall, he could hear the water below. A dirt and gravel path with many steps led down to what was called the Waters. Near a small wooden bridge, curators and technicians were installing a large bronze sculpture in the middle of the stream.

Given my lack of interest in anything right now, I found it quite interesting, Rudi said. He was in shirt sleeves. His forearms were large and pink.

What does he say?

It's a rumination on the power of objects. Art objects included. He rattles on about Mayan stones, scold's bridles, the really rather exquisite Madonna col Bambino by Agostino di Duccio in Perugia, the Orthodox icons of course, the meteorite in Mecca, fragments of the true Cross, inkwells, the capstones of the Pyramids, that kind of thing.

Inkwells?

They were under the cool of the riverside trees, wending their way down, step by step, to the water. Newhouse could hear voices and a tapping sound. In the shadows of the branches he could see clouds of midges amid the nodding weeds and nettles. Colliding and rising like sparks on the shadows between the span of the leaves.

Ja. Martin Luther, my favourite German, he threw an inkwell at the devil.

I thought Mahler was. He saw the devil?

Mahler was Bohemian. And your Reformation knowledge is lamentable, George. When he was translating the Bible into German, Satan appeared. Herr Luther threw a pot of ink at him.

That rings a bell, Newhouse said. He was hot. Sweat gathered under his jacket. His skin prickled.

That Douglas Gordon made a work about it, you know. But you probably have never heard of him.

Actually I have. He was hot and he was bothered.

He is pretty good, as they go. I guess, Newhouse said.

Well, well George. I will pass your in-depth analysis to the director of contemporary art.

So what was Wycliffe's conclusion?

They left the trees and walked onto the bridge. Down below, in the shallow river, several people in boots and waders were standing around a bronze statue of a featureless woman. It was a new commission from a sculptor. The sunshine wove ribbons of white light on the water as it sped towards a weir downstream.

Well, you know he has always had some Neo-Platonic notions.

Meaning?

'Some objects, when made under certain conditions – war, close to death, amid madness, perhaps in sorrow – appear to act as vessels or reservoirs for the feelings of the maker.'

Christ – and is that presented as an original conclusion? Newhouse said. Who printed this? Didn't Wycliffe lose his job?

The Journal for Contemporary Analytics. One of their chapbooks.

Hmm, Newhouse said.

He tripped on loose wood and his body was jolted.

What piss, Newhouse said. He knee had been jarred, and he rubbed it.

I'd love to see his evidence, he said. Dreams and hallucinations.

He has some interesting ideas. It's not some fucking bullshit I am talking here. You should just bloody read it, Rudi said. Get your head out of your 17th century arse for a change. Bone up on your quantum physics, string theory, bubble universes, interpenetrating dimensions.

Sounds formidable. You can lend it to me, Newhouse said.

Yes, of course. It's theory, George, it's not an academic study.

Theories, who needs them. The world is being destroyed by theories.

Rudi stopped and put his hand briefly on his friend's shoulder. The German shook his head.

I'm sorry George, I haven't been sleeping well. Too many lucid dreams. Too many strange wanderings in the night. I think I may even have a haunted house.

Really?

Yes. There are cold patches. Strange intensities in the air.

What does Iona think?

Who knows. I never know what she thinks. She may be the ghost herself.

They both leant over the handrail of the bridge. The people were now wading back to the riverside. The statue stood upright, facing downstream. Newhouse recognised a curator from the modern art collection, technicians from the facilities department, and also, in white shorts, he saw Tyler.

Her hair was up in a messy bun, she was wearing blue plastic gloves. She spoke to her colleagues as she sat on the riverbank, pulling off the gloves, smiling about something.

Who is that young lady? Rudi asked.

Who, Newhouse said. Her face was open in the sun. He could hear the melody of her voice but not what she was saying.

The one you are staring at, George.

George looked downstream.

I might have met her somewhere or other. I am not sure.

Do you meet people? Real ones?

Sometimes.

Tyler looked up at the bridge and saw Newhouse. She raised her hand to wave but then just held it in the sun. She was not smiling but her eyes flashed in the sunlight.

Newhouse looked down at her. He nodded.

One of the crew below spoke to Tyler and she turned her head and responded.

He wanted to go down and see her, speak to her. But only alone, not in the exposing sunlight, not among all these people.

Let's go back, he said to Rudi. I need to work.

I might stay, Rudi said. I might sit in the sun and have a sleep. I think I need the rays.

Newhouse saw Tyler packing some things into a bag. She looked up at him again. She raised her hand to an ear, as if talking into a phone, and smiled at him.

He nodded and waved a short wave.

His chest was tight and it was painful.

OK, he said to Rudi, who was leaning on the bridge with his eyes closed.

Newhouse turned and walked back across the bridge and into the shadow of the woods. Walking quickly up the steps, he was nearly at his office before he said: For fuck's sake.

Newhouse turned on his heels to walk back to the river. Then he stopped and turned again.

THIRTY TWO

Gavin opened his mouth as the coffin was lowered into the ground. His eyes were screwed up, and his hands were held to his newly cropped hair. His mouth was wide open. His mother, small, clad in black fur, moved to hug him.

The priest said his lines and the crowd, all in black, swayed in silence as a light rain began to drop on trees, on gravestones, on the plastic tarpaulin on which the earth that would bury Martinu sat in a neat pile. A cry eventually came from Gavin's mouth. Newhouse stood beside Rudi and Iona, and stared at the grass at his feet.

He could see every blade, every line of every blade, every shadow of every blade, cross-hatched and cumulated like wickerwork.

A spider spun a web, silently and speedily, somewhere, somewhere on the window of a door in an abandoned room, a lost room somewhere where insects curled, caught in the silken sieve and weave. A wave broke silently at sea, an expanding circle of foam that glittered, bubbled and sunk into itself again. A pebble was knocked by a child's trainer, and rolled, and fell from the cliff, past chalk and grassy outcrops, past the orange beaks of baby birds, past black rocks, and fell into water, silent, and was lost until it was sand, pressed into wetness by a foot yet to be born.

Newhouse knew he was crying and then wiped his eyes, turned away, and let the funeral continue as he walked back to Rudi's large black German car, parked under a yew tree, by a broken gate.

Colebrooke, before the service, had passed him a file.

It had been written by Martinu for Colebrooke, and the board of the Public Gallery. It concluded The Blue Horse did not exist, or may have never existed.

George, he said quietly, make sure we have Venice all tacked down, budget-wise. Especially with this unpleasantness right now. Read this document and be impressed by its conclusions, George. Don't waste your time with Doelenstraat any more. It won't help with those Ardrashaig so-and-so's and that is our priority right now. Martinu knew what he was doing. It's over.

Now Martinu did not exist, and never had, except in memory and in the memory of Gavin's now empty hands, his empty chest.

And the skin was now dust, dust on his plates, cups, and floorboards. Crystalline sugar-dust on the spider's death trap, nest, graveyard and home.

THIRTY THREE

Hello George, the voice said. He half recognised it. He was in his office, looking through Martinu's notes, through Gillian's notes. They seemed to be dispatches from different worlds. Why had Martinu given him the Russian file, and then written another for Colebrooke which denied The Blue Horse ever existed? He wondered if Martinu had written it at all.

There was a meeting with Colebrooke to come, and another dreaded Venice budget meeting. There was a press conference in the main gallery about a new work by Matthias Stomer which had been donated in lieu of inheritance tax. The painting was so ordinary, so bad, he could not concentrate on his notes.

On the office wall, Jesus was raising the dead from hell.

His telephone rang. He picked it up.

Hello George, it's Foster from Melcombes, a woman said.

Hello.

There was a silence.

Hello?

Hi, he said.

You don't know who I am, do you, she said.

I'm sorry, I'm...

It's Foster, Foster Flintergill. I'm calling in a business capacity, George. Wearing my Melcombes gloves, if you like.

OK.

Ah yes, he said. He thought of her, long and silken in

her blue ballgown. She did not look much like her uncle; his face was all jowls and whiskers, his eyes slippery between two oyster shells of wrinkled flesh.

I was wondering if you might want to meet for a coffee sometime, discuss this Van Doelenstraat problem we have.

Is there a problem?

Martinu's strange file concluded that The Blue Horse was a misinterpretation, a fumbling and fudging of disparate evidence. It ran against much of what he and Martinu had talked about over years, and months. It was almost written purely to pursuade Colebrooke, alone, to not think about it any more, and not to pursue it. Dr Martinu was among the most respected Golden Age scholars of his generation. The Rembrandt quote was 'troublesome', Martinu had written. The documentation over the many years was confusing, contradictory.

Yes, well, we have a mutual problem, George, Foster said, and went on to say she would like to meet Newhouse after work, discuss an idea she had.

An idea, he said.

A proposal, she said, Without wanting to sound too dramatic, too cloak and dagger.

Can we talk about it now?

I would rather not.

OK, he said, but I'll be working late so is nine fine with you?

Of course, she said, and named a pub in a Georgian crescent near Newhouse's flat. He put the phone down.

He read Gillian Santopietro's papers again.

'Due to this unease and unhappiness in the residents of the Vlamingstraat, Jol performed his prayers over the

*belongings. All were saved, but the vexed painting of
the Equine Spirit resisted even appeals to Michael and
the Blessed Virgin. The town's men and Jol submerged
this most black item into the sea, where it will reside
with the wrecks and the ruinations.'*

The sea, the sea.

He opened Dr Martinu's pages again. Martinu had
spent much time discounting one link to the Blue Horse
which had confused both Martinu and Newhouse over
time. The paper came from a find of papers in London,
when an ancient auction and dealing house, Henry &
Dee, had been wound up, due to a police investigation
into money laundering, five years before. The expert
working on the auction house's historical papers had
known Martinu, and had discovered 19th century sales
and ledgers which mentioned large quantities of Dutch
art. He had shown them to the Doctor.

Martinu studied references to many sales of Golden
Age artists there – many of the sales fitting into the already
established histories and provenances. Some mentioned
paintings that were unknown. Others concerned paintings
that were known, but were now lost. More intriguingly, the
Henry & Dee papers mentioned a dealer, Halfhouse, who
had bought a painting called A Blue Horse from a man
called Langebeck in 1890. Halfhouse had sold it on, and
was never mentioned again. Langebeck died in 1913.

Newhouse had looked for information about Michael
Langebeck, a Dane, before. He vaguely remembered
something. He stood up. His computer screen hummed.
His mobile phone buzzed and buzzed. A missed call from
a number he did not know.

He found his box, still unfiled, of his Blue Horse research. He hesitated before opening it. He pulled off the lid. He flinched, expecting, he thought with a wince, a blossom of Ruth's perfume. But there was none: just dampness and the flat wind of paper, dust and a puff of mould spores.

He kneeled and looked through the papers. He found his own typed summary of the Henry & Dee documents. Newhouse clicked his tongue. His notes were often bad copies of papers which were probably now lost forever. He looked for the brief information on the Langebeck to Halfhouse exchange. He found it:

> *S Halfhouse (contract) from M Langebeck (York) – 13 pictures including The Flottila in a Storm, L.Bakhuizen (1696), Ship Cannon, WW van de Velde (1671), A Blue Horse [!!] (damaged, undated), v Dolenstraat. Langebeck of Langebeck, Armstrong and Swinburne, Deighton, York.*

He took the paper to his desk. He knew a scholar who had studied the provincial English art dealers of the 19th century. They had studied together. One of many who knew that area, he thought, but David had brought out a book on it, English Art at the Edges. It had some good reviews. He had a good little book on the Golden Age too, *Minor Dutch Painters*. He knew both subjects well. He was a minor authority.

Newhouse looked through his contacts book, a black notepad stuffed with loose pages, post-it notes, blue and black and red with scribblings and crossings out. He found the name – David Sherbone and a number.

He rang it, and Sherbone answered.

Hello David, it's George Newhouse.

Jesus Christ! George. Wow, great to hear from you. Sherbone had a loud voice. He had been born with a split lip.

They talked.

Sherbone asked after Ruth.

She's fine, fine, Newhouse said.

Any sprogs? Sherbone said.

No, no, Newhouse said.

Not blessed? Got three myself, Sherbone said.

They talked more. Newhouse wanted to ask about Langebeck. After Sherbone had asked questions about the galleries, about the loss of the Ardrashaig collection, Newhouse cleared his throat and asked.

Ah yes, Michael Langebeck, 1854 to 1913, Sherbone said. Then, his voice seemed to leave the receiver.

Strange you ask, because I was looking at the Yorkshire and Lancashire provincial sales recently myself, his faint voice said.

Oh really?

Yes… from 1894… nothing amazingly Dutch though, sadly, so calm down, not a clog in sight. Let me look, be back in a tick.

Newhouse waited.

Here we are George, Sherbone said, returning to his phone. Newhouse could hear children playing in the background. A girl was yelling. Things were being dropped and thrown. A kettle boiled.

M Langebeck, 1855 not 1854, born in Copenhagen, moved to London 1874, to York five years later. Had a minor job at Henry & Dee in London, seemed to have got a better offer from Isiah Armstrong in York, who was cleaning up with the factory owners.

Right, Newhouse said, writing notes on the back of the press release for the Stomer donation.

Where did Langebeck live? Newhouse asked.

He had a couple of places, they did terribly well with the competing families up there, Sherbone said. They cleaned up on furniture, tapestries, and so on. Because of Langebeck, they sold a lot of mediocre Scandinavian stuff, and Dutch paintings too. So he had a place right in the middle of York, of course, Sherbone said, and one in Scarborough.

Scarborough?

Yes, well it was the spa town of its day. Langebeck was ill a lot with digestive problems, which got worse as he got older, and finally killed him. His recorded death was choking on his own bile. Which isn't nice.

No, Newhouse said.

So… yes he had a place fashionably on the south cliff in Scarborough, on the site where a hotel was built. Oddly enough that hotel, The Charlotte, slid into the sea a few years ago. But these are all my slightly hazy notes, you know – all the Langebeck stuff is in London at the Thorn Library, not sure why. Do you know Williams at the Thorn? Odd chap. Anyway. There's more there – Langebeck wrote a memoir for the Danish audience, before he died. There's an English edition at the Thorn. It's very, very wordy and boring, I must say. He loved Yorkshire, though, he built a school and so on.

Thanks David, I knew you would know all this, Newhouse said.

He had to go to London and read the book.

I didn't really go into Langebeck much for the book

George – Armstrong and Swinburne were so very much more interesting.

OK, thanks.

Newhouse said good wishes to his family and that he had to go.

I'll email all this over to you old thing, Sherbone said. Love to Ruth. We must meet up if you are up again.

Of course, Newhouse said.

THIRTY FOUR

Foster sat alone, pooled like a shadow in the corner of the pub. Newhouse walked from the dark and cold of the street to the clamour of the bar, wincing. He had turned his phone off. He had spoken to Hayley, arranged the trip to London. He would fly down in a few days.

He moved around the bar, avoiding bodies, avoiding pools of bright light. His head was full of fuzz and noise. The press conference he had been dreading was, in fact, fine – a cheery photographer from one of the papers was present, and a sullen reporter with a heavy cold. One of the press officers had posed with the painting. He had given some earnest quotes. He avoided saying the Stomer was a minor work, an ugly painting, one destined for the stores. It was all over in twenty minutes.

Worse, leaving a hollowness above his bowels, a tightening in his guts, was the brief meeting with Colebrooke.

Colebrooke said the Ardrashaig association with the PG was definitely to be brought to an end, after more than 100 years of that collection being at the centre of its Galleries. The heart of the PG collection was to be taken down, boxed up, and sent 'to the Arabs'.

A cold black coffee in his hands. Colebrooke was pale. Newhouse realised what a disaster this was for the Public Gallery, for the nation – even, in some vague, wider sense, for the art world itself. But his new life was resting on smaller, more delicate beams. He lived from day to day as if his body and his mind were blown from glass. When he was with Tyler, there had been the hint of a warmth from which he flinched. At the bridge, he had moved away. And he could not quite count or list the reasons, but he could not bear to see her again.

Colebrooke had said, at the end of the meeting, that the Government had found enough in its capital funds to buy the best of the collection – three pieces. He laughed.

What a joke, Colebrooke had said. He went on: I will stand down in the New Year, I think you should know. I do feel bad for you George – I have brought you here and now I am leaving. But my position is untenable and the Honours will be kind to me. You should think of your own position too, George. Try the National Galleries, they might need someone as talented as you. And make sure you enjoy Venice.

Colebrooke had looked over the gardens and houses of the city, up towards the lumpen castle on its rocky stump. His shoulders had started shaking.

And now Colebrooke's niece sat before him. She was dressed in blue and had a glass of white wine. She was acting as if she was checking her phone, but Newhouse had seen her notice him as he stumbled over legs and bags and chairs in the noisy bar to get to her.

Ah George, she said and smiled. Her cheeks rose and almost covered her eyes. She had very red lips, red nail varnish. Her hair was pulled back over her ears. She had a small red leather bag.

Shall we… he shouted.

Go somewhere quieter? Yes.

They walked down the dark street, past a few bars, until she suggested a hotel in a barely lit square. They walked to it.

I don't know if you have plans for tonight, she said.

I don't, he said.

I am going on to a party. It's members only. But I'm sure I could slip you in, she said, with no tone to her voice. Newhouse looked at her. She was striding forward, her face in profile.

What kind of party? He said. I'm not sure...

It's a get together, she said. I'm a member of the club, but we can just grab a drink and talk, or call it a night and leave if it's not your thing. I just thought I'd mention it, she said, with a sudden hard tone. I am duty bound to attend. It's a place where people meet to do business. I am sure you can imagine.

What kind of business.

Government business, financial business. Show business. Business business.

Show business?

Melcombes have all kinds of interests. We like to open dialogues and re-assert shared interests.

OK, he said. He wanted to turn around, walk back to his flat.

She turned into the hotel lobby. He followed her.

They went to the bar and ordered drinks and sat in the corner of the long, dark room. Foster apologised and stalked to the toilets. Newhouse looked out at the black square, the three globes of white light that hung like eyes in the trees, and above the branches and roofs, the blue night, the singe of the moon on gathering heavy clouds.

So: George, she said. She sat down and crossed her legs. She did not seem to breathe, she could have been made from moulded plastic, ivory, white bone.

Yes, he said.

I know this may seem a bit sudden. I don't know how

to say this without sounding a little bit melodramatic, she said, and took a sip of wine. It wet her lips.

Go on, he said.

Are you alright, George? You look a little pale.

I'm fine. Long day.

Yes, I'm sure. The Ardrashaig situation is a calamity.

He raised his eyebrows.

Of course Uncle Thomas told me, she said, smiling. Not that it's surprising, anyway. He's taking it hard but then it's 'on his watch' as he said. Look, they'll keep a few and the rest will go but there will be some kind of round-robin loan deal and really, that's the best solution for all concerned. I'm just so glad I'm not involved in public-facing activities.

Right, he said.

She put her glass down and squinted her eyes and squared her shoulders. Newhouse looked past her, to the bar, to avoid her. A bar girl was slicing a lemon with slow, deliberate strokes.

He thought of Tyler. He saw the face of Ruth, and then she passed and he saw the silver blade of Foster before him. Faces looming and fading as on a carousel, lit briefly in darkness.

His gut clenched. He realised he was hungry.

Melcombes need your help, George, she said.

Right? he said. He had the sudden urge to take off his suit. He resisted it.

I don't know how to say this correctly, she said, tilting her head.

She started again. She blinked slowly and lowered her voice.

Yes, it's a shame about Dr Martinu, and I know you

knew him fairly well, she said. You may need to know, now, that he was doing some work for us, as a consultant, on your friend Van Doelenstraat, and that painting. He came to the conclusion, which may upset you, but I don't know how else to say it, that the painting does not – did not – ever exist.

Right, Newhouse said. He tried to show no emotion at all. He kept his face solid. He did not blink. He realized he was grinding his teeth.

Now I know you're shocked, she said, nodding.

Hans knew his stuff, and he was the best scholar, the finest researcher I ever knew, we ever knew, Newhouse said.

Yes, she nodded.

He looked down at his drink.

Do you think he was right?

He could see she was tense.

Well if he thinks, sorry, thought that – although it leaves me a little confused – I must see his research, see how he came to that conclusion, he said.

Well, that's business, and confidential, she said.

Newhouse was waking up. He felt an itch in his mind. He was beginning to feel agitated.

Are you sure?

I'm sorry, she said again. You can't see that report, it's confidential. She pursed her lips and sat back in her seat.

I actually know he held that opinion, he said. But Hans never told me he had come to that conclusion while he was alive. It's slightly surprising, given he thought almost exactly the opposite for so long.

It seriously and fatally undermines your position of course, she said. Your scholarship.

I would say, really, that it's pretty undermined already. I am aware of that. Nobody has found The Blue Horse, seen it, touched it. I am happy my work has brought to the fore a major Dutch artist of the Golden Age. Van Doelenstraat is now mentioned in the same breath as Fabritius, de Hoogh. His Absent Period, some say, parallels Vermeer's interiors and some say rivals them. The Blue Horse is a puzzling part of his history. I think that is what it is: a puzzle. I loved and respected Hans, but his papers are not definitive.

Foster nodded. Her eyes had lost their focus. Darkness moved behind her. Blurred figures shifted in shadow and haze, in gauzy electric light, the heavy square of black, the door to the bar.

To sum up, she said quickly, he thought that much of the Blue Horse scholarship and articles, yours included, was a misreading of history, a wishful reading of what in fact were mistakes, coincidences, misapprehensions. He basically thought all those references and quotes and ledgers refer to quite different paintings and...

Well I would... If he were still here, I would disagree with him, Newhouse said.

We know that, she said. I know that. Which is why we are here. I, we, would like to offer you a small commission.

To do what? Newhouse said, leaning forward. To write a counter-argument? You can just pull up my articles from somewhere. I stand by every word, given what I knew and how I knew it. Nearly every word anyway. And Rembrandt's words in his note. The master himself: why would he write about something that didn't exist?

Foster Flintergill shrugged.

I am not an academic. No, it's not that, she said, shaking her head. One of our clients, a very close, well-supported and acquisitive client, has found an interesting painting. It's Dutch, from the 1640s we think. It may be your painting.

He looked at her again. Her pale blade of a face.

Oh really, he said.

Yes. I mean, I am not convinced, or even half convinced. I prefer Dr Martinu's thesis. But Professor Adams, our Dutch man, says he is excited.

And how did this client find it? Newhouse said. He knew that this painting was not The Blue Horse. The Blue Horse was somewhere under sea, silted over and silent.

He is a very private man, she said.

So? He said. Who isn't?

Well, we don't really need to know how he found it do we, George? The paper trail is non-existent, I've heard. But as I say, Andrew Adams, our...

Yes, I know Adams.

Well he has seen the photographs of its reverse, and its unusual frame.

The reverse and the frame?

Yes. But out client will only let visitors see the actual painting, the image, in the flesh, so to speak. He wouldn't send us a picture.

How strange, Newhouse said. Is he charging entry?

Maybe he should.

Where is it then? Newhouse said. Here?

Currently somewhere in the Mediterranean, on one of his boats.

Right.

But it will be accessible soon. It will be wherever the yacht stops. The client is looking for a new home, somewhere to dock his boat and spend the winters.

Ok, so... Newhouse said.

So, when he and his people have found the new home, he would like you to view the work in its new gallery.

Newhouse sat back. He imagined a large black yacht. In its guts, a black windowless room, a black painting, hoof marks on the floor, the ceiling, and a curtain of lead.

Right, he said. How did Melcombes get involved in this?

We organised some of the logistics of the buy, shall we say, but we are still unsure who sold it. The vendor is anonymous even to us. One of our couriers secured the deal. It was, they say in London, one of the trickiest purchases they have arranged. But there were no leaks. In the meantime, we would like a counter argument. Yes, and a summary – an executive summary if you will – of all the work you have done on the question. There's a generous fee, compensation for your time and effort.

OK, I'll think about it, he said. He suddenly wanted to leave. He stood up. He looked down and realised he had not touched his drink.

OK, business over, Foster said, and stood up too. She moved close to Newhouse, he could smell her perfume, her make-up. Her face was heavily made-up, he realised. Her hair was thick with some kind of spray.

Let us know as soon as you can, she said, but now: the party? Do you have the time?

Against the gathering gloom of the bar, the darkness outside, she seemed to be a bundle of white sticks and hair, floating in a black space, tethered by clear twine and set with reflecting, unblinking eyes.

He agreed, and she ordered a taxi. In the back of the cab they sat silently. Foster checked messages and emails on her mobile phone. Newhouse looked out at the blank, elegant city streets, the lines of flat Georgian terraces, neat railings, long rectangular windows. The city was empty, glowing under the black night.

The taxi took them to a street that moved down a steep hill, to a crossing where a tall church stood, and moved into a crescent of houses with heavy porticos. It came to a halt and the driver turned around and pointed to a cobbled lane that ran between two of the high, dark houses.

Foster paid and turned to smile at Newhouse.

You may need to keep your wits about you, George, she said.

He followed her down the unlit lane. Muse cottages lined one side, high windowless backs of houses the other. Foster's ankle turned slightly as she exited the car. She hopped and then walked down the lane. Newhouse followed her. He heard the taxi move off.

There was a light ahead, an electric lamp fashioned like a gas lamp. A man in a heavy winter coat stood, his face a mask, beside a door, set into a large, flat-roofed building at the end of the lane. Newhouse could hear music leaking from somewhere, the sound of voices.

Foster said something to the man and he opened the door. Newhouse followed her into a dimly lit hallway. Coats hung on hooks, red walls leaned inwards, fake and real candles flickered. There were some stairs leading upwards, and doors, slightly ajar, either side. Bodies moved in the murk. He could smell body heat, rubber, perfume. Low male voices, a sharp female giggle, the tinkling of music.

A drink? Foster said. Newhouse nodded, and he followed her upstairs. There was a red velvet bar, a barman in a uniform. In alcoves, pale-faced men sat in suits, murmuring to each other. Slow orchestral music was playing. The light was soft and gauzy, it melted into the bottles behind the bar, the brass and the gold, the red velvet and the thick carpet. Newhouse realized he could smell semen, a whiff of sea salt and sterilizer.

They clinked drinks. In the dusk-light, he could not see her eyes. She smiled over his shoulder at two stout men drinking shots.

Ah, there's Mackie and Copthorne, she said.

He looked at them, but could only see neck rolls of fat, well cut suits, eyes like stones chucked into mud.

George, you must get to know the city, you know, she said, smiling, her canines flashing, there are some interesting people here. I will introduce you. This is the place to meet them. Everyone is here.

No, he said. It's OK.

The counter-argument, she said to him, turned her hips to the bar. It need not be much, not even three or four pages.

Fine, he said.

Is that a yes, she said.

Maybe, he said. What is this place? It smells.

Just a gentleman's club, she said. With entertainments which may appeal to you. Have a look downstairs.

I might do, he said. He wondered how close he was to Tyler's gallery from here. Maybe a ten minute taxi ride, through the dark.

There was a symposium in two days with academics and curators from across Europe, meeting to talk about his Dutch catalogue. A day of talks and papers, round table discussions and dinner in the gallery restaurant – rubber chicken in white sauce, bad breath and pricking egos. He had work to do. But he did not feel like doing it. He looked at his mobile phone. He had a missed call from Rudi.

Do you mind? Foster said, and brushed past Newhouse to talk to Mackie and Copthorne.

Newhouse looked around the bar. Something had changed.

In a far alcove, he saw a thin, moustachioed man, his trousers around his ankles. A young woman, dressed in red underwear, red as the velvet on the bar, on the floor, was between the man's legs, sucking his dick. Her head bobbed between the table and his groin. The moustache man put his hand on the girl's head and pushed it.

Newhouse looked around and Foster was laughing with the two men. He looked to the barman, who was drying glasses. He looked back at the girl in the alcove, her lips on the man's balls.

Newhouse moved down the stairs, holding his gin and tonic. He felt a low electrical charge in his blood, his heart began to pulse. The hall was dark, singed by the light from both doorways. He turned to the left and moved to the door, which was partially open. He moved to it. He could see a gathering of men's backs. Suit jackets and crumpled shirts and red necks. There was a fireplace, he could see, and rows of books in heavy shelves: green and brown and red. There was moaning and a rhythmic slapping. He moved into the room. He could see two women, kneeling on the carpet. They were circled by men with their dicks out. The women were red-lipped, dark-haired, topless and wearing thin red knickers. They were sucking the dicks, one by one, moving around the circle of penises. The men were close-eyed, or staring. They wore suits and shirts and ties.

Newhouse left the room. He felt light headed.

He moved across the hall to another door. He opened it and looked into a well lit room. There were tiles on the floor and threads of steam snaked from under a glass-paned door in the corner. Three young men in towels sat talking in low voices on a bench. Soft pink skin and short hair. One had an arm covered in blue tattoos. On a table under an elaborate mirror there was a bowl of condoms, a stack of mints, pale blue tubes, small packets of wipes.

Alright big man, one of the boys said.

He backed out.

Newhouse moved up the stairs. The bar was full of men in suits, talking in low voices, their eyes barely blinking, the orchestral music louder than before. Leaning against a wall, he saw a man whose lionine face and hair seemed familiar, from television, from a flickering screen. He had his hand on the shoulder of another man he also recognized, but he could not remember where he had seen his bald head, his hooded eyes. He looked around the now busy room. He could not see Foster. A group of women and men, their faces distorted, as if under water, sat in an alcove, a half-naked girl serving them drinks as they smiled and nodded.

Newhouse left.

He found himself in the dark alley. He moved back to the living city. He found a taxi and took it home.

THIRTY FIVE

The press conference was coming to an end.

Thomas Colebrooke was sitting behind the table, elbows on its green top, moving his shoulders from side to side, staring into the long, busy room, flanked by the Minister for Culture - a gaunt man in a suit - the thin body of his deputy, Carver, and the Public Gallery's head of marketing and press relations.

The room had been hung with the best of the Ardrashaig Collection. It had also been filled with interlocking plastic and metal seats, and on them sat the press – from national papers, from the city papers, from the BBC and other broadcasters. There were a couple of film cameras, and several photographers from newspapers in jackets and jeans, kneeling on the floor or off to one side, with large black lenses, clicking, every flash splashing on the gilt frames, the glass of the paintings, the pale surfaces of busts, the dull grey pillars.

Newhouse was standing off to one side with some of the other curators, with Rudi Hessenmuller, sombre and large in a new three-piece tweed suit, with board members, with the chair of a sponsoring bank. No one from Ardrashaig Holdings was present.

Colebrooke officially announced that the bulk of the Ardrashaig Collection was being moved to Dubai but thanks, he said, to the 'incredible generosity' of the government, three paintings were to remain at the Public Gallery. He launched a new public appeal to raise funds. He beseeched the business community to support the galleries and the nation. He made no mention of his own imminent resignation.

Colebrooke answered questions from the press as the cameras snapped, crashed and whirred. He leaned forward, to speak directly into the uneven row of dictaphones and digital microphones which had been placed on the table.

He said: I would say, of course, that this situation, could be painted in the light to which your question alludes. However, I think we, and the Minister, believe that in fact it is a challenge, to the gallery, to the people of this city, to our supporters, to our board, to our trustees, to...

Pens scraped on paper. Electricity hummed in cameras and voice recorders. Newhouse looked over the press, the table, the people behind it. On the far wall hung a Dutch church interior, sheer and pale and clean. Pure lines and sparse architecture. A black hymnal, an empty pulpit, the smell of damp, rain lashing on the colourless window panes, quadrangles and chevrons, lined by silvery lead.

Let's get a drink, Rudi whispered to Newhouse.

...and what is more, this deal, as I have said, is not the end of these paintings being seen at the galleries, and the public will be able to see the highlights of the collection once every four years...

Newhouse slid backwards through the press of bodies at the door to the gallery. Rudi followed him. They walked silently. Rudi seemed glum, his face heavy. There were large blackheads in the creases of his nostrils, his eyes were watery. He walked slowly.

They found a pub in a back lane next to a bookmakers. They ordered in brief words, a pint for Rudi, a glass of port for Newhouse. They sat near the fire. Rudi began to talk of gossip from the offices, of minor intrigues and petty squabbles, of new faces and old faces.

He talked to Newhouse as if he was not a member of staff. Newhouse felt he had not seen his friend for a long time. He had been away, or out of the office, in the last few weeks, and even when he was in his office, had not seen or spoken to Rudi. Newhouse had also been busy. There had been meetings and lectures, and a week in the PG stores working with archival staff on the remains of his Dutch survey.

Newhouse now realized he had become accustomed to living alone.

He saw the Public Gallery and knew what it was but could not feel its weight, its heft, their place in a continuum of time or experience. He moved through buildings and rooms of what significance, he did not know. He did work, of what import, he did not know. He spoke of histories that could not be touched, concepts and ideas that no one could prove or disprove. The world itself, this clean cold city, this ancient and sometimes beautiful city, seemed a backdrop, a solid weave of shadows laid over something empty.

Sometimes his mind found itself thinking about his mind. Memories rose and fell. Ruth appeared in dreams. And he woke alone.

And so Newhouse thought of Tyler, and was thinking of calling her. He thought of their kiss. And if it had even happened. At the bridge: perhaps she did not know him, and he did not know her. She had not waved. He had not gone to her.

At least now he was thinking about his life.

Oh my darling.

He had boxed the photographs away, he had parcelled their possessions away. Dust, spindly and soft like hair, rolled on the green shoeboxes. He took down the pictures from the wall, from the shelves. Their wedding day: Ruth transfigured by camera light, her eyes and lips gleaming with something new and bright and depthless. He looked scrubbed and alert: his hair cut short, new suits, tie and boots. New smile, and a new posture in his back, in his chest, his arms and legs. He was holding her hand, her nails painted and iridescent. The photograph went into the box, the box closed, brown packing tape shrieking as it is ripped over the hinges.

And the nights of those empty days after her ceremony, counting money, his mouth smiling at people, drinking port and wine. And the dateless nights. Unpaid bills and dust.

Under his duvet at two in the afternoon. Food cans and jars, going out of date, long after she had gone.

I don't want to be dramatic, he had whispered one day into a phone propped up by a pillow.

You're fine, George, the German had said. Carry on.

I feel cored out, he said.

Tears ran into his ears.

It's natural, Rudi had said, his voice huge in the telephone. It's normal. Come and stay with me. We will go in the mountains and howl like the wolves.

I am howling like the wolves.

There was silence and shadow. But not real shadow, just the shadow of a shadow.

I wanted to protect you, she had said. And he had held her hand until she was dead.

My darling

...and anyway, it seems, to cut a long story short, that my show and so also my book is well and truly fucked, Rudi said, staring into his dwindling pint.

What?

The manhood of Christ, Rudi said, nodding, his eyes dopey, almost closed. Ja. Kaput.

Your show, they have... Newhouse swum back into the now.

Indeed, Rudi said. Fucked like a big anus.

Newhouse stared at his friend's heavy face.

I can barely bring myself to tell Owen and Grace, Rudi said.

His assistants had done much work finding the paintings and arranging the loans for the show.

I mean, the Uffizi, Rudi said, staring Newhouse in the face. They had agreed to loan the Veronese, the Holy...

Family with St Barbara And the Infant St John? Newhouse said.

Yes. The fire in the pub was now burning, sparks floating up into the darkness. It flicked red and amber lines on his friend's fleshiness, and bronzed the whites of his low-lidded eyes.

What a piece, Rudi said. That chubby infant Christ holding his manhood, just like that, showing his mortality and his masculinity, his new un-circumcised Covenant and his sinless body. And such perspective.

Wow well, Newhouse said. I think, Rudi, we can now safely say the whole place has gone to pot.

I won't be around to see it go into the pot, Rudi said.

What?

Iona made some calls for me, Rudi said.

In what way? Newhouse felt his heart beat faster.

Have you heard of Highrigg House in the north of England? Rudi said.

Yes: an El Greco, two Cannelettos, a Constable, a mechanical lamb.

A beautiful St Michael by Theotokópoulos, perhaps the best, Rudi nodded. Anyway the chair of that Trust is some family friend of a family friend of a cousin of an aunt. You know how it is.

Newhouse nodded.

Perhaps that is a bad thing. Anyway there will be an interview but it's but nothing but a crisp formality, as we German bastards like to say.

Jesus, Rudi.

Yes, a provincial museum in the middle of nowhere. I have become Nietzsche wondering the streets of Turin, howling after beaten animals. I did not want to tell Iona about my show at first.

Why not?

Women hold failures against you. I know this. You may not. They like to be sympathetic and caring, understanding and all those things. The hugging and the encouragement. But they store away your failures and then use them against you when you are weak.

Right...

In our father's day, men did not talk about work, for that reason. They didn't bring it home. Now we have to talk all the time, about everything. And it weakens us. So this favour from Iona will be remembered, be sure of that. But she's a nice girl. The first six sexy months are over now, though. No more sexiness. Sex is something we do now to remind us we are together.

You are marrying her.

Nothing is permanent in this world George. You know that. We are sand in the hourglass.

Newhouse nodded.

It is strange, isn't it. When you see a pretty girl in the street. Or in a bank, or at a concert. You never actually meet them. You never talk to them. They may look perfect. It's not something that ever happens.

No, Newhouse said. It's not.

You never see them naked. The pretty girls in the street. The pretty girls in the parks.

No.

Do you know that song: One fine day in the middle of the night.

Two dead men got up to fight. Yes.

Back to back they faced each other, drew their swords and shot each other.

Yes, Rudi, what of it?

I did not realize until now that the men are the same man. That they are the same.

I hadn't either. Are you alright?

And what about you, George? Rudi turned to his friend. The flickering shadow of the fire cast shadows on his stony face.

Well I have so much to do. I have the Dutch...

Oh my God, that survey will be ignored, belitttled, patronised: and fucking binned. Rudi snorted.

I have Venice to oversee.

Rudi snorted again.

Oh Venice. Yes of course. Eight oils of coupling strippers by that idiot Brick Macpherson.

Is that what it is?

Rudi looked at Newhouse, his eyes wide. Come on now.

Is that…? Newhouse asked.

You don't know what the show is, George? Man. You don't…

Of course I do, Newhouse recovered. Yes of course. It's called *The Man of Sorrow* and it's a video piece. It's quite fascinating, really.

Right right right, Rudi said, staring into the fire.

Tell me, have you seen anyone yet? Rudi said, looking down at his hands.

Seen?

You know, George, had any dates with women, any sign of that kind of thing…

No, no, Newhouse said. Nothing. I have been working, he said. Becoming familiar with the city, and the country. I have been into the hills quite a lot. You know. Um. Hiking.

Really? I left Germany to avoid fucking hiking. Rudi laughed. He turned his bulk to Newhouse. He looked at his friend tenderly.

You must George, you must try and meet someone. You must at some point, try and at least date someone. Maybe just a drink, a concert, a meal. Take a nice lady. A walk in the Botanic gardens, or down on the beaches.

A sandy fumble in the dunes with a stranger, Newhouse said. He shrugged.

Come now, Rudi said. Let's face it, we all know you are a good man. You have that distant way about you, but I have seen you play the game alright. Reach out to someone – in your own time. You can meet someone off the internet, too. I've heard there's all kinds on there. Remember how you fancied that girl from the bridge. Someone like that.

I'll see, Rudi, I'll see.

I know that tone, George. You mean: fuck yourself.

Another drink, my abandoning friend?

Of course of course. I plan never to set foot in that rotting edifice again, Rudi said.

As Newhouse moved to the bar, his mobile phone buzzed.

Tyler: *What you up to?*

He texted back immediately.

Nothing much. Want to meet an old man and talk about enamels?

THIRTY SIX

Newhouse worked for two weeks on the final document of his Dutch survey, long hours during daylight, and long hours at night. He oversaw the X-rays of three contested paintings. He linked a sketch, long in the stores, with an oil in a collection in Atlanta. Emails were sent, answered, forwarded, deleted in a silent dance of acceptance, debate, discussion and denial, white lies and negotiations, half-truths and honest brokering.

Life became clearer, harder-edged. Decisions were made at work, and he made decisions outside of it. He sent a strongly worded email to Carver about the paucity of archival IT and, the same day, he walked to a Turkish barber and asked for a wet shave with a razor. Sweet oil on his cheek and chin, soft hands on his neck and mouth.

He had started ironing his shirts again, he had taken four suits to the dry cleaners. He bought fresh vegetables and fruit. They lay there now, the green peppers dimpling, white fuzz on the carrot, the bananas brown and shrunken in their plastic bag.

At night, when he dreamed, he dreamt of ruined cities, of shattered walls, the serration of mangled glass, the hush of collapsing buildings.

He dreamt of smoke tunnelling and barrelling, blasting black and noxious through tree leaves, through foliage and broken masonry. He saw a distant forest, engulfed in white heat, shimmering in a haze throbbing from within.

He thought of Tyler, he had even dreamed of her, and had responded to her text, but it was something he needed to put off. He could not confront it and he could not confront her. So he was ignoring it, and her. He thought of the way he had replied so quickly to her again, and was annoyed. He had given something away.

She had replied again, but he had not.

Shall we meet for a coffee? she had asked.

He moved to delete her number. But he did not.

Newhouse now sat in the dark of his living room, his hand on a bottle, the TV on with no sound. He reached for the handwritten letter that he had received. It lay on the coffee table. It was written by Ruth's brother, John-Joseph, the priest.

Newhouse read its second page again:

The great wound of life is the passing of time. People and events, love and experience, all pass and die, with memories remaining as ghosts, ghosts that haunt but fade each day, until they are lost like air into air. You are lucky George, even in your terrible loss, because you live in the world of art, humanity's great gift to itself. Art works to halt the loss, to stop time, to harness it and fix it. Art is the closest humanity gets to answer the great possible sin of God, the creation of time, the unending tyranny of past, present, and future. Maybe God had to sacrifice to time in order to create the universe. But on this earth, there is a great compensation. For in our human lives, art is the great net, or the great hunter, gatherer, and curator, the nurturer, of humanity's loves, its dreams and desires. And through art we can always see love. Art flows like blood from our minds and our bodies. It is the human mind's amber, and love can be caught in it and be seen forever, transformed but not lost and it can stay – even frozen, imperfect, fragile and denuded – with us, as long as humans can see, and read, listen and feel.

The television glowed and hummed blue. It flickered and shook on the white walls.

Newhouse put his head back on the sofa and remembered, in clear light and defined lines and shapes, a winter's day.

He remembered.

The car rattled and bumped up the country track in the winter mist. All around was white. Shadows of trees faded away from the rutted road, yellow with ice. The road rose up into the hills, past farmhouses slumped under heavy snow, white-washed lodges crowned with icicles, black-rutted fields icy in the mist.

He came to a junction, by a cattle grid, and he slowed the car. Newhouse had parked beside the gate. The engine grumbled and stopped. Ahead the woods rose to the hills. A tree stood beside the gate, bare and black, tiny berries of ice on its shorn branches. Beyond, the winter field of frozen snow.

He left and locked the car, opened the gate and closed it, and walked across the white field. The sky was white, the ground was white. The snow squeaked and broke under his tread. His new beard warmed his cheeks and chin, his neck. His eyes began to water. He walked slowly and eventually he reached the hem of the forest.

He put one foot onto an icy stile and peered into the trees. Silver birch stands, the shadows between, bars to mark the way, their branches and twigs, a net of shadows.

He crossed the stile, into the forest, and the snow

crunched beneath his boots. His legs pumped through the snow, his breath billowing, flickering over the whiteness, like the fluttering shadows of a fire, dancing over the frigid cold.

He walked in the silence.

As the hill beneath him rose, the sun began to dimly heat his neck. It glittered on the frosted snow, on the melting icicles.

He stopped. He was in the heart of the forest. He looked at the track ahead and scratched his beard. He looked into the snow ahead. He saw her in his mind, her cheeks in the winter, red and blushed. She liked to snap icicles from branches.

Wouldn't this be the perfect way to kill someone? she had said, holding a long icicle, a razor-sharp shaft of ice. They had been walking beside a river, which ran blue and cold through naked trees. She rolled the icicle in her black-gloved hand. She stabbed it into the air. The blade would just melt away, she said. Her sly eyes were swirls of green and gray. She had held the weapon in her hand and swished it through the air as they walked.

And on their wedding night, hot and sweating on the hotel bed, the red wedding dress up around her belly, her tights rolled at her ankles, her makeup blotched and smeared, both their breath a stink of alcohol and smoke, she lay her arm across his hot chest, and whispered to him.

Promise me, she said. My darling.

Enough promises today, he said. Surely enough for today.

Never betray me, she said. Never let me down.

He walked on. His legs were tiring. His skin was reddening, his back was aching. He came to a bridge, clogged with snow and hanging ice. He brushed his hand along its rail, and snow fell in a white drape, with a whisper, onto the frigid stream below.

Up ahead, he knew, the folly stood at the top of the hill.

They had visited it in the summer and eaten a picnic in its courtyard.

They had sat on a blanket and eaten, on clacking plastic plates. He had thrown stones down the well and she had walked amongst the battlements, on the broken walls, around the trees which crawled over its pavements and cobbles.

She had loved the snow, in the few winters they had spent together, crunching snowballs in her hands and throwing them at the silent silver birch trees. She loved the way snow sat, perfect, on her red raw hands. She loved to sit still with one hand outstretched, and watch the crystals slowly come to clarity on her hand, melting just as their patterns were revealed. She loved the crunch of it, the fine-cut prints left where she had walked. She loved waking to snow when it transfigured the land. She loved the world under snow: reborn and clean, erased and empty.

Newhouse looked up, his breath a cloud, and saw the folly up ahead, broken and black, gap-toothed on the high white hill.

He looked into the endless forest, standing still to catch breath, his shadow as long as the trees. He felt wires in his arms. He reached the end of the path and the icy steps to the folly. Its rock and weight hung above him, its stones, battlements and turrets.

There was an inner courtyard, where the well stood.

He stood back and looked down, over the valley.

And as he looked down he saw his tiny car.

Snow lay thick on the ground, and he held his head. His face was solid, grey. His hands were blue, his nails purple, his eyes open and pale. In his ears, the tears from the night before, froze into jewels, into balls of tiny ice.

He saw black figures walking across the field to the forest, a dog leaping over snowdrifts.

He turned and walked to the courtyard.

He looked into the well.

He took off his wedding ring, and held it between a finger and thumb. It was on fire in the snow light.

He closed his eyes, and dropped it into the well, and it did not sound, once it fell.

THIRTY SEVEN

It was 2am and something buzzed. His alarm clock glowed crimson. Red numbers throbbing in the darkness. Something had woken him. His head was heavy, his eyes open or not open. There was the buzz again, cutting through the thick darkness of his flat.

He swung his legs out of bed. His bedroom had changed. He had put his clothes in the cupboards. He had put books on new bookshelves. They stood heavy in the night.

The telephone was still ringing.

Fuck sake, he said. He staggered through the dark of his flat. Who had his landline? Who was calling? He wondered if it was Tyler. He reached the receiver in the blackened living room as he remembered Tyler did not have his number. And why would she call anyway.

He lifted the handset and put it to his ear.

Hello? He said.

George Newhouse?

Yes?

George Newhouse, the voice said.

Yes, he said.

There was a whining noise, like wire swinging through wind and rain.

Yes, it is me, Newhouse said. It's four in the morning.

We are very, the voice said.

The voice sounded muffled, distorted.

Can you confirm you George Newhouse of the.

Yes? That is me, he said.

Good maybe we have miscalculated.

There was whistling and whining. There were clicks and scraping. He thought he could hear waves, and enfolding, collapsing walls of static.

Maybe, he said. Can you call my office number in the morning? Or write to me at george.newhouse@...

We want to talk yes the painting. Deepdale. Mr Vardoger.

Right, he said.

Blue horse.

The Blue Horse.

The blue horse the blue horse verify complete confirm for Vardoger.

What?

Deepdale here. We need you inconvenience Professor.

I don't understand you. I am not a Professor, he said. Look I am sorry, this line is terrible, it's the middle of the night.

No no no. The voice said. We will be in touch we will write we will call you in the.

The phone was put down, somewhere far away.

Newhouse sat in the darkness. His hands were clammy.

He packed for London.

THIRTY EIGHT

He was crossing the river. Light fell on the water and the bridge, fell on the flats and the offices, on the rumbling red bus that groaned past him, the cyclists thinly wobbling, the dispatch rider with his dark hornet-head.

Light fell on the wet tarmac, the rainbow oil splatters, the gentling shaking green, green trees.

He walked off the pink metal bridge and turned down to the water, to a path that ran past new red-brick flats, squat and cramped. Past a large silver building, the shape of a donut with a bite removed, its balconies decorated with green plants, sun loungers, its windows hung with translucent blinds, with billowing cotton. Dark barges hulked down beneath the walkway.

He was walking to meet Fr John-Joseph, Ruth's brother.

John-Joe. He was a priest at a church in Battersea. John-Joe looked a little like Ruth, her skin, a little reminiscence of her eyes. He had been abroad, in South America, when Ruth had died. But he had led the funeral, he had led the wake.

In his bag Newhouse had photocopies and folders, notes and notations from the Thorn Library. There, he had found the papers of Michael Langebek. Sale books and business papers. His long, tedious memoirs. Long Victorian sentences, from Danish to English and back to Danish and into English again. Bad writing.

'It was in the length of these years the mightiest chance of luck and Providence that laid its hand on my unworthy shoulder...'

He sat at a long dusty table for two days, on a chair like a bar stool, going through the Langebek papers, under low light, under brown wood and ochre shades, with soft feet padding in closed rooms above him and beneath him. No computers, no electricity, it seemed, in the library, the buses of Trafalgar Square outside, rumbling past the National Gallery and those wide backstage corridors he had paced as a younger man. That morning, shortly after a brief phone call in the cold, bright day with Fr John-Joseph, he had returned to his seat, and the librarian had padded over, hushed in the feathery gloom, and said there was another box with Langebek materials, part of the 36 boxes belonging to the archive of Henry & Dee, the now defunct London art dealers of the 18th and 19th centuries.

Langebek had worked there for a short time, but did not mention them in his memoirs. None of his business papers dated back to his H&D days. Henry & Dee were based on Sloane Square, at an office that was now a bank. And of course, Dr Martinu had mentioned them. A Mr Halfhouse had worked there, and bought A Blue Horse by a V. Doelenstraat in 1890.

Newhouse thanked the librarian, who floated away. There were sale books and ledgers deep in the box. Two were dated 1889-90 and 1890-91. The first mentioned Halfhouse securing a De Heem, a selection of works by Adrien van Ostade. Nothing more. Halfhouse seems to have been a junior in the firm, with most of the business through Julius Henry or Jonah Bynders-Dee, the grandsons of the original Henry & Dee.

Then, as the pages flipped over in the low light, Newhouse reached October 1890, among a list of thirteen paintings bought by Halfhouse from M Langebeck of

Yorkshire. He already knew about some of them. The writing was crisp and clear in black ink. Last on the list was *A Blue Horse, PV Doelenstraat 164- on RV Study 'The Empty Hand'd 1646. Damaged & repaired.'*

Reverse: The Empty Hand: Newhouse read it over and again. Damaged and repaired. Perhaps it had, indeed, been in the sea. Surely the sea would have destroyed it.

The depths and the shallows. Narwhales and leviathans. Sunken ziggurats.

He left his bag and coat on the high stool and walked out of the heavy library doors into the London light. He thought of Dr Martinu. He wished he could call him. He turned on his mobile, found the number for Gilda, and called it. The number rang out, and he left a message. He asked her to find any reference to a Van Doelenstraat called The Empty Hand. He could not think of one and he had left his files behind. It could be the description of another painting, it could be misnamed. He said urgently to call him soon. He walked back inside the library and back to the long desk. A heavier paper was stuck underneath the page of sales and acquisitions from 1890. He turned the page, and it was an envelope, attached with paper glue. The envelope was dark, as if stained. Inside was a folded piece of paper. He took it out.

JH - Mstr Halfhouse has noted in 13 Oct. Langebeck, Armstrong & Swinburne group, curious V Doelens-painting incl/gratis & so no fee entailed. 2/11/90 JBD.

He photocopied the note and packed his bag and left.

Now the sun was a blazing crescent on the silver building and beyond, it illuminated a white church, which sat in a small graveyard hugging the course of the river. A service was over and people were leaving. Old women in padded coats and purple hats, old men in baggy suits. A tall man with a jagged gait loped away, wispy hair dragged across his pate, eyeglasses black and broad. At the door, John-Joseph stood, clasping the hands of a man, talking quietly. He looked up and saw Newhouse by the gate and nodded before returning to the man.

Newhouse walked to the wall of the churchyard, and looked down to the river. A man sat reading a book on his barge, smoke slowly spiralling from a small chimney on its roof. A small white dog lay at the man's feet. The Thames water slupped heavily at the barge, gathering polystyrene cups, plastic bags, dark matter between barge and wall. Newhouse looked around and John-Joseph was standing at the church door, waving one loose hand at him.

Newhouse walked towards him. John-Joseph smiled and they shook hands. The priest's face had greyed, so had his eyebrows and his whiskers, and his hair was retreating. His eyes were blue and he had a scent of clear water.

His black clothes were sharp and neat.

Hello George, he said. How lovely to see you again.

John-Jo, Newhouse said. How are you?

Oh, you know. Still waltzing with the Holy Ghost. Coffee?

That would be lovely.

They moved inside.

I'm not sure you have been here for a while, John-Jo said.

No, not for a while.

Have you been to London at all?

Only for work.

Best thing, perhaps. It's becoming rather cramped.

How is Edinburgh?

I feel I don't quite have a sense of it yet.

As you know my first church was in Glasgow.

I didn't know that. I don't know it either.

Wonderful place. More beautiful than its more conventionally pretty partner, I often feel.

John-Jo looked Newhouse up at down and said, You are looking tired, George. Are you working too hard? You have always worked so hard. My sister would say that.

Newhouse looked away, up to the altar, the Victorian stained glass, the modern Stations of the Cross. White flowers were massive in silver vases, white petals lay curled like pale solder on the tiled floor.

She worked harder than me, Newhouse said.

Through here, John-Jo said, and walked to a door. In the kitchen, modern and clean, a woman was sitting at a table, smoking and reading a book.

Mrs Mulholland, this is George.

She stood up and stubbed her cigarette in a saucer.

How nice to meet you at last Mr Newhouse, she said.

Newhouse stood and nodded.

I am sorry for your troubles, she said, and looked around the kitchen.

Could you bring us coffee and some of that wonderful tiffin, please Maggie, John-Jo said. We will be in the living room. George, just drop your bags there.

In the living room, windows looked over the river, across the darkening water to an old factory. Newhouse saw the full bookshelves, a print of Turner's Rome over the fireplace, the worn throws on the settees, an old expensive writing desk and chair, an old white plastic television. By the west window, a framed dark Dutch scene, a nocturne by Aert Van der Neer. He wondered if Ruth's book was in the room. Then, by the north window, he saw her mirror. Her brother must have claimed it. Red framed, circular, with a design in gold: three fish around the glass, three stars between them. The glass seemed to be filled with light.

Mrs Mulholland brought in black tea and slabs of black chocolate cake on a black tray. John-Jo asked simple questions and they chatted. In the slanting sunlight the edges of the pictures and the books, the furniture, the stray hairs on the priest's head glinted golden and copper. Simple questions and easy answers ended and they sat in silence. John-Jo sat further back on his sofa and his head entered shadow.

And how are you, really, he said.

Newhouse wanted to run out of the room. Down to the river and the city. He shook his head.

Can I trouble you with my theology, George?

You can try, Newhouse said, attempting to smile.

I have to believe, John-Jo said, his eyes closed, that our love for each other as human beings is a fragment of God's love for mankind.

Silence flooded the room.

I want to talk about my sister, John-Jo went on.

Newhouse felt his body stiffen. His eyes were suddenly painful. He closed them.

The Empty Hand. An empty hand on a clean sheet lit by fluorescence. An empty hand on his stomach, warm and breathing. An empty hand rolling inside the wood, rolling into the final flames.

Do you believe in the possibility of life after death? the

priest said.

I don't believe in ghosts. If that's what you mean.

I did not ask that, George.

I'm struggling with life before death, right now, Newhouse said. He closed his eyes again.

I have to believe in the eternal life, the priest said. And oftentimes I do. Oftentimes, I must tell you George, I do not. His mouth moving in the shadows. Sometimes when I hear the Late Quartets. There seems the possibility they are divine hints of what could be. Someone once said that all that exists in nature is nothing compared to what is to come.

Newhouse opened his eyes. He took a draught of coffee. John-Jo moved forward, put his cup down, rubbed his eyes and kept them closed, his hands clasped together.

You are honest, Newhouse said at last.

Christ was all about the truth. He only spoke the truth.

Truth, Father, and its consequences died many years ago.

You cannot believe that.

Newhouse looked down at the black circle of coffee in his hand. Rings within rings of shaking, subsiding light inside it.

My life is art, John-Jo. And a life of art is, essentially, however beautiful, a life surrounded by lies.

You need a good memory to lie all the time. To tell the truth requires no memory, the priest said.

I know. You know I do not share your beliefs, John-Jo.

Did not a great artist say that art is a lie that happens to be true?

He may have, Newhouse said. He shrugged.

We... I have to also believe God made the entirety

of existence, George. Or created the conditions for its creation. Not just the earth and its inhabitants. But the atoms and the molecules, the planets and the stars, the dark matter and the light.

I know.

I have wondered why, George. Indeed it used to obsess me, even as a novice. I would watch programmes, I would read books, even science fiction films. Why, God, my Lord, why make so big and baffling a universe, too big to comprehend, which mankind will never see. Its limits are so limitless, its vastness is so vast. I have begun to think maybe when we die, we can see all of creation, not only as one, but as it is.

Right, Newhouse said. I didn't know you felt so strongly about astronomy.

John-Jo was smiling. Imagine George. To travel into and through the Horsehead Nebula, how unbelievably wonderful would that be?

I can't imagine, Newhouse said.

When we die, George. When we die. The universe is open to us. We used to call them the Heavens. They are heaven. That is what heaven is.

I had hoped death might be more restful or peaceful than that. I hope it is just sleeping.

Maybe I am over-excited, John-Jo said. I confess I didn't sleep well last night. And I am happy to see you.

He looked at Newhouse.

When I saw Ruth, just before she passed, she said something that has lingered with me.

Really?

She said, and I think she meant this, even though she may have been emotional, that she knew, even in the difficult times, in the bad times, that you loved her entirely. That this was certain and she never doubted it, even if she doubted many things about this life, this world.

The circles inside the circles shifted again. The rings entwined and interlocked.

I do love her entirely, Newhouse said. That has not gone away, he added. It has never gone away.

The priest nodded.

Let us not talk theology anymore, John-Jo said. But, George. Remember two things. One, you have been loved. That is why we are here today, I might say.

Newhouse nodded.

And also this. God made us in his image. He is a creator, and we are creators. And the greatest thing we make is not art or industry or science, it is love. You, from your own free decision and choice, fell in love and Ruth fell in love with you, and that love is the same love with which God loves the Universe.

John Jo, why are you telling me this.

We will never talk of it again. But that love is real.

I find that a very difficult concept.

What, George? He loves the entire universe. If he did not, it would all cease.

I loved her.

You still do. And she still loves you.

Newhouse shook his head.

She is dead, John-Jo. I cannot move on from there.

Love is as strong as death, the priest said. It is an equal power.

No.

Yes, George.

No. Newhouse was shaking his head.

But you do love her.

To what end? Newhouse was irritated now. What does it matter? No one cares, he said. If I have learned one thing: the world does not care, he said.

You care. God cares.

God has not told me of this.

I have to believe he does.

Does he care about pain? Newhouse asked.

Well, the priest said, sitting back. Let us not get into the Problem of Pain, George.

Newhouse shook his head. He had said too much. He felt like an adolescent. He felt embarrassed.

We would be here all night, the priest said.

Indeed, Newhouse said. Your letter, he said.

Yes…

You mentioned something that I should see?

The priest stood up. He moved to his desk, and took a piece of paper from it.

He handed it, the paper shaking in the light, to Newhouse.

I found this in one of her books, John Joseph said. It's a poem by Ruth I don't remember seeing before. I thought you may want it for the collection. I appreciate its theme, but think, indeed, I know, it is a love poem, for you. I think it's a first draft. Certainly, I don't think anyone has seen it before.

Newhouse looked at the folded paper in his hand.

'1 Corinthians, 13:12'

Lover, in this smoky glass is my face too,
reflected: the cooling bones, the eyes, the sea.
Shaking inside a mirror's bilocated space.
But if you find it, you find me.

He stared at it for a while.

Newhouse felt tears come but they would not fall.

I am sorry, the priest said.

Newhouse opened his mouth to speak but said nothing.

Now, the priest said briskly, would you consider taking communion?

RUDI

Rudi was leaning, poised and concentrated, in the gallery.

He was looking at the face of a horse. Its body lean, its long eyes black. The horse stood square and firm. But it was under-painted, its tones slightly translucent. As if it was unfinished.

The Stoning of St Stephen by Adam Elsheimer. Rudi had not seen the painting for some time. And he had forgotten why he had left his office, and walked across the city, to enter the National Gallery.

In the foreground, a pale, young martyr was being stoned. His flesh was mauled and battered. A youth stood near him, a large rock above his head, about to deal the death blow. Men on horseback watched. A crowd stood and stared. And in the dusky eaves, that strange horse stood. Its eyes firm and black. The horse looked at him. The horse moved its hoof and a horseshoe was stamped into the painted mud.

Rudi stood back.

A couple with a baby in a light buggy moved noisily into the small gallery. Rudi looked at his watch. He was running late. Work was done, but he had to buy some food, buy some wine, go home to his fiancée. He moved away from the Elsheimer. The horse stood, motionless. Its left hoof suspended in air. Its eyes were blinking.

Rudi slung his bag over his shoulder and moved through the velvety gallery rooms. Oh how he wanted to work at a gallery as well run and supported as the National Galleries. He knew he was not good enough.

That day, at his own institution, some of the Ardrashaig paintings had been removed. More were going soon. On the red walls, pink rectangles and small holes stood where the paintings had hung. New cardboard information signs were tacked to the thready walls. Rudi had been involved, with Carver, McCormack and Laird, in attempting to re-arrange the ground floor of the galleries, inferior works were being brought out of storage to hang in corners and passages, whilst other works – 19th century civic landscapes, and, in his view, acres of Pre-Raphaelite tosh – were being 'promoted' to the main rooms to cover for the loss of priceless works being lost. Rudi had six weeks left. His exhibition on the Manhood of the Christ had been cancelled. Iona was looking for a house south of the border.

He was not only leaving a job he had long desired and worked for, but a city he loved – its parks and concert halls, its clean lines and smallness, its mild and polite atmosphere, its modestly restrained but overt self-importance (so much like Vienna!).

He was leaving George Newhouse too. His friend's youthful beauty was older and slightly bedraggled now, but that profile, those eyes. Sometimes George would appear, his trousers crushed, bewhiskered. Sometimes his clothes looked unclean and unironed. He would disappear, not attend meetings. He was distracted. Sometimes he eyes were dead, his voice a monotone.

Other times he was the George he had known since college: handsome, funny in his stiff way. And with that memory, such a good memory for everything. How beautiful he had looked with Ruth. Poor George. He has come so far, Rudi thought, as he stepped into the darkness of the night, the city lights a garland of blushed neon, the grainy wind whipping around the columns of the gallery, his reddening ears, his exposed neck.

Poor George. He remembered the scenes in Chelsea. The report of the naked man lurching in the Thames mud, prostrate in the silt in the early wintry hours, a silent open mouth.

The days and nights smashed and deranged in Notting Hill. The ambulances and police cars, the polite doctors and the quietly spoken coppers. Lights swinging and revolving on red brick, on slippy concrete. Stomach pumps and clagged pots in his destroyed kitchen.

The deranged woman in the bed who would not leave, who George could not name, and who she could not name. The bonfire of papers and photographs. The expensive replacement teeth, the compacted wall plaster, the half dome of his head, smashed into it. Naked poor George, his body hairless and lithe, sobbing and shaking. Blood leaking in tiny bubbles from opened skin. Poor George. The lonely funeral among the oaks and elms. And the silent crematorium in the winter mist. White faces and black clothes. Wet petals on black marble. George clinging to his sister, a dead tree and its living vine.

Rudi walked into the old town to buy wine and cheese and ham. He entered a bright, noisy delicatessen. He stared at the wall of dark wines. Special offers scrawled on fluorescent pieces of card. The shop seemed to suddenly empty. It was quiet. The radio music had stopped.

He felt calm. George would be OK. This Highriggs House deal would be OK. He liked the countryside. He would hike again, he would take up golf, perhaps. He might buy cars again. Iona might have a child. The job would not be hard. He could have an affair with a barmaid.

Two dead men in the middle of the night, he sung under his breath.

The wall of wine glinted. Dark red wine stood silent in its bottles. He saw the lights of the shop, bent and straightened and then bent again in the glass. He looked from side to side and realised none of the bottles had labels. The offer signs had gone. The wall became a sheet of glass, a red wall of solid wine. In it he saw his reflection, his head massive, tottering on a tiny neck. His body ill-painted, translucent. He felt a shoulder of hot hair rub his head. In the reflection of the glass, a black shadow stood beside him.

A hate from outside mankind.

Christ, he wanted to say. But no sound was made.

The radio music was loud. A man was singing a slow song about crashing in a car. A young man with acne pushed past him with a pizza in a box. Rudi rubbed a hand over his head.

He picked a bottle of rosé and paid and left.

Rudi walked quickly, skipping over roads, nipping between cars as lights changed. People bustled around him, with their hats and coats, their bulky bags and shiny faces, their eyes flicking here and there.

The dark sky like a lid slipped silently over the city.

Rudi bustled on, thrusting himself through the crowds, down the thin streets to the bridges over the railway station, down past the hotels and the statues, down the long road to the empty, rusting docks. He stood at the dockside, and wondered where he was, why he had walked, sweaty, head down, all that way. He was two miles from home. He walked back, he hailed a cab at a crossroads, told the driver his address. The dark cab growled through the darkened streets.

Rudi thought of his mother, washing soil off new potatoes in a clean white sink. He thought of Astrella, her golden hair, her head asleep on his naked stomach. There was music wasn't there? A radio tuned in, his favourite music, and her lovely hair on his stomach, caught in the small curls of his belly. Oh the weight of her lovely head. You never forget or stop loving the one woman you really love, he thought.

I will dream of you for years, yet, my gorgeous Astrella. Those don't go away, these feelings. They have nowhere to go. His mind turned and turned. The wound in his mouth, still, from her bait and hook, which she had lowered, and then ripped from him. Men only love once, he knew, once apart from their mothers, and that one love is always the first, the last and the worst.

He thought of Saturday morning, when, still sleepy and hungover, he and Iona had made love. She had that look on her face. Her warm and vigorous body.

He got home.

The flat was empty. Its rooms were dark. Iona was not home.

He felt light-headed and he paced the large apartment. He put the food in their large steel fridge. He drank a glass of water and stared up into the Venetian chandelier. Pinks and purples, puce and violet lights, spangling and sparkling in ugly fronds and lumps, ribbles and tubers. I don't know why we bought this, it is so ugly. They had it sent over from Venice in pieces. They had spent tense days assembling it. It hung like a jellyfish.

He walked through the flat. There was no one in the

large empty bed. He walked into the dark living room, the huge sofas, the large paintings. He sat down, and thought of that horse in the Elsheimer. He stood up. He turned the lights on. He sat down again. Elsheimer, 1578-1610. Too early for those endless fucking Netherlanders.

That phonecall, he thought.

He had received a phonecall at work. From Gilda, a woman who had worked with Newhouse on his exhibition. She had asked a favour. She knew Newhouse was away, working in London. Could Rudi help?

He had said yes, of course. Always worth putting down a deposit on a future fuck.

He had not known she was English, he thought she was Dutch. Wasn't her surname Van Gaal?

There is a file on his desk, probably, written by Dr Martinu. Could he photocopy the summary, fax it to her?

Sure, sure he said. Of course. Where are you these days?

He had found the file in Newhouse's clean, ordered office. Closely typed. He found not a summary, but two pages of numbered conclusions. He photocopied it and sent it to her number, somewhere in Italy.

Poor George. The Blue Horse was something George hardly mentioned, but when he did, he talked with an intensity he never mustered for any other subject. Apart from, maybe, his need to sleep.

Newhouse usually spoke coolly, even robotically (especially lately). The only mention, recently, of The Blue Horse had been another discussion of that 'Rembrandt note'. Rudi wondered whether that note was written by Van Rijn at all.

Rudi snorted as he pulled off his shoes in the dark.

He wanted to ride that horse, feel it, hold its bone head in his heads, taste the bile on its stone lips, encircle and accept its power.

The night after his exhibition was cancelled, he had dreamt of a wide black beach. The sand was made from tiny rotten teeth. The horse had stood by the waves, and he had gone to it. Its face was soft like mud. He had put his face into it and woken up wet.

Where was Iona.

Iona was probably buying food and wine. They had not spoken all day. Dr Martinu (and what had happened there? What had happened to that fat smug coot?) had encouraged George to chase that fucking picture.

Rudi looked around his dark living room. The lights were out. Had he not put them on? He looked at his mobile phone. Its battery was nearly gone. It was two in the morning.

He stood up. He was alarmed. That's not right. He walked through the dark flat. He looked down as his feet. They felt odd. He had trainers on, not his work shoes. In the bedroom, someone was asleep in bed. It was Iona, she was snoring. She was on her front, the duvet pulled back a little. He could see her naked back, her neck.

I must have fallen asleep, he thought. She must have fallen asleep.

I will check those Dutch files in the morning, see if I can help, he thought cloudily, lost in the misty warm darkness of the room. There must be things to know. Newhouse had read so much, read the files over and over again. Newhouse had blinded himself. The words meant nothing now. He could not see the Horse, the real animal, what was really there, amid all the theorising, the abstruse debate, the thicket of dates and names and theories. The story had been coated in lead, thrown into the sea. But it was there, somewhere. Soft and hot.

Rudi thought: I have a cool brain. I am dreamy now but not all the time. I can think these things through. Fogginess now, but not always.

I will read those notes, I will write poor George a paper for when he returns from London. I could send it to him and Martinu. See what they think. But not Martinu. Martinu is dead.

I know things George does not. I could help, he thought.

I could find it and claim it.

With a snort, Iona turned her head from under the sheets. It seemed, in the dark, that her entire face was covered in hair.

And then, he was suddenly outside again, on the way to the Gallery in the 3am darkness.

He wiped his wet hands on his hair.

His bare feet on the cold wet lawns of the black gallery grounds. The key in the lock, and his fingers sure but cold on the security combinations. 678-456-901. The red light turning to green.

The heavy security guard at his station, dead, his head caved, both eyes burst like egg whites strung with chick's blood.

And then he was padding through the blackness and silence of the darkened gallery. Past black paintings and black sculptures, past closed doors and silent stairs.

Then his handle was on the heavy door. It turned and he entered. He was in George's office. He turned on the light and sitting in George's chair, was a large heavy man in a tweed suit, reading papers.

Rudi turned to him, and saw Rudi, himself.

Guten Tag, he said to the other.

Rudi said: Nails, feathers, pins, coins, coal meat cloth and hair. Here comes the young prince. To see his young Astrella again.

Under its curtain of lead, the Blue Horse lay dreaming.

BATTERSEA PARK

Sunshine lit the window, gilding its frame, making the curtains billow with heat and glow golden. He woke. Her arm was over his chest, her long fingers limp and warm. He could hear her breathing heavily into the pillow. He slipped out of bed and pulled on jeans, a sweatshirt, some trainers and walked into the kitchen. He pissed in the loo and looked at his face in her circular mirror, framed with blue metal, swimming fish swirling around its edges.

In the small shop in the square, he bought some bagels and some orange juice, some cream cheese, some salmon, some tea bags. The flower shop was opening. He walked inside and smelled roses, tulips, sweet lilacs. He bought some small carnations, wet and green.

She was still asleep when he returned, an arm bent under her head and hair, like a small wing.

He put the food away and put the flowers in a vase of water. He sat on the sofa and then lay on the sofa and the heat glowed through the window and onto his skin, and he fell asleep again.

She woke him with a kiss on his eyelids and he reached up to her head and felt her mussed hair and her cool skin. They sat together on the floor by the coffee table and watched the news as they ate. They decided to go for a walk along the river, to the park.

On the riverside, joggers jogged and couples pushed milky babies in prams and strollers. The sun throbbed on red brick and glass, on cobbles and black metal and cool white concrete, and the slowly rolling river.

They walked, holding hands, between the trees. It was warm on his skin and her skin, on his neck and her neck, on his eyes and her eyes. Her hand left his hand and moved around his waist and she leant her head on his shoulder. They walked down a green colonnade of trees and reached a wide lawn where a van was selling ice cream. They bought two cones and walked to grass under wide elm and sat down. People passed by. Children on scooters and trikes. On the playing fields, young men were arriving and pulling off sweatshirts and jumpers, kicking around footballs, throwing rugby balls, shouting at each other. The brown tarmac glittered between the fields of grass.

I had a horrible dream last night, she said.

A nightmare?

Yes.

You seemed happy this morning.

It woke me up. You didn't move, you were snoring.

I don't snore.

Yes you do. I pushed your face.

Did you?

Yes.

I couldn't find you.

You have terrible eyesight.

I couldn't find you. Then you were in this pub, with a girl, and you had got her pregnant.

He looked at her and smiled.

This sounds more like a nightmare for me than you.

And you were shrugging, saying, 'So what, she's pregnant, I don't care, what's it to you, I will sort it out.' You were being a dick, really unpleasant.

I can't believe that.

I ran out crying and then I woke up.

Well, it was a dream, he said. A piece of cheese.

I know, but it was still exhausting and upsetting, George. But I feel fine now.

Well it was a dream. I haven't made anyone pregnant.

I know I know, she said. I have so much work to do today. Form filling.

Not now, he said.

They sat under the tree and ate the ice cream. She leaned her head on his shoulder and rubbed a finger up and down his stomach.

Do you think we should try again?

He sighed.

Don't sigh.

Yes, probably, he said.

Probably?

Yes, let's.

Good, she said. That's good.

As long as I can choose the name.

Not some Dutch name.

He laughed.

Carel, he said.

Carole is a girl's name, she said.

Well then it works both ways.

Shall we walk into town?

No, let's go home and start mating.

Well, OK then.

They walked past her brother's church on the way home. Fresh fruit swung in a blue plastic bag from his hand.

Maybe we should get a blessing, a good luck in our endeavours, he said.

Maybe, she said.

Did I read somewhere that women are born with all the eggs they need?

I told you that.

Oh.

Do you listen to a word I say?

Pardon?

You're hilarious.

Did you say something?

They walked back to their flat, and emerged in the evening, walking silently into the city. They found a bar and drank wine and smiled and laughed. Foreheads leaning into each other, each other's weight balanced on each other's temple.

In the red skied sunset, they rambled slowly home. They sat on a bench looking over the crimson river.

THIRTY NINE

What, he just left?

Newhouse was surprised.

Yes, said Hayley. He said he had told you. He said he wasn't working his notice out.

He never said that. Not to me.

Are you sure? He sent an email around last week...

I didn't get it. I tried ringing him...

We took his Gallery phone back. He said in the email he would pass on his new number. Although he hasn't done that yet.

OK, Newhouse shrugged. I'm sure he will.

I'm sorry George, I thought you had spoken to Mr Hessenmuller.

No, no. I was in London.

How was it?

London is London. Most people overrate it and I underrate it. I can stand it for a short while.

I suppose you have heard about McKie.

No?

One of the night wardens. Was found in the Waters.

No. That's awful.

Yes. Police think it's a suicide. There's an envelope going around for his wife. Remember the Venice meeting at two, George.

How could I forget, he said, and walked back into his office.

The papers on his desks were neater than he remembered.

He had stayed in London for a few days longer than planned. He had visited the National Gallery, and seen new shows. He had bought a book of posters for Angus. Found a book that Ursula would like. He had drunk coffee in the members bar of the Tate Modern, watching a red sun set on St Pauls.

He had eaten good dinners with nice wine, quietly alone. He had visited his bank, moved money around, and spent some. He spent time on the Underground, comfortable in its thrumming business, its emptiness at night and in the afternoon, its frenzy in the morning and at rush hour. He had met an old friend from the National at the Royal Academy, drunk coffee, had light conversation.

The friend, the acquaintance, had aged, seemed thinner and lighter. He had left public galleries, moved into the private world, running a gallery near Pimlico. He suggested Newhouse do the same.

The clarity of money, he said, is refreshing. No public to deal with. No public funds to hamper you, no social inclusion strategies, no education projects needed. Just art, the artist, prints, prices and sales.

I love working in the public sphere. If the public cannot see it, what is the point of my job at all? Newhouse said. You want to return art to the era of the Borges, of courts and princes.

Nonsense. Art is competition, like everything else George, you know it is. Think of the future. There is no future for public galleries. Only stagnation and decline.

You could say that about the whole human race.

You were always a pessimist, George. You think civilisation peaked in 1789.

Not always, Gerry.

His friend paused.

I know. I'm sorry. I heard. I didn't mean that. I'm terribly sorry.

They looked at each other. They put sugar in their coffees.

So how is this extraordinary farce in Venice looking for you? I hear you are trying to rescue the Brick Macpherson mess. I was talking to a friend of mine at the British Council... my, my.

Newhouse shrugged.

I have never curated an exhibition before where no one knows what the final work will look like.

Welcome to contemporary art practice, George, Gerry said. I heard the budget has been exceeded and capped twice already.

Oh you don't want to know about it. It's actually the most amateurish project I have ever been involved in. Are all Biennale shows like this?

All 145? Or whatever it is? I don't know.

We are not even an official show. We are some ancillary thing. It's a Byzantine process.

We tried to work with Macpherson you know, his friend said.

We could never find him. Impossible man. Apparently he owns an entire island. Made a fortune in Russia, selling that awful porn to murderers. When are you going to Venice?

In a couple of weeks. I haven't been for years, Newhouse said.

Last Biennale, I was there... those oligarchs, plutocrats, pulled up these gigantic yachts beside the entrance to the Giardini, huge black things right up against the Viale dei

Giardini pubblici. Disgusting, really. But Venice is Venice.

Full of ghosts, Newhouse said. Full of shadows and reflections.

Now George was sitting in the Public Gallery's conference room, waiting for the Venice discussion to start. Someone had removed two of the light bulbs from the light above.

The door opened and a red-faced Carver and some others walked in. A woman and man that Newhouse knew but could not name. Celia Brussels, the new head of marketing. The previous woman had left or been fired, he could not remember. Papers were handed out, many of them copies of printed emails.

The meeting was short.

Terrible about McKie, someone said.

Yes. Awful. Gambling debts, Brussels said. Press release is done.

Carver tapped his finger on his papers, and said that oversight on the whole project was close to a disaster, looking at Newhouse.

I am not the manager of this project, Newhouse said.

No, Carver said, unconvincingly. Not officially.

Well, Brussels said, we all know that Robert Hill has now left, which is probably for the best, and we have to carry on and get this show on the road.

She had almost yelled. Her voice echoed around the room.

What happened with Hill? Newhouse said.

Well, it's an HR matter, Carver said, cracking a sheet of paper.

It's definitely an HR piece of business, another man said.

Poor man, someone said.

Yes, awful, quite awful, Brussels said.

What I heard about what he did with the…

Yes.

Carver coughed and looked up and out at the group around the table, his almond eyes wide.

Damned thing is, he said, we have little evidence this Hill has even spoken to Macpherson. At least not in the last few weeks. All we get is emailed invoices for video kit from his blasted agents. The closest we have got to Macpherson, as we can see here, is through a girl called…

He looked at his notes.

Ivy…

Ivy Boyd, Newhouse said. And she is not a 'girl'. I've met her, she is the most capable person on this project. This room included. She has given me budget updates, technical updates, as far as she is able.

Yes well at least she seems to pass messages to and fro competently, Carver nodded. We don't even know if Macpherson has even been to Venice. Or even seen the pavilion.

They talked more about the project, the exhibition.

It seemed Macpherson had cleared the interior of the Biennale pavilion, which was itself an undistinguished 19th century Palladian block with one main room and two side galleries, wedged as an ugly lump between France and the official UK buildings at the end of the Giardini gardens. Macpherson's team – mainly his brothers and sisters – had repainted the interior and installed sound baffles. The video screens were being erected on a large, cross-shaped scaffold on a false floor at the end of the main gallery, with theatrical lighting in the ceiling.

Photos emailed from Venice, via Ivy, showed an extremely large Cross, made from the flat-screen video screens. A snake's wedding of black wire hung from the back of the screens, tangling on the marble floor. Large, flat white speakers were being attached to the gallery walls.

We do finally have a title, *Son Of Man,* Carver said, looking at his notes.

Hill was right about something, someone murmured.

So, Carver said.

Newhouse looked at the photocopied papers.

Each screen shows 2000 images – taken from men across the world of various ages, races, creeds, social status, etc etc etc – of various parts of the crucified form. He has videoed or photographed, in order from top to bottom, hair, forehead, eyes, nose, mouth, cheeks, ears, beard, Adam's apple, neck, shoulders, sternum, ribs – either side, stomach, stomach 2 – what does that mean for God's sake? – hips…

Yes, Brussels said. We see.

Forty-five body parts in total, including hands, feet, Carver added.

Each screen will show these parts in sequence, of some kind, and after a period of time, as following the Synoptic Gospels, the rapidly flicking phalanx of screens will, in strict co-ordination with each other, show the death of Christ on the Cross, the Seven Last Words, etc etc etc.

Carver began to mumble.

With attendant sounds and so on, Newhouse said, reading out the same email from Ivy.

Yes, someone said.

Newhouse, Carver said, suddenly bright. I've spoken to Colebrooke and he thinks it's best if you take over, see this horse past the finish line so to speak. You know Venice, you know this Ivy girl, and let's face it, Hill has left a mess you can clean up.

OK... I was appointed as an advisor, I am no contemporary art person, Newhouse said.

Well, the commissioning and idea phase is over, Carver said. You just need to make sure it works and doesn't embarrass us all too much. You've mounted a show before, have you not?

If you've seen any of the Biennale shows, you needn't worry about embarrassment, someone snorted.

Newhouse looked at the faces around the table. They looked to him.

What the hell, he thought.

Well, Newhouse said, suddenly feeling light. I should go out soon then.

Good, good, whatever you think's best, Carver said, standing up.

Good good good, he said again, and walked out the room.

Nice job, someone said, curtly.

The other people filed out. Newhouse looked down at his papers.

He had drawn something dark and tangled with his pen in the margins of his notes.

He wandered back to his office. He closed his door.

Something buzzed in his pocket. He pulled it out: his mobile phone. There were two messages. One from Foster Flintergill: *Hello George: Have you prepared that argument for us? Just email it if you have thanks, FF.*

The other was from a number he did not recognize.
Hallo the Rudis here. I split. I have been on the hunt. Away

now. Met something who will interest you. talk to me. R.

He deleted the message. His friend was drunk. But at least he was in touch.

Newhouse prepared for Venice, putting files in his bag.

He put in his diaries, his notebooks. He heard staff nearby turning off the lights. He looked around his office and wondered if he would see it again.

Before he switched off his computer, he looked at the book of Ruth's poems for a while. He put the book back, and wrote an email.

From: G. Newhouse
To: UrsulaNMcDonagh
Subject: Canal surgery

Dearest U,
Tomorrow I travel to Venice for the wretched Biennale.
I am sorry I haven't called. There's been hell on.
The artist we have chosen for our show is a mercurial type, a guy called Crawford 'Brick' Macpherson – I don't know whether you have seen his stuff, I hadn't before I took this doomed project on. In fact we are not sure what the hell he has planned for the exhibit. Light a candle for me.

Work… well, my new job here wasn't what I thought it would be. In fact I am not sure how much longer I can stick it. More radically, I am wondering whether 'the art world' is for me anymore.
So maybe when Venice is over we can compare calendars, and I can take you up on your offers and come and see you for a while.

Do you remember when we were little, living in that draughty house in Newsham, and I would have all those nightmares? The owls at the window?

Father, and I am sure he was trying to help in his own way, would sit there and tell me about the nightmares he had suffered when he was young. He would dream that the world was melting, or that he was being squeezed into a crack in a huge wall.

I ended up having those nightmares too.

I feel I am back there again, scared of someone else's nightmares, adding their terrors to my own.

Let us speak soon.
But first – La Serenissima.
Love to the little guy.
x
G.

He was closing down his email and a new one arrived from his sister, an instant reply.

He smiled and opened it.

George,

Hamish here. I haven't read your message: I just thought, given you are awake, to let you know - Ursula was taken into hospital last night.

She collapsed at home. I was working, but believe it or not, Angus raised the alarm, he used her phone to call 911. Clever little guy. Thank F– !

Ursula seems to have just fainted. She is OK now, under observation – she is now complaining of splitting headaches and toothache but the worst is over.

I am relaying a message from her: that she has been thinking of you! She said that she had a strong dream, the night before her collapse, of you on a boat, somewhere at sea. You know what she is like! I am just passing it on.

I will print out this email from you and take it in to her.

Thank F— I wasn't away, and that Gussy is such a brave, resourceful boy.

Call me if you like. Don't worry about Little Bear – she is in the best place.

I hope she will be home soon!

best—

H.

Newhouse sat back in his seat.

He called Ursula's number.

It rang out. He called her home number. It rang out.

FLIGHT

The sunlight shone on the red brick. Glitter trails in the fine mortar. On the high walls and white plaster. And across the parkland, the sun grew shadows from the newly cut grass. The trees stood hung with leaves, and as they walked, the shadows turned around the trees, although the trees remained still and the black lines moved around and shifted and lengthened across the grass. New bowers were unveiled under the branches, new safety under their armoured interwoven leaves. And there was no sound within the parkland, between the earth and the wood and the still green grass.

Over the hill.

And water fell silently from the new fountains and the paths and gardens, and the new flowers nodded and dipped.

Above the writhing canopy, there was red brick and sandstone, and above that, blue sky and teased threads of cloud all interwoven in nodding braids, from side to side and side to side. A light breeze was in their hair and a light wind ruffling the edges of the lengthening shadows.

At the collonade, on clean cotton, they ate the fresh white fish and drank sweet wine as the sun rose to its height and stayed there, for a while, and then began to fall, and the shadows of the trees moved again like many clock hands on the face of the silver grass.

He had seen in his dream, the columns and the arches. And from beyond the columns and arches shone pure golden light, warmer than the sun, and as he turned his eyes to the light, the light would fade, and as he turned his eyes to the columns, the arches, the alcoves and the towering ruins, the light would return again.

I look in death, she had said, for what I cannot find in life.

FORTY

He arrived in Venice in the dark.

The night rolled over the waves and the water.

Wanting to arrive in the city by water, he carried his case past the waiting buses and out, past the concrete pillars of the airport, into the calm cool air, past the inky water's edge, to the jetties.

A private water taxi sat bobbing there, its engine grinding. The night was black, but in the distance, a fluttering swarm of lights floated golden on the black lagoon.

San Toma, Newhouse said, and the man nodded, and Newhouse climbed into the taxi, its smooth wooden roof glinting in the electric lights of the harbour. There were already people inside it. He saw a head turn, and realised it was Ivy.

Well hello, she shouted at him. He moved to greet her. She looked healthier. She introduced him to three young men. One was tall, hunched over in the cabin, with a red beard. The other two were dark and small.

I wondered when you would be coming over, she said.

Me too, he said.

Where you staying? I'm in some flat near the Rialto with Henry and Donald here, she said.

Near Frari, he said. You coming to the meeting tomorrow?

Yes, I guess so, she said. She was suddenly uninterested. She was angry about something. She looked around the cabin and sat down.

I need some air, I'll get this fare, Newhouse said, and the artists and Ivy thanked him.

He moved outside onto the unsteady deck, and the water taxi moved away from the light of the airport and into the lagoon.

The roar of the engine in the darkness covered the slapping of the waves, the waters all around them. The driver was silent, standing at his wheel, looking down the motorboat to the distant lights ahead. They passed wooden posts stuck deep into the velvet lagoon. Other lights moved in the dark; other boats, receding and growing then moving away, liquid and evasive.

The artists and Ivy sat chatting on the white leather seats inside. Ivy occasionally looked up at Newhouse, who was standing near the pilot, looking out over the passing, churning waters. She seemed different, her hair shorter, her eyes made-up, wearing leather and colourful cotton. The artists laughed and passed around a bottle of wine. The pilot throttled down and the boat groaned. White waters rumbled around the stern. Nearby, lit by low floodlights, Newhouse could see a villa in the murk, rising alone on the waters. A small boat berthed at the bottom of pale steps. The house was alone, its windows shuttered. A watery stench in his nostrils, Newhouse's eyesight was blurred and gauzy in the nightlight. The glow of St Marks and the Dorsoduro lay ahead as the taxi moved closer to the islands.

Slowly, buildings came through the dark, moving like banks of black clouds

The canal city, in its floating dream, was asleep. The windows were closed, doors were closed. Some lights shone dully on the Dorsoduro shoreline. Starlights hung around a winery door. And then the taxi swept right, moving down into a thin canal, high crumbled buildings on each side, the water sloshing and gulping in the restricted space. The sky above was flat and black, the water road behind, flat against the night. The buildings moved by, depthless, as if they were only one inch thick, theatre scenery pulled by on casters and ropes.

The engine churned on and the taxi moved through the canyon of buildings, under bridges, and then swept right, into another channel. Past walled gardens and black iron gates, under empty balconies and silent roofs, and then suddenly it was on the Grand Canal, the wide slash of sea, and powering up to the Rialto bridge, before braking at the vaporetto stop at San Toma. Newhouse paid the driver. He ducked his head inside the cabin, and saw Ivy kissing one of the artists, the other two talking.

He moved away and took his bag and walked into the silent city. Silent and empty. He walked under an arch, and up an alley to an empty street. A cat slunk off a wall and down into the shadows.

He stopped in the light of a shuttered bar, and found the details of his rooms, off the Calle Saoneri. It was a short walk, his feet echoing off brick and stone. He found the door, set into a steep wall. He pressed the buzzer and was let in. He walked up a dark stair, and at the top a golden triangle of light slipped into vision. An old lady in a blue nightgown stood, and ushered him in. The flat had a cracked marble floor and seemed to be full of dark furniture.

Mr Halfhouse, the woman said.

Newhouse looked at her. Her eyes were open and blue. Her hair was dyed red.

Newhouse, he said.

I'm sorry yes Mr Newhouse.

She handed him keys, and a small map of Venice. She said she lived on the floor below. She wished him good night and left the flat.

On the table, under an upturned plate, was a lump of breaded chicken, some cold pasta, some salad. He had the flat for the week. He ate some of the food and looked at a guide to the Biennale that had been left on the worktop. Under Brick Macpherson's show, the guide said:

The title and contents of this show have yet to be announced. Macpherson's seminal and inventive career speaks for itself, from the profane to the sacred, from the fields of sport to the pinnacle of the Renaissance, from the valleys of California to the bedrooms of the lost, Macpherson has remained...

He dropped the guide and walked to the bedroom and turned on the light. A large fan in the ceiling began to turn with creak and a swish. He put his bag on the bed and went to the window and opened its large slatted shutters. The cool night air flooded the room. Down below was a canal, roofs and a walled garden, balconies and a long marble jetty. Churches and towers floated somewhere in the dark. He could now hear high voices and shouting, laughter, and a shriek. He wondered if it was Ivy.

He used the clean white bathroom with its unused beday and had a shower, the hot water very hot. He moved to the bedroom and his mobile phone was bright on the bed.

There was a message from Foster.

Glad u are here too: meet me at Accademia 10am?

No peace. No solace. Not even here, in this graveyard.

FORTY ONE

He dined alone. The restaurant was in a tight alley, the walls close, no hint of sky, no breath of air, just the wet flagstones and the red brick, the ricochet of feet, and the dragging smells of standing water and churned foam.

The food was over and he sat in a corner, drinking the last of the wine. He fiddled with his phone. He had tried to call Ursula again, but only heard beeping noises and a solemn recorded Italian voice.

At the bar, a drunk woman in a tight white skirt, leather jacket and heels was lolling on a high chair. She was talking in French into a mobile phone, another lay on the bar top. The bar man was smiling at her, pouring wine into her glass. She was talking louder now, almost shouting. She twisted on the seat and, with a swift twirl, suddenly fell to the floor. Her head hit the tiles with a hollow knock. Newhouse stood up. The barman leaned over the bar and peered down. The woman lay prone, her legs crossed, the skirt ruffled up to her thighs. The barman walked around and knelt at her side. She raised her upper body, put a hand to her head, moved it away and stared at it. Newhouse sat down again. He drank more wine.

That damned painting vexes my minds eye.

No one doubted the writing, the ultimate authenticity of the letter. Maybe van Rijn had been the last man to see the Blue Horse. Nothing seemed to remain, now. He had not written the file for Foster and her client, who had probably been fooled into buying something worthless. Maybe Martinu had been right, and the Blue Horse was a phantasm. The smoky threads of its history shifted and moved like the hint of a lantern moving through distant stormy woods.

He paid for his meal and walked past the now upright girl and the smiling barman.

He walked down alleys and through empty squares and plazas. Black coverings lay over disused wells, graffiti stained bridges and heavy water slopped in dead ends and abandoned waterways. Above the dark sky and the roofs and walls, there were barred roof gardens and silent balconies.

His feet on the slabs and bricks the only sounds. He came to the Rialto bridge, its shops covered, its attendant squares and markets locked up and silent. He had gone the wrong way, lost as he had been times before. He walked up the wide steps to the high point of its span and felt the canal below shake and slide and churn. He saw water taxis cutting smoothly through the water, yellow lights shifting on unstable waters below, and the wide grand canal stretching away into darkness, its long slow left-turn hidden in shadows.

In the boiling field of water, the world was repeated as it was above. The city was doubled. The water churning above and below, and somewhere in the churn and the foam, he was doubled too.

He walked over the bridge, past a glowing cafe, and through streets and lanes. The slosh and dank, the trapped stink of the canals. His footsteps tapping off brick and plaster. He walked and walked. The passages opened up into a square, and beyond, the black bulk of a cathedral, squatting in the murk. Something was moving over its steps. Newhouse could not see what it was. It crept. It was heavy and halting. It turned its head, something flashed, and it moved into a darkness that matched its own. Masked and obscured.

He was suddenly aware of music.

A bar was throbbing in the dark, beats leaking from its whorled glass windows. He moved to it, as if in a dream, floating, and was at its bar, ordering a beer. There was heat and sweat, the bar was packed. Artists and collectors, gallery people and journalists. There was food on a table, and some literature: it was a party for one of the national pavilions. Flyers and magazines on the floor, some kind of banner draped along one wall. He drank his beer, jostled and bumped by the party. Voices were loud, laughter was loud. People were shouting at each other, yelling over the music. Boom boom boom throbbed a bass drum. People were bellowing and hollering. In the din, something sounded different. Metallic and sonorous. It was a voice he recognised. He looked to the corner of the bar. Near a corridor to the toilets, he saw Rudi, large and black, his face staring at him. He was grinning. Newhouse stared back. Something was wrong with his friend's face. His eyes. His teeth looked awry. Newhouse shivered. Rudi was gone. No shadow on the red wall.

Newhouse drank his beer. In the press of bodies, he saw Ivy and her friends. They were dancing near a DJ, who was standing playing music on a CD player, heavy headphones over his small head. Ivy had her eyes closed, her fingers in the air. A man came close to her, put his hands on her hips. Her head rocked from side to side, her eyes closed.

He put down the beer and left some money on the watery bar top. Splintered light in his eyes, throbbing in his ears.

He moved to the door.

He reached the door, and felt a soft hand on his shoulder.

George? a woman's voice said.

He moved forward but the voice hardened.

George Newhouse, she said loudly. Well hello, she said. She was smiling.

Hi, he said. He saw her breasts, ill-contained, moving around. Moles on her cleavage, brown and black.

I heard you might be here, she said. Her eyes wide open.

Yes, here with the…

Yes, yes, yes, she said, smiling, I know.

He nodded.

Do you want a drink?

No, no, actually I'm just off. Been a long day. Must go, he shouted above the din. Someone dropped a glass, it rolled and smashed. A landslide of laughter and shouting seemed to collapse across the small bar.

I'll come with you, the woman said, I must go too, she said, and they walked out together, into the cool night.

He realized he had walked a few steps with the woman's arm through his. He turned to her. She had red glass beads in her hair. He stopped and looked at her.

She turned to him, her eyes closed, her mouth open, to receive a kiss. He could not remember who she was, or if they had met before. He put his hands to her face. It was warm in the cold night. Her mouth open, her eyes opening.

Kiss me George, she said. He looked in her mouth. Something black on her tongue. Blood sluicing around

Philip Miller

her gums. Her breasts were bare, purple nipples hard, one of her hands rubbing them.

He dropped his hands and moved away, his heart pounding. She stared at him.

George Newhouse, kiss me, she said.

No, no, he said, and she pulled up her top, rubbed her hand through her hair.

Look, he said.

I am not being myself, she said, this isn't me…

I'm married, sorry, I am married, he said.

No more, she said.

What?

The cat ate his eyes, she said.

She stepped back into the bar.

He turned and walked quickly, walked fast back the way he had come, through the alleys and canals. He walked over it quickly, the unreal city whirling around him in its brick and water. He found his way from there, almost running back. He was soon lying on his bed in the darkness. He turned on a small bed lamp, and pulled the mosquito nets around him. They slithered on his head. He fell asleep.

He woke. His phone was buzzing on the side table.

It was a message from Foster.

See you soon George, it said. Keep the pills for the party.

He looked around the room. It was morning.

He remembered the woman.

What the fuck, he said.

He showered, dressed, put the tube of pills in his pocket, and left the flat then walked, light headed, light footed, through the city again. Darkness had risen from its streets and alleyways. The day before had gone. The sunlight was flat and cool, rising from nowhere, not from the sky, not from the water. He walked past the university, past a museum, and then he was at the Accademia bridge, its wooden span dark and hard-spined over the churning, gulping lagoon.

A vaporetto, bulging with people, barged and bumped against a wooden jetty, then churned, and chugged uncomfortably towards the Rialto. He saw a figure standing at the centre of the arching bridge, a woman dressed in a red coat, a red hat: it was Foster. He walked over flagstones and bricks to the foot of the bridge. The sunlight had risen now, to the sky. It glowed on red plaster and ochre plaster, on marble and brick, it slit the water's waves.

In his mind, he heard her voice, soft and gentle.

Good morning George, she said.

Morning.

Welcome to Venice.

Yes, he nodded.

Which hotel are you staying at?

Not the Gritti, he said.

No.

Danieli?

She smiled. Well of course. Shall we get a coffee?

Sure, he said. I have a fuzzy head. But I need to get to the Giardini by 11am.

You meeting your friend?

No, the Brick show, I mean, the staff… he said. He didn't know what she meant.

I saw him last night, she said.

Who? Macpherson?

Rudi Hessenmuller. I didn't know about his accident.

Right, right, he said.

They were walking now, over the bridge, down to the city, past a church and into a wide square.

So, how has your report gone? she said, as she sat at a table outside a cafe.

Newhouse sat too.

I have it on a data stick. But I've... left it at the flat. Sorry. And why are there pills in my flat from you?

Ah, she said. Well, perhaps you can meet me later?

Yes, yes, he said. He had not finished the report. It was not on a memory stick. She had ignored his question.

I take it you have taken the right line for us, she said.

A tall waiter arrived and she ordered in Italian, her long left index finger spelling out each syllable in the air.

Well, I may be in a minority now, he said, looking across the wide piazza. In that I think it exists and that there is a Blue Horse out there.

Our client will be pleased, given he spent so much money. Were you at the US party last night?

No, he said.

Oh, I heard you were spotted.

No, I had a quiet night. Brick's plans can give anyone a headache. We have a lot of work to do.

Yes, I hear, she said, raising an eyebrow. I understand he's leeching electricity from every generator in the Giardini.

It's resource-heavy, Newhouse nodded.

The coffees arrived and Foster said: So the gossip is you were in a clinch outside the party.

No, not me.

Ah, shame, she said. It would be nice to think you were in clinches. Even with a succubus.

He looked at his phone. No calls. No messages.

So: the painting, she said. Your horse.

I'm a believer. I'm not sure what Martinu was getting at. I wish he was here to explain. There's enough evidence, more than enough. *The Red Army* report itself is a wonderful document. I have recently found something from Henry & Dee that is also informative. I wouldn't be surprised, given what we know of its history, if it was in Eastern Europe. Somewhere out there. Perhaps your man has lucked out.

There is another image on its reverse, she said, firmly.

Yes, he said. I understand there is.

She had seen it.

A crude thing, she said. A card game, a family sitting around a table. The children with blank cards. The woman's face is unfinished. It's very 15th century, pale faces and ruffs. It's curious. Maybe not a Van Doelenstraat. Perhaps a re-used canvass. It's rather ugly.

And the horse? he said.

Well, I think you probably know. It's obscured by lead, she said, looking at him in the eye.

So how?

It is clear there is an image is underneath, she said. It is in relief. It is clearly some kind of three-dimensional image, perhaps plaster, a very severe impasto.

Impasto through lead? he said.

She shrugged.

It's a thin layer of metal, almost as if was sprayed, she said. Which of course it cannot have been.

Hm, he said. He sipped his coffee. He wanted to see it. The idea of it opened something. Ruth's face suddenly flashed into his mind. Her eyes like knives.

Are you free tonight? Foster said. There's a party. I have an extra ticket. We can see the painting together.

He did not want to.

Is this party like the last place you invited me to? That revolting place?

Irrumatio? No, that's just a cock-sucking club for ageing bankers, businessmen, and, I might say, members of your parliament, she said, evenly.

I just thought, what the hell is this place. To be honest.

Oh gosh, toughen up, George. And wise up. My client will be there, as will the painting. It's on his boat, The Old Man. You will see it berthed by the gardens actually. You can't miss it. Meet me by the fencing at the entrance to the Via Garibaldi at 10pm.

What's your client's name?

You won't have heard of him.

Well?

Mr Vardoger. He has interests and investments.

Newhouse's mouth suddenly felt dry. The coffee bitter at his teeth.

Not a Russian then.

Oh yes, but not the kind you're thinking of, I would think.

Right.

Don't run away this time. And bring that report. He needs reassurance, and you're the only single fellow he trusts, George.

She stood up and left money in a silver dish.

See you later, she said, and walked off, a thin red spear bobbing through the Venetian haze.

It was after she left, and he drained the coffee, that he wondered what she meant when she spoke of Rudi's accident.

FORTY TWO

He had been pushed and buffeted on the packed vaporetto. It was suddenly hot. Light glinting on the green-blue water, on dark glasses, on sun-drenched skin. He had stood by the gate onto the waterbus, looking ahead to the stops to come: Salute, San Marco, Zaccaria, Arsenale.

The engine churned and people took pictures of the brick and marble landscape, the pale faces of the buildings in the water, the domes and steeples, the palaces and jetties, the insect gondolas, and the tower and palace of St Marks.

The crowds left the waterbus at St Marks and Newhouse left the boat at the Giardini. The trees were moving in a light breeze, the parkland stretched dark into the distance.

He walked to the garden's gates, He passed through the ticket barrier with his curator's pass. He heard children's laughter from a playground hidden somewhere in the trees. There was a wide, sandy path. His feet crunched on it. In the trees stood the squat buildings of the Giardini, the permanent exhibition galleries of countries. Up ahead, on a small rise, stood his show, flanked by France and the UK, Germany and Canada. The sounds of the canals receded, the waters passed away. He heard engines in the water, but could not see it. Beetles and ants moved underfoot, amid large dry leaves and grass. A park in the middle of the swelling waters. The trees were brown-tipped, it had been dry for weeks, no aqua-alter, no rain, no downpours. Curators and technicians walked around, artists on mobile phones. Shows were getting ready, the last touches to exhibitions were being made before press views and reviews, parties and receptions. Young assistants carried large brown boxes full of literature and guides, tickets booklets and posters.

Birds sung in the dry trees. He could smell flowers – red and white roses grew in ornamental beds.

Slung between two trees was a large red sign marked by a golden lion carrying a flag: La Biennale di Venezia: ALL SECRETS ARE TRUE.

Sounds leaked from the other pavilions. Video soundtracks, rumblings of bass and tinny treble, laughter and shouting. A bass boomed from near the Venezuelan pavilion, its concrete crumbling. Flutes, clarinet and trumpets from Japan. Running water from Scandinavia. A loud recorded voice intoning from somewhere in the taut neoclassical bulk of the German building.

He stopped before the pavilion of the Public Gallery. It had been built in the 1920s, now it was shadowed by ageing, parched trees. Its bricks were crumbling. Inside, through the heavy portico, he saw people moving.

A large sign read: SON OF MAN. He walked up the steps.

The three rooms of the pavilion had become one, the walls between were now arches. The walls were covered from floor to ceiling with soft, white, pyramidal sound baffles. Sound stopped and the air felt dead. The floor was painted white. Ivy was on a stepladder with some technicians in T-shirts around a base, pointing at a large speaker, also white, which was attached to the wall. More speakers were fitted around the now cavernous gallery. The ceiling had been covered in a silver, reflective material. On a dais at the centre and back of the room stood a monstrous crucifix made from dozens of smooth video screens. The screens were turned off, and loomed, matt grey. The cross of screens nearly touched the high silver ceiling, the wide white, spongy walls. On the wall beside the door was attached a metal folder, with printed material inside. While Ivy talked to the technicians, Newhouse took a booklet and read it.

Son of Man was written in small uncapped letters on its red cover. Inside were two blank red pages. On the back, at the bottom of the page, a small credit to the galleries, and 'Inspiration: Edward Cornelis Florentius Alfonsus Schillebeeckx.'

Newhouse looked through the open doors to the steps, down to the bone-dry gardens, the trees and the galleries. He could smell the lagoon but not see it.

Hello there, Ivy said.

She was standing beside him now. He smiled at her and said Hello.

How is it all going? Looks good, he said. He adjusted the bag on his shoulder. It was warm. The gallery was enormous, the cross gigantic.

There're some electrical issues, she said, and the windows need to be blacked out.

Electrical issues?

Just so many wires, and the wiring in here is awful, she said. We've borrowed electricity from Canada. France have complained about their trip switches... tripping. The UK pavilion isn't very happy either. You will need to talk to them.

Germany?

Their thing is all acoustic and lit by those tree candles made from something organic or other.

It can't be all acoustic, what's that voice?

It's some kind of speaker made from rubber. She's intoning.

Oh yes, Maud. I liked her earlier work with resins. But not sure anyone needs a Venice retrospective after only ten years.

They were pulling round a real horse earlier, Ivy said.

Newhouse looked at Ivy. There was a bang from behind the silent crucifix. A technician said Fucking hell. Another one laughed. The cross was giant. A real man nailed to it would be dwarfed by its scale.

A horse?

Yes, the Russians. They were leading a horse into their show. Or out of it. Something else.

God, Newhouse said.

A horse, Ivy said.

Ok, well show me the wiring. Not that I know anything about wiring.

Oh now you tell me, Ivy said and smiled and she walked down the long white room to the banks of screens.

The huge cross of screens loomed over them. It felt precarious, even though, now, he could see they were firmly attached to the stone beneath the spongy walls.

At its base, from close in, Newhouse could see a mass of screwed up, messed up and coagulated black, red and grey wires bunched in a plastic ball of tumbleweed behind the cross. Three technicians in black jeans and T shirts were straightening out wires, testing ampage with small instruments, changing plugs and transformers. He could smell their sweat. The wires from the top of the cross fell down like vines.

Shit, what a mess, Newhouse said. Who in God's name installed this? I have seen better in a degree show. My nephew makes neater things than this.

I know, I know, Ivy said, biting her lip. Look: Brick did it in the last three nights. He wouldn't let anyone else help. He and his fucking brother. The Biennale Council are furious. In the way they can be.

I'm not amazed and thrilled myself, Newhouse said. This looks like a dog's dinner. When's the press view... it's tomorrow... fuck sake.

Tomorrow at 11am.

Can I speak to Brick?

He's thrown his phone into the lagoon. Ivy laughed. Or may as well have. He says the exhibition is finished.

Does it even work?

Yes, she said. She moved to the wall and pressed a switch. She asked the technicians to stand away from the cross, which they did.

Of course, the windows... she said.

But then a noise filled the gallery, throbbing from the speakers. It was thick and in waves. White and brown and dizzying. The room seemed to shudder. There was a throb that moved through the tiles at their feet. Ivy and Newhouse quickly stood back from the cross, which flicked into life, dozens of screens whirring with white energy. There was fizz and crackle. Swirls and stars, black holes and galaxies flashed and fuzzed, turned and cart-wheeled.

Suddenly the room shook with the smashing crack, a sudden bursting dam of noise. Even louder than the first. Like a popped sound barrier. A thundercrack. Newhouse jumped.

The screens were warping and weaving. Fingers appeared at the edges of the cross, wriggling and flailing. Then toes at its bottom: black toes, then white, then short, then long, then toes soaked in blood, then dry with blood, then smeared with mud and then calm on cool grass. There were pebbles under the toes, and then grass, then concrete, tarmac, sand, sea, a stream, a path through woods, a road over a hill.

Gradually all the screens filled with constantly flipping, rotating, scrolling body parts, which made up the whole, a collage of a multitude of fragmented bodies, people, men. Hundreds of men and boys, crucified, becoming the one body, tethered, nailed, tied, hammered, to a cross – or a pole, a tank trap, a stone pillar, a police cordon, a crash barrier, a tank, a car, a mountain. The body changed and the instrument of his death changed, but the crucified collage of Christ stood at all times.

Around his ever changing, permanent face, a sky and landscape which also changed, were clouds, rain, fire, mountains, clouds, stars, city lights, trees, scrubland, waves, rivers, hills, car parks, motorways.

His eyes were blue, then brown, then green, then black. His eyes were clear, then milky, then glass, then blue, then white, then black. His glimmering torso was a mosaic of flesh, of brown, yellow, black and white. Blood appearing and disappearing, blood flowing, blood in gouts, dried blood and pale washed blood, lash marks and tattoos, operation scars and diseases, burns and fat, coloid scars and scrapes and scratches, muscle and bones. Music played: percussive, melodic, momentous.

The Christ head turned left and right, through its changes, through its tortured repetitions and alterations, its mutations and differences, and then faced the viewer, as the background solidified to a scene of an empty desert, an empty sky which was then a city, ablaze with electric light, a wall of light. He closed his eyes and the body, in changes, slumped, and then screens became, one by one, drenched in darkness. The music stopped.

OK, switch it off, Ivy said quietly to the technician.

There was a splintering electric crack through the speakers, which hummed and then fell silent.

Jesus, Newhouse said.

Exactly, Ivy said.

How long is it? Does it repeat in a cycle?

Its fifteen minutes.

Is it? Newhouse said. He had felt no time had passed.

Yes, and it goes round and round, there's a setting where the mouth says Eli, Eli…

Eli, Eli, lama sabachthani.

Yes that's it. Very loud.

Well, it seems to be OK, Newhouse said after some time. Yes, yes it's fine.

Ivy started talking about blacking out the windows, fixing some speakers that were not arranged properly, making sure the party organisers knew what they were doing. She was talking but Newhouse just looked at the massive cross.

What you doing tonight? Ivy said to him, as he began to leave.

I have a party.

Oh, the Russians'?

Yes, yes, that one, Newhouse said, but he was distracted – his mobile phone was buzzing in his pocket.

See you later, good job. Get the windows fixed…

Thanks George, guess I'll see you later.

There was a sudden noise, a crack, and one of the technicians swore again. We need some fucking help back here, he said, in a shaking voice.

The phone was buzzing

He knew it was Ursula.

He smiled. He looked at the phone. But it was a British number, one he did not recognise.

He moved through the door, and stepped outside onto the terrace.

Hello?

Hello, is that Mr George Newhouse? A female, formal voice said.

Yes, yes it is.

Sorry to bother you sir, I understand you are abroad.

Yes, I am in Italy, in Venice – sorry who is this?

The female voice said she was the police. Mr Rudolf Hessenmuller had been reported missing, his fiancée had also been missing but had now been found.

My God, Newhouse said.

I have to say, Mr Newhouse, that we have been told Mr Hessenmuller was a close friend of yours, and you may have known of his whereabouts. There is no need to return to the UK immediately.

And what of Iona?

Ms Gillespie is critical but stable at the Royal Infirmary. She was found in an advanced state of exposure. Her family is with her.

My God.

Sunlight on the Giardini, the tall trees, the dappling leaves and the distant waves. Newhouse sat down on a step, warm sun on his neck and arms.

I have no idea where he is, Newhouse said. I haven't spoke to him for a while, indeed he has quit work, handed his notice in.

Yes the Public Gallery informed us.

He was moving south, down to…

…Yes Mr Newhouse, we understand. We have however found his mobile phone. It was left at his flat, albeit in some condition of disrepair.

Right?

The last text he sent was to you Mr Newhouse.

Right?

It was arranging to meet you there in Venice.

No no, I never got that, Newhouse said.

He heard another banging noise from inside the pavilion. Something heavy dropped and echoed around its walls.

Mr Hessenmuller is German?

Yes, yes.

But the text was in Dutch.

Really? Newhouse said.

Are you meeting Mr Hessenmuller in Venice, Mr Newhouse?

No, no, not at all, he said.

But his message.

I know. I know. But I don't know that he is here. I didn't receive that message.

Our colleagues in the Italian police would like to interview you, if that is at all possible, Mr Newhouse.

Yes of course, although I am working. When?

The woman said that afternoon, and gave him an address in Santa Croce.

Ok, Ok, he said.

She thanked him, and the conversation ended.

He noted down the police address in his notebook and walked heavily through the Giardini. Newhouse left the gardens, and walked towards Piazza San Marco, the lagoon blue green on one side, the city on his other. He walked over a bridge, and he saw a huge black motor yacht, berthed on the Riva Degli Schiavoni. Massive and black, like a giant's anvil in the sea. It cast a shadow across the bricks, the stones, out into the churning water.

Written on its vast, sleek, unblemished side: The Old Man.

FORTY THREE

Once he had imagined he might see her again.

That in a street, in a field or airport, she would be there. Her body, her face.

For a time, he lived as if she had just gone away. On a sabbatical, a holiday. They had another row, and she had fled. She had met someone else, and was taking some time to herself, away from him, their life.

These ideas lay, for a time, over his mind, shrouding the reality of her death, which would not fade or move. Other times, he saw her beside the sea, perhaps in her green anorak, in jeans, in boots, looking back at him, smiling. Maybe she was skimming stones. Maybe she had a rod in her hands. The waves beyond, and the mountains beyond that.

Now he was drinking coffee in a cafe in Venice, and remembering how he had once called her from there, telling her he had at last found a city as beautiful as her.

What, Birmingham? she laughed.

The day was getting on. He had wandered for a while, his phone off. He had eventually eaten a quick lunch – a poorly warmed sandwich – and attended the main Biennale show in the Arsenale.

He had walked through its many long chambers and spaces in a daze, thinking of his sick sister, of Rudi, of poor Iona, of the night ahead, of the Blue Horse, which he might see, at last. And beyond: nothing.

He thought of Martinu, and, in one dark room that smelled of pine, he thought of Tyler, and her lovely almond eyes, her eyelashes. His stomach had at last turned, and he had rushed to a toilet, and his bowels had opened.

He staggered, hot and wet, down the long, windowless concourse, to the doors of the Arsenale, where a press of journalists were waiting for their Stampa passes, and turned on his phone again.

He had a message from Ivy: *Please call me.* He had a missed call from the police. He had a voicemail call from the Public Gallery.

He called Ivy.

George, she said, breathless.

What's the matter? I've been...

I'm, so, so sorry, she said.

What?

About your friend.

Who?

Rudi? Is that your friend? Hessenmuller? The British Council called me. The cops have been trying to get you.

What of him?

They found his body. In the river. I'm so sorry.

Newhouse felt weak. He leant against the stone doorframe of the Arsenale entrance. People pushed by. The sun was setting. Its dying clouds bloodstained the tight military walls. The nearby canal smelled of eggs.

Which river, where?

Back home, down by the sea.

What Ivy, what?

I'm so sorry.

Her voice went on.

Newhouse took the phone away from his ear. He looked at it, and switched it off.

Everything was coming to an end. He had felt this way

before. The collapsing walls, the tumbling masonry. He felt like the blood was bending in his veins. His arteries hurt.

He went looking for a bar, and a drink.

He found one, and ordered spirits.

He found the pills in his back pocket, and one by one he took them all.

FORTY FOUR

Newhouse was staggering.

He had a line of vomit behind his gums. His cock was sticky, stuck to his pants. He had left her in the toilet, pulling up her knickers, wiping herself. Her mouth marks on his neck, his chest. The bar was busy. She had been too much for him. There were confusions now: large plants in his way, flagstones replaced with glass, below only bottles of wine, amphora. He did not know her name. It was the woman from the night before, but this time he had given in.

His dick had only partially worked, but it didn't matter now. There was blood and shit and cum. Black things moving in her mouth. A patch of long black hair in the small of her back. Her body had not been hot. She had been cold.

He could not think of her. He needed to be sick again. He had lost his bag. He walked out into the dark canal street and leant over the water. A brown gush of vomit shot from his mouth. He coughed.

Holy hell, he mumbled.

He walked and walked. He saw signs and landmarks. In a glass doorway, he looked at his reflection. He straightened his clothes, his wiped his face, his hair. On he went. The sea churned, the lagoon was dark and turbulent.

He found himself by the black bulk of the The Old Man. Foster was there, by the metal fence on the causeway, dressed in white, gold jewelry, heavy make-up, her hair on top of her head. Lights and music throbbed from the boat.

A man in uniform stood beside her.

Hello George, she said as Newhouse approached.

She reached out with both hands and straightened his collar. He felt her fingers brush his neck. She pulled his jacket down. She laughed at him.

OK, this way, she said and nodded at the man in the uniform, silver buttons shining in electric light, and ushered Newhouse through the metal fencing, onto a wide platform that led to the boat. On the wide deck of the black boat there were many people, drinking drinks, fizzy wine, champagne, devil-red spritz, white and gold and honey and red. There were women in dresses and men in black tie, in white tie, in suits. There were shouting and laughing. Beyond them the black lagoon and the distant rocking lights of the unreal city on the water.

How do you feel? You look shocking. Foster whispered into his ear.

Music was booming from a DJ's deck somewhere on the boat. A large flag was hanging low from a mast. The lights and the sea, the black boat – plastic, steel, wood – rolled around him. The lights, the shapes, began to spin around his head in a carousel. His mouth tasted of salt and metal. His back was aching.

Fine, he croaked.

I meant, not your obvious parlous state, George, but being so close to seeing your painting.

I don't know who she was, he said. I don't know what that was.

I'm sorry?

I don't think that happened.

George?

I don't know. I'm sorry. I am not myself. A good friend

has died, he said.

She turned to him. Behind her he saw buckets of ice on a table, waiters dressed in red livery, pouring drinks, large silver salvers filled with drinks and food. Mouths opened and closed on liquid and solid. A wretched world. This flesh, these bricks and mortar. The concrete of the jetty and the rotting bricks of the dying city. Its flat horizons and fetid canals.

What?

My friend is dead, he said. He sounded drunk. He was slurring. His tongue had doubled in size.

Hessenmuller?

The body in the river.

No, no, she said, smiling. He is here in Venice, he wanted to see the painting too. I sent him away with a flea in his ear.

Rocking lights and swirling glow, the swinging electric glow of thousands of points of light, and laughter, and from somewhere, the sounds of flesh slapping on flesh. Laughter and music.

No you are wrong. I feel rather unwell, he said.

I'm sure he will be back soon actually, she said.

She was looking at him. In her white and gold, tall and thin and pale, she looked like an elaborate lamp. Her hair on fire.

Newhouse suddenly laughed. He looked at the crowd. Women and men dressed in lingerie, underwear and wearing Venetian masks were walking among the crowd, pulling guests gently by the arms, leading them inside the boat.

Mr Hessenmuller seemed a little distracted. He was here for more research, she said.

I don't— Newhouse said. He felt like jumping from the boat and into the lagoon. The water would be fresh, clean.

The water would be rotten.

He said he was working for a Prince. Why on earth did you think he was dead? she asked. You have been drinking.

I don't know. That girl gave me some pills, he said. You gave me those pills.

He had sucked the pills from her mouth. He had crunched the pills between his numb teeth as his fingers pulled down her knickers. It had been all wrong. Her heat and her sweet smell. She had been in the bar. She had put her arm through his arm. Her hair was thin and floated, like sea grass under the waves. He had been thinking of Tyler but then she had kissed him…and he had fallen into her.

I didn't give you anything. What are you talking about? Come on, to business, Foster said. Before you collapse.

What else was there for him? The Blue Horse would be a fake, or a mistake. He could see it, and go down into the sea.

Ok, he said quietly.

He looked into the crowd. He saw a man like Martinu – fat, bearded – being led into the boat by a women in a mask, her bottom bare. Red marks on her buttocks. The bearded fat man unzipped his trousers.

What kind of party is this? Newhouse said.

Mr Vardoger has hungry friends, Foster said.

She was calling someone on a small silver mobile phone. A man with large black glasses, tall with a closely shaved beard, emerged from the crowd, in a pale suit, his head bobbing to the beat of the thumping music. He said something to Newhouse that he did not hear. The man then spoke to Foster. Someone put a slim glass of something red into Newhouse's hand. He drank and it bubbled up inside his sick-choked nose. He looked at the lights lining the jetty, down to Saint Marks, over bridges and ramps, down to the heart of the city. He felt cold. His knees weak. He smelled burning.

OK, George, Foster was smiling. Come with me.

She opened her hand and he took it. Cold and clammy, her fingers more human than his own. They squeezed through the crowd.

She whispered to him. Her body close to his.

I trust you brought the memory, she said.

My memories, he said.

The memory stick with your report, she said.

Yes, yes, yes, he said, as they squeezed between bodies of men and bodies of women. Between the music and the sea. He felt enclosed and hemmed in. He felt suffocated for an instant, and then they had moved, she leading him by the weak hand, her body white and silver, through a door and into a metal corridor inside the boat.

Her voice echoed in the grey metallic hall.

This party has some events that people have paid a lot of money for. Don't worry you don't have to take part, she said, and laughed. You just need to see this painting and you can leave. We have to go through rooms, some stages, before we get to the owner.

Another door opened. Newhouse felt disembodied. Something was taking hold in the dark of his mind. His legs and arms were swimming in a thick darkness. His eyes focusing and unfocusing. A thickness at the edges of his sight. They passed into a large, dimly lit room. Foster led him through. They stumbled around the room's edges.

There was a crowd. It seemed they were many people there. The crowd was looking at something in the centre of the room, something rolling, turning while it was being beaten by two men dressed in red. They raised their arms and brought them down. The crowd murmured and mumbled.

Foster led Newhouse on. They stepped through a bulkhead door. The suited man came with them, looking at a device in his hand, flicking through message and images. They entered another corridor, lined with wood and carpeted. Women with masks on their chests were kissing other men. Music was playing.

Newhouse passed an open door. A door to a dark room, a large black cube. Windowless and stinking. He looked in and saw a heavy animal of some kind, suspended from the ceiling in a series of straps and buckles. Dark and rotund and hairy. People in the shadows, clapping and drinking. Some of them laughing. A body lay beneath it. He heard a bellow. The press of bodies and the sounds of heaving flesh. On the floor, black pools and animal pelts. Piles of clothes and possessions, and in a further, larger room, a pile of ashes, coals, a pile of burnt wood, silvery with ash. On the walls, skins and furs.

His legs felt wet, felt weighted. He looked down: there was water. They moved on. Down flights of metal stairs and then flights of stone stairs, across landings and hallways. Past red curtains and black curtains.

He was led by the hand into a dark space with red and gold furniture, a large mirror that reflected tiles and marble, windows and stairwells. And there was a picture frame, suspended in a vast room, its corners fastened by wires that held it to the distant corners of the chamber.

There was a figure like a man, pacing back and forward.

He was floating. He felt light. Only Foster's hand on his hand held him in place. He held on. He closed his eyes. He was stumbling and falling.

Not long now, she said.

Foster, he said. He felt darkness cover and smother him. His body was alone in the black.

Are we still here? he said, his voice muffled. He felt his arms and legs being held, he felt his head being held.

No, someone said. A sound from beyond his ears. Stars wheeled and darkness revolved inside a kernel of itself.

George, he heard.

It was a voice. He realised his eyes were closed. He clenched them tighter. He saw veins and blurring lights. He opened his eyes again.

George, the voice said. It was a woman's voice.

He was not on the boat anymore. He was alone.

He was in an alleyway, bricks and walls, high walls and windowless, and above, a strip of sky. He was slumped at a door. There was a sign and he stood up and read it.

VEDOVO

He turned and walked down the alleyway. He walked through it, and came to a plain square, walled with shuttered buildings, with a silver tree at its centre.

Beyond it stood a church, a cathedral. It had broad steps, and a woman stood at the top, before its opened doors.

He walked forward, through the thick air. He looked up and his heart moved.

It was Ruth.

It was her face, and her body. She stood still, in the night air. She was lit by starlight and leaping firelight. Her eyes were closed, her body still.

She was bright. She was all red. She was a deep red, red from hair to feet. Blood ran from her face to her fingers, from her legs to her toes, and rolled down the steps, unfurling slowly like a dropping crimson robe.

He moved up a step. He looked around. He was still in Venice.

Ruth?

Do not touch me, she said. Her mouth was black. Her eyes were closed.

Follow me again, she said. Not far now.

She turned and walked, red and naked, into the darkness of the door.

This way. Not far now.

He felt as if he was being carried up the steps, with hands under his shoulders, under his legs. He looked down, and the steps were pale and marble, and clear of crimson, clear of blood.

He moved passed the opened doors into the darkness.

Pale still figures sat at a table, with pale cards in their hands, with smooth featureless faces. And he passed them, and moved into something else.

His feet sank into black sand. Wet and black.

He was standing on a beach, a dark beach of black sand, and the sea ran from it, breaking from it to the flat horizon. From side to side the beach ran, from horizon to horizon, where the sea met and became the churning clouds. And there was a horse, a blue horse, blue as lead, blue as copper, strong and massive. He could smell it. It was lapping at the roiling tide. It's body was hot and steaming. And it turned its head. Black eyes. It kicked a leg. At the horse's feet lay the body of a man, black and burnt, smoking like a charred corpse.

The man's head snapped at the neck and rolled away, rolled down to the endless tide. Then, out of the body's neck, a small head slid, and then grew, and a head was on the neck again, and it turned around and around, its eyes opening and closing.

Over the sea, he could see clouds and shadows, and in the distance, shapes like curtains rippling and waving.

He heard a voice but not what it said.

Ruth stood before him, her back to him. And she was clothed now, in blue jeans, in a T-shirt, in trainers, her hair up in a bun. She turned. Three fish, red, were swimming around her face.

You can never betray me, she said. She took one of his hands, and wrote on it with her fingers. She showed him the hand. There was writing he could not read. It faded into his skin.

She smiled, her eyes like light, and she pushed him.

He was falling.

Hard marble on his back, his head, his back. Back, back down the steps.

He groaned on the flagstones of the square. Sharp pain in his elbows, his knees, pain in his back, his ribs. Pain in his lungs, burning in his chest.

Oh, he said.

Oh my lord, he said.

Fuck, he said. He was sitting now. Pain in his body. Everything working again, his body alive again. Soreness in his head, spikes of shivering in his arms, in his shoulders.

Foster was there, and the man in the pale suit.

They were standing and smoking cigarettes and he was lying on hard pavement beside a closed and shuttered well.

So, she said. What did you think?

FORTY FIVE

You need to go home, the man in the pale suit said. You're still a mess and it's morning.

I mean seriously, Foster said. She was tapping her foot.

Unbelievable, the man said.

The boss was not amused by that at all, Foster said.

Not answering questions like that, so rude. So disrespectful, the man said. You looked like you were in a coma. I thought you were having a fit. Catatonic, the man added.

Shut the fuck up will you, Foster said to the man. Come on Newhouse: what did you think?

I'm sorry, Newhouse said. He was shaking. He pulled himself up and sat on the edge of the well.

Your friend was a little more... engaged with it than you, Foster said.

Right, right, Newhouse said. He could still see Ruth's face. He could still smell burning. The massive heat of the horse. He looked at his empty hand.

I think it is fair to say that Mr Vardoger is not particularly happy with his purchase, Foster said, quietly, as if to herself.

The pale suited man shook his head. He took a long drag of his cigarillo. Foster was blowing blue smoke through her nose.

Why are we here? Newhouse said.

Foster cocked her head.

Are you OK?

Yes, but the boat... Newhouse said.

What of it?

We were there.

Yes, and you fell asleep below decks, she said. We got you in a boat and brought you to Vedovo. Then you went into the viewing chamber.

Fell asleep, the pale suited man snorted, shaking his head, that's one way…

Where are we? Newhouse said.

The Palazzo Vedovo, as I said, she said. Jesus George, whatever you've been taking… thank God you woke up in time to see the painting.

The Empty Hand is worth something, the man said, eventually. Newhouse noticed the pale suited man's teeth were covered in thick braces. They glinted between his lips.

The new day was clearing darkness away. There were stars in the sky, but the sun was rising. Newhouse could hear water sloshing on buildings, canals moving amid the buildings.

I'm very sorry for everything, Newhouse said.

It's been a lot of work and time for you, Foster said. She dropped her cigarette and stamped on it, turning her heel. She had let her hair down.

Deepdale here, he doesn't know. I was never convinced. Like you said, Martinu never believed it existed. I mean, what can you say about a few bumps under solid lead?

Yes. No, Newhouse said. The flagstones were clear beneath his feet.

Can you hear that? The man, Deepdale, said, his braces clinking.

No, what? Foster said. I'm fucking cold.

Sirens? Is that sirens? Deepdale said. He was craning

his neck. He was looking in the direction of the Grand Canal.

Something moved in Newhouse's jacket. He looked inside his pocket and there was a silver phone, not his own.

met harisbar, 10.thirtypm, Rdi.

Jesus. Where is Harry's Bar from here? Newhouse said.

It will be closed. You're in no fit state. No fit state, Deepdale said. Is that burning?

There were sirens definitely now, somewhere in the city. Wailing and honking. Booming off close walls and water.

That way, ten minutes, Foster said. Don't you want to stay with us? I could get you some food…

No, no, no, Newhouse said.

The woman on the beach was still behind his eyes. Her face and touch. Like Ruth, but not her.

I definitely smell smoke. There is smoke somewhere, Deepdale said.

I will be back, Newhouse said. I will see you.

Foster looked at him.

Perhaps I should apologise, she said all the work you have done, that Dr Martinu did. I know how much it meant to you. But now…

I know, it's gone, Newhouse said. He was feeling clearer, less confused. He was in a bare square in the heart of Venice.

What did Rudi think of the painting?

Mr Hessenmuller?

Yes.

He had a funny turn, Foster said, lighting another cigarette.

Deepdale laughed.

He saw it. He put his hands to the lead. I got a bit upset

about that, and he ran away. Just like that. All flapping and flopping. Ridiculous.

I too was upset, very upset, Deepdale said. The lack of respect, he said. And you, being silent. Such manners in you people.

Newhouse was standing now, and looking down at his rumpled clothes. He had stopped shaking. He wanted to see Rudi. He moved to Foster and reached for her elbow.

Thank you, he said. She nodded.

I'm not sure why, she said.

I am, he said, and waived a hand at the man, and walked down another alleyway marked with a large yellow sign and a black arrow: S. MARCO.

FORTY SIX

The bar was empty, pale furnishings empty, leather and cotton, empty. Rudi was sat at the bar on a tall stool. There was no barman. The glasses glinted in soft gold light. The windows were black, like fish tanks filled with ink.

Newhouse stood at the end of the bar. Rudi looked at him, his pale big face uneven, one of his eyes large and black, like a kidney laid in an enamel bowl.

Hello, Newhouse said. What is going on?

Doe quam den edelen prince daer, Rudi said.

Pardon?

Drinking again George? Rudi said. He had red lips, as if he was wearing lipstick. His suit hung long and short. Half way up one leg, over his wet shoe on the other.

Bellini? Rudi said.

What happened to you? Newhouse said, and walked slowly down the bar, holding it with his left hand.

I am an empty man. Nothing man, Rudi seemed to say.

Are you OK? I had a call from the police, it was very…

Ah yes my wife my fiancé, Iona, her face so hairy, her face so furry. Like a horse, like the vole, the field mouse. There were 12,652 demons in one body in 1584.

Rudi, it was serious… why are you here? The police…

Did you tell them I was here? I'm not here, I could tell them that. My head is in the sea, coated in plaster of Paris.

Rudi was drinking a pint glass but it seemed to be full of a pale green spirit, shards of salt like broken glass along its rim.

Do you know your history Poor George? Rudi said.

Rudi? Newhouse said. He noticed a tooth on the bar top. A string of skin from one of its roots.

Rudi was singing and then he stopped. His eyes were normal, his eyes were fine. His clothes were normal, his clothes were fine.

Did you hear about the seven Venetian martyrs, picked at random. The captain died and they were taken and executed, have you heard them? About them.

Yes, yes I think so, Newhouse said. He wondered where the staff were. He thought he heard footsteps above. He sat at a stool, one away from Rudi, whose hair seemed different, whose ears seemed larger or smaller. Newhouse looked at the walls of the bar, and there were pale oblongs where pictures had been removed. Torn wall paper and nail holes.

What's happened to the maps? he said.

The teeth are the first to go because they are the hardest, Rudi said,

Rudi reached into his mouth, slumped over the bar. He pulled out a tooth and laid it beside the other. The teeth moved together, as if magnetized.

Newhouse rubbed his eyes. The boat had been a dream. The church had been a dream. This is a dream. And I will wake and she will be alive.

No, that's not going to happen, Rudi said. I am afraid I supped from the sup you cannot sup. And you did neither.

Rudi, you're drunk. I'm drunk. Let's go, Newhouse said.

I said hello to your mentor, Mr Martinus, Rudi said, wiping a bloody finger around his mouth. The cat got the cream.

Rudi, let's go. I'm not sure what this is.

I have gone on this long and now you know how, Rudi said. And it started before then. The cannibals in the Ukraine, the timber in Manchuria, the babies at Wounded Knee.

George Newhouse looked at his friend. His eyes were black, teeming with something.

I don't know who I am and neither do you, Rudi said, pushing a glass along the bar top to Newhouse.

It looked like a bellini, it was pink and swirling with something.

The world we are in, Rudi said, it's slipping away now. This art, it's all nothing, and nothing will be missed. Dust and rocks. Sand and dust. Sand and ashes. An empty hand. The only way out is sideways.

Rudi reached into his mouth and pulled out another loose tooth, he put it on the bar top, alongside the other two. A small puddle of sandy brown liquid gathered. More sandy liquid was at the corner of his mouth.

Rudi, I have to go, Newhouse said. He felt nauseous. He felt his guts quake. He saw in his mind the boat, and its inhabitants. The beast in the ropes. He saw Tyler and her face. He wondered where she was.

Rudi was still talking. His mouth empty of teeth, his gums open like wounds. You will see her, that's for sure, he said. I saw her. They took me for you. You on this chair, not me. But she was there, she was writing the rules of the exchange.

What do you mean? Newhouse said.

Now I go to wander his earth. And our numbers will one day outnumber. We sing: *The living are conscious that they will die, but the dead, they are conscious of nothing at all...* Rudi said.

Newhouse looked at the jawful of teeth, white on the bar top. The sandy liquid gone, the blood gone. His glass was empty.

He looked around and the pictures were hanging on the wall.

The door to the city was open.

...for there is no work nor devising nor knowledge nor wisdom in the grave, the place to which...

Newhouse moved to the door. Rudi had gone. Harry's Bar was empty.

...the place to which you are going.

And out into the clean night air, and the lights of the boats, the clanging of bells and the rumble of engines. Human voices speaking, and behind him, a closed locked door. He heard sirens and hooters, shouting and roaring, and smelled burning and smoke.

FORTY SEVEN

The Giardini was on fire. The high trees were burning. Red and orange flames and sparks shot up against the sky, and the flashing strobe of police and fire boats, the lights of torches and rapidly erected beacons, the coiling, white and grey smoke, covered them. Newhouse walked quickly along the path beside the lagoon. People were gathering and coalescing into one large crowd. Tourists and locals, police and men and women in uniform, Biennale staff and gallerists, workers and artists.

More fire boats and police boats shuddered past. Two ambulance boats surged through the night's waves, their prows bumping and jumping over white caps.

There was intense heat and smoke rising from the red heat of the burning trees. There was a hubbub of voices, some shouting, a scream.

Fire reflected on the black sides of the silent, empty, berthed Old Man. It seemed to throb with red and orange, sheer yellow and crimson. Men in uniforms ran back and forward. Newhouse stood on his toes and strained to see more. He could see people being hustled out of the gardens. Women and men, near the entrance of the gardens, lay on the floor, with plastic masks on their faces, breathing oxygen from cylinders held by medics. The green gardens had been repainted in black and red, fire behind the black silhouettes of the trees and the pavilions, the throbbing firelight revolving, turning and moving like a children's lantern.

There was a boom and a crackle, and a sudden sheer

curtain of red high flames shot up into the sky. The crowd murmured as one. It swayed and briefly surged. A woman next to Newhouse screamed. The trees were ablaze. Inside the gardens, Newhouse could now see the pavilions standing firm, a roof or two alight, sparks flying around them, and then his eyes became sore, his head sore.

He was being jostled and pushed. A policeman spoke through a loud haler in Italian. People shouted back and waved their hands and fists.

What did he say? people were asking. What's happening?

Something exploded in the Giardini. There was a rapidly expanding ball of flame, deep in the trees, towards the Lido. Flames rose higher.

A high tree collapsed. Slowly, and with a boom and crackling crash the tree fell, and landed, as if softly but with inevitable crushing weight, onto the café that stood at the edge of the Giardini. The building collapsed inwards, as if made from paper, string and felt, not stone and metal and tiles, and then, suddenly, with a flash, something inside it exploded, and the walls falling inwards burst outwards.

The waves, as if dipped with blood and orange, yellow and silver, flashed against the walls of the burning park.

People were screaming now, the crowd surged back. Newhouse felt his legs move under him.

The expanding ball of flame, blue and white and red, rolled over the fence of the gardens and slapped against the black sleekness of the The Old Man. For a second it seemed as if the flames had extinguished themselves on the great ship's matte slopes and angles, but then something on the boat popped with a loud crack, and like a wrenching seabeast, it shook and bucked in the water. A terrible tearing noise shrieked as it grinded against the seawall, and it lurched suddenly to one side. Furniture toppled and slid from its decks. Then with a rumble, something inside the guts of the craft detonated. Its graceful lines buckled and crumpled. A silvery cascade of glass burst onto the path and into the sea. People at the front of the crowd fell down. Police ran to their aide.

As if caught in a breaking wave, Newhouse felt the press of people moving, as one, away from the gardens and the ruined yacht. Black smoke was pouring from its burst interiors. People turned as one and fled. Some fell, others were shouting and screaming.

Newhouse ran too. He was jostled and banged and bumped. He realized he was closest to the line of hotels and shops facing the lagoon. He cut in front of a young couple to his right, and ran, his head thumping now, into an alleyway.

Hundreds of feet slapped as people ran from the flames.

He looked at his phone. It was his again. Was it not silver? No. That had gone. All that had gone.

He rang Ivy.

It rang and rang. He left a message. He hoped she was alright. Give me a call, he said.

He stood at the entrance to the alley. The crowd surging past.

Smoke was moving along the edge of the lagoon. Sirens and lights, revolving and flashing on the churning waters.

One of the shows, an American and his girlfriend said as they pushed past Newhouse. I hear it was one of the shows.

Newhouse, slumped and empty, sat down. He watched the legs and the feet move past. He saw the police boats, the fire boats, the motorboats and helicopters move to the

Gardens.

After a time, the pathways and bridges along the edge of the lagoon became empty.

Police had set up a cordon, marked in tape, from the door of the Danieli hotel to the waterfront. He walked towards it, feeling light, and lifted the plastic line over his head.

Newhouse walked away from the cordon, over a small bridge, and back to Saint Mark's. He felt empty and clean. He sat down on a stone at the foot of the Doge's palace. He could hear sirens and horns, the rumbling churn of boats, launches, water ambulances and vaporettos. He heard shouting and talking, and the footsteps of many people. He closed his eyes. He fell asleep in the shadow of the old palace. He dreamed of nothing. Newhouse slept soundly and deeply.

He woke. Someone had put a silver emergency blanket over his shoulders, and a bottle of water beside his knee, a rolled clean green blanket and some bread.

There was clear light on the palaces and churches, the domes, bricks, windows and spires, the moving water and the waves. The air stank of smoke. Of burnt timber and scorched stone.

He stood up and felt unsteady for a moment but walked past the palace and across the square.

He looked at his phone. There was a missed call from Ivy. He would speak to her later.

Newhouse looked at his store of numbers, rolled through names and figures, and found the one he was looking for.

The name flashed up on the grey screen.

Newhouse wanted to talk. He was happy that suddenly

he felt happy to talk.

He looked up to the sky, the rising light blushing across the white and the blue, the empty day brushing away the darkness. Singing birds danced in patterns on the gleaming stones of St Mark's.

He called her.

THE END

The whereabouts of The Blue Horse by Pieter van Doelenstraat is unknown. It was last seen at the Palazzo Vedovo, Venice, Italy, in 2009.

ACKNOWLEDGEMENTS

Special thanks to:

Nicola Atkinson, Adam Brannen, my mother Susan Brannen, Jonathan Carr, Jacky Copleton, Freya Davidson, Alex Dickson Leach, Roanne Dods, Allan Donald, Roberta Doyle, Rodge Glass, Rosemary Goring, Simon Groom, Rohan Gunatillake, Deborah Haywood, Lucy Luck, Samantha Miller, Thomasin Miller, Alison Rowat, Daniela Sacerdoti, Adrian Searle, Helen Sedgwick, Mark Stanton, Simon Stuart, Scott Twynholm, Teesdale Comprehensive, Alison Watt, Gutter magazine, Fish Publishing, The Hobsbaum Memorial Writer's Group.

And love: Hope, Frank, Teddy.

In memory: Christopher John Miller (1936-99)